# *Bequeath the W...*

## The A

... Series.

You will be transported into the life of Ian Bishop. Travel with him, from the summer theater in the Ozark Mountains to Rome, Italy, across the Mediterranean Sea and experience exotic Ports of Call. Share in the shipboard romance and Trans-Atlantic Cruise to South Texas for the winter.

Is Ian being followed? Why would anyone want to follow this simple, yet complex man who is just following his dreams? Ian stumbles into a plot of international intrigue and before he is finished, he will have to die.

This fantastic epic is based on a true story. It will envelope you with mystery and suspense that will take you and Ian Bishop to London and Germany with major players out of South Africa and the movement of large sums of cash money across three continents.

Sherlock Holmes had nothing on Ian Bishop, who also gets involved with The New Scotland Yard, Metro (Fraud Division), London, as well as The United States Secret Service, and F.B.I.

Leonard Landerfeld is Ian's "Watson", and his best friend. Leonard and his wife Laura are members of the J.C. Foundation Board of Directors.

IAN BISHOP IS THE CHAIRMAN OF THE BOARD!

# BEQUEATH THE WIND

*A Checkmate Adventure of Ian Bishop*

By Jan Douglas Bish

ISBN 0-7414-3532-2

Original Photography by Jan Douglas Bish

Cover Design by Jan Douglas Bish

***Published by:***

***1094 New DeHaven Street, Suite 100***
***West Conshohocken, PA 19428-2713***
***Info@buybooksontheweb.com***
***www.buybooksontheweb.com***
***Toll-free (877) BUY BOOK***
***Local Phone (610) 941-9999***
***Fax (610) 941-9959***

***Printed in the United States of America***

***Printed on Recycled Paper***

***Published September 2006***

Jan Douglas Bish is the author of the novel:
***Bequeath the Wind***

Other books by Jan Douglas Bish:

*A New Revelation of Israel*

*So This is the Garden of Eden*

*Trump Your Trouble*

*Light and Shadow*

"Spanish Village" original painting by Jan Bish on page 25
24"x36" canvas in full color........................................................$ 3,000.

"Alfama Fountain" original painting by Jan Bish on page 62
24"x36" canvas in full color
Cover painting for *Light and Shadow*........................................$ 5,000.

Welcome to
my life!

07

# FOREWORD

This is a true story!

Well, maybe not true, in the biblical sense. The author has taken liberties with the story line and sometimes the characters themselves. He has embellished upon the truth to make the story easier to follow and more entertaining.

Sometimes the author took a few diversions down a different path, a path of fantasy. Life does not always take us the way that we want to go. It can be interesting to see where that other path may lead.

The writer allowed this story to lead him on occasion, and the conclusion is where he wanted this story to end. The names have been changed to protect the guilty. On all of the original documents displayed in this book the names were changed, to that of the author, in hopes of protecting Ian Bishop's privacy. The author doesn't mind that you know who he is.

This is one more chapter in the life of Ian Bishop.

Please allow this tale of Scams, Frauds and Deception help you to stay far away from getting involved with people that would prey upon you as a trusting, caring individual. Your life and the lives of the people you love are at stake, as well as your financial future.

As it was stated in the beginning, this is a true story.

Ian Bishop lived it from the beginning to the end.

Step by step, you will be able to see how these scams are laid out, to pull you in deeper, to where there is no alternative in the end, but to kill yourself.

If you follow this same road, it may lead you to financial ruin and destruction."

~

"Always remember that it is not money that defines the man. It is the kind of man or woman that you are, that defines your life. It is the things that you do and are doing for each other that defines who you are. "

Signed:

Ian Bishop

# CHAPTER 1

*Ian had no idea that his death would create such a stir. After all, this is the first time he had ever died. He had been through a few close scrapes before but this was a new experience for him.*

❧

The women that knew Ian Bishop well, would say; "Ian is like the wind. He moves about quickly and confidently. He is even sometimes motivated by unknown origins. You were never really sure where he just came from or where he was going. But, you knew that he was there, because his presence was felt."

Leonard and Ian were like kindred spirits, and close friends. They understood each other and could talk about things that no one else would understand. Leonard was over at Ian's house. Laura, Leonard's wife, had gone shopping with a friend, as our story unfolds.

They were lounging in Ian's living room with their shoes off. The background was being filled with easy listening and they had just opened a bottle of white wine. They were sipping from the hand blown glasses, that Ian had purchased while he was in Israel. Leonard asked, "Ian what is it like, when you get in touch with the spirit realm?" They were always relating on a deeper level than anyone else around them, either that, or they were being totally foolish, like a couple of over-grown kids.

Ian had so much practice, that he could just about will himself into a spiritual state.

“Well, Leonard, it’s kind of like self hypnoses. Hypnoses takes you right out to the edge of consciousness, to a place where you lose inhibitions and open yourself to suggestion.” Ian continued, “To take it one step further, is what some people call ‘Out of the body experience’. You see, you have to leave your body behind because you have to be in a place where gravity is not going to hold you down and time is of no importance.”

“Wow! How do you do that, my man?” Leonard asked in awe.

“It’s like exercising your spirit to reach new levels, or dimensions.” Ian explained, “When you were a kid, did you ever have any nightmares?”

Leonard answered, “Yes, sometimes when I was a kid, I was almost afraid to close my eyes because I would slip into a light sleep and see terrible things.”

“That’s what I am talking about.” Ian said. “That’s a place I call the fifth dimension. It is at that point that you leave your body behind and travel weightless into the spirit realm. That is the lowest spiritual realm. As a kid, you just stopped too soon. You have to travel on to the sixth dimension. That’s the place in the spirit world where you find dreams and visions.”

“But, how do you know how to get there?” Leonard wanted to know.

“Leonard, you know that I don’t talk about such things with most people because they will think that I am either crazy or have a wild imagination.” Ian said. “But, this is how you know. . . .You need to be at peace and you have to be still. As you are drifting off to sleep, you find yourself with one foot in the physical realm and one foot in the spiritual. You begin to feel light headed and just a little dizzy, but that is a good feeling. You can still smell the smells of this world and hear the sounds of this world, but they will become distant. That is where you step out of the physical and into the spirit. Time stands still and gravity does not hold you down. It all seems surrealistic. That is like stepping into the Light."

"Is that what it is like, when you receive the spiritual messages that you talk about?" Leonard asked.

Bishop answered, "Yes, you don't ever want to stop in the fifth dimension. The fifth dimension is where you find spiritual warfare. Continue on through that dimension into the next. You see, we live in a three dimensional world with gravity, and we are going through the fourth dimension of time.

I figured that if we can travel through that fourth dimension of time, as we are, that maybe I could also travel through other dimensions as well. I have only been to the sixth dimension. I believe one has to be invited to the higher dimensions by a Higher Power."

"That is so amazing. I love the talks we have about so many different things. You truly are a voyager through time and space. I have never known anyone like you before." Leonard said.

"The future always comes back to haunt me" Ian said. "It is like I can look into the future and know what is to come, not all the time, but enough to where I pay close attention when I receive these thoughts."

They had been playing a game of chess, while talking. Ian said "Checkmate! You should pay closer attention."

Leonard said, "Ah, that's okay. I was more interested in what you had to say. It is like you are in touch with your spiritual side, kind of like a prophet in that sense."

Ian responded to that, "Sometimes I feel like this is more a curse than a blessing. There are times when I just know that trouble is around the next corner, times I feel oppressed and heavy inside. That is a feeling I do not like. Once in a while I get a feeling of depression. Yet, I am not the kind of person that ever suffered from depression. I feel that way, for other people, like I just stepped into their body."

"Then at other times I have a joyous feeling and know that good news is on the way. And, I feel very expectant, but this time I just do not know what to think."

Ian continued,

"This time I could actually hear the unspoken words rattling around in my head. I was like a fly on the wall."

*"The last time I was this angry, a deal had gone wrong and it was up to me to make the problem disappear.*

*That man was just like Bishop! He just would not follow proper protocol !!*

*I sent you guys after him. I told you that he had ten thousand dollars in cash, but you killed him before you got your hands on the money. You made me look bad in front of the organization.*

*THAT WAS REAL SMART !"*

*The man in charge yelled at them, sarcastically.*

*'But, It wasn't our fault. He was going to go to Scotland Yard. We had to stop him.' said the larger thug that looked like he could have been a pro wrestler."*

Ian said, "And then I get this message". . . .

*"I am happy to inform you that I have concluded with the WILL. I am hereby sending you a copy of the duly signed and notarized WILL.*

*The Will makes you the beneficiary/sole executor to the estate, which is worth*

*Twenty-five Million, six hundred thousand*

*U.S. Dollars."*

"Was this spiritual communication tied in to the one before it?" Ian could not be sure. Bishop was used to receiving spiritual messages, but this dispatch, he was not ready for. "Who had died? How can this be? What would I do with that kind of money? I don't even know anyone with that much money! Money has been the ruin of many fine men in the past."

Leonard asked Ian "Did these messages come to you from out of the future, because of something that you had done in the past? Was it a warning, or an omen of things to come?"

Ian answered by saying, "I don't know. But, this communiqué sounded very ominous and foreboding, to me."

"These words just came to me last night as a dream."

*"They would be ready for Ian Bishop's return.*

*The scene was now prepared for Ian Bishop to set foot on stage.*

*The Queen was going to take this Bishop out of the game!*

*A man was telling his people, "If Ian Bishop knows what's good for him, he will play by my rules this time."*

Ian Bishop continued, "I heard this message in my head as clearly as if I was standing in the same room with these people. And, I did not like what I was hearing. The last time I had a message like this, it almost cost me my life."

☙

Leonard Landerfeld was a friend of Ian's and knew him quite well because they were two of a kind. They had met at the Summer Playhouse last season where they were both actors. They worked together so well that they were like two Bishops in the same chess game, brothers in arms.

☙

It was only fitting that Ian's friends and family had come together in this Grand Ballroom of the Crescent Hotel, to say a few parting words about Ian Bishop's life.

Leonard stood behind the podium and said, "Ian was a dreamer, but Bishop liked to live his dreams. Some people don't dare to dream, and some **only** dream. Ian lived his life to dream and then pursued his dreams. This philosophy took Ian Bishop down a lot of roads, across oceans, through the friendly blue skies, and some not quite so friendly. His dreams took him through many adventures and even to a few dead ends. But, what a journey it was !"

Leonard would always tell anyone who would listen "It was really fun to be around Bishop because you never knew what he would say next or even do next."

"If Ian Bishop was still with us today he would say; 'Life is a chess game. You have to be able to think or imagine several moves ahead in this game or you might miss your boat and get left behind.'" Leonard was Ian's number one fan, and Ian had been Leonard's mentor.

Ian's son shared that his dad had told him; "Never gamble more than you can afford. Never take a sucker bet, but always gamble with all that you are. Live each day to the fullest, as though it were your last. You may never be wealthy, but you will have a rich life. Where there is an open door, explore. See what is on the other side. Where there is a mountain, cross it. If you see a river, swim it. Always stop long enough to smell the roses and tell someone you love them. Follow your dream and find out where it will lead you."

Leonard knew that Bishop was a romantic. "Ian's love for the fine arts was very apparent in his paintings, he loved good music. Bishop became enveloped by his own writing and gave his stories the freedom to lead him."

"It is said that time stands still in the face of creativity, and Ian found that to be true. That is why at the age of eighteen, he lived as though he was sixty-five and at the age of sixty-five he lived as though he was eighteen. At the speed of light, time stands still and Ian always lived within that light!" an artist friend of Ian's added.

Leonard was remembering that Ian had told him once; "Don't ever settle for just living in the three dimensions of this world and traveling through that fourth dimension of time. Sometimes you just have to live outside of that four sided box. In the chess game of life a Bishop is a very important and powerful piece, capable of moving from one side of the board to the other in one move. Always keep an eye on the Bishop."

He missed Ian Bishop already and wished he was still around.

If you have not guessed, Ian Bishop was Leonard's hero, the man he always wanted to be.

Actually Leonard was that man also, because they were two of a kind. He would always think of Ian Bishop as an adventurer, explorer and world traveler, a true voyager. A few have called him worse. "He vowed `to himself many years ago that he never wanted to get to the end of his life and discover that there was something that he wished he would have done, but never got around to it."

A woman that worked with Ian was saying, "He went to the places that interested him and did what ever he liked. Do you think that sounds selfish? Maybe so, but he would give anyone the shirt off his back and had a tendency to trust the whole world. That is, unless you ever crossed him, and then watch out. Ian never made idle threats."

A person came up to Ian one time and told him "You are silently aggressive." Ian's reply to that was "Thank you." And, the other person said "Oh, You thought that was a compliment?"

Ian Bishop's daughter, Dorinda was remembering, "My dad was a hard working professional actor. His acting jobs were during the summer months. He authored four books, three of which are sold out editions. Dad was a professional artist (painter). His publishers have sold over 800,000 fine art prints of his work internationally. I even traveled with him on occasion when he went out on his many adventures, and gathered subject matter for his books and paintings. People expect you to be a little strange when you are an actor, artist, writer and musician. My dad did it all. Jack of all, and, yes, master of some. He never wanted to disappoint anyone, so he was just as strange and crazy as they wanted him to be."

Bishop's older daughter said, "I miss all the trips we took together as a family across the United States, Mexico and Canada. I feel like I was born with a wanderlust, just like him. I am part gypsy because of the love for adventure that he instilled within each of us."

Yes, everyone had come together in this Great Hall of the Crescent Hotel to honor a man's man.

He was a man who was not afraid to say what he thought, a man who was in touch with his spiritual side.

Ian Bishop was a man who gave everyone who knew him a zest for life and even more important than showing them how to die, he showed them how to live a more abundant life.

☙

# CHAPTER 2

This episode of Checkmate begins last October. The Summer Playhouse where Ian Bishop worked the summer seasons for the last twelve years, was drawing to a close. Fall was approaching with a gentle breeze. There was a morning and evening chill in the air. You could smell the scent of the pine logs burning in the fireplaces and hear the rustling of falling leaves, as you walked down the country lanes. The Ozark Mountains are a wonderful place to spend the summer, and the Fall Season is beautiful. But, when the leaves started to change color, Ian began to wonder where he would spend his winter and that itch needed to be scratched.

Maggie was Mr. Bishop's house keeper. One day she was caught up with her work and engaged Bishop in a conversation, "I have noticed that you seem to be such a loner, but then again, you really enjoy the company of others. You do like your quiet times for reading and listening to music with a glass of fine wine, but why have you not remarried?"

Ian said, "I would prefer doing all those things in the company of a beautiful lady. But most ladies my age remind me of my mother, and I don't care to date my mother, as wonderful as she was!"

"So you fill your life with beautiful women because you are an artist? What is the deal with you?"

"The actor in you requires that your ideal woman be intelligent with a touch of drama, but when you come home at night after the theater, you are always alone." stated

Maggie.

"Please Maggie, give me a break." Ian pleaded.

"But, Mr. B, you have to understand that there are a lot of beautiful gals out there that enjoy the company of a wild and crazy guy like you, especially one who is MATURE. It is a wise lady that chooses to be with an older man who is settled and established, emotionally, spiritually and physically." This seemed to be Maggie's favorite topic with Mr. B, as she sometimes called him.

"Maggie, my days are full, my nights are full. Why do I need someone to tell me what I need to do? I have a GPS system that literally talks to me and tells me where to go. When I have any time left over, I always have computer games and email to attend to. My virtual life is more interesting than most people's real lives. Just don't ever send me 'spam' or 'forwards'." Ian requested.

"Mr. B, you are hopeless. If you have nothing more you need of me today, I will go home to my husband, and TELL HIM WHAT HE NEEDS TO DO and WHERE TO GO !" Maggie said, good heartedly. "I will see you, day after tomorrow." She only worked for him two days a week.

Mr. Bishop said "Oh, contrary to that, I am not 'hopeless', I am always full of HOPE."

It was the last of October and he found himself wondering what to do in November.

Just then, all of the sudden there was a "pop-up" that half filled his computer screen.

"That's interesting," Ian read aloud "CRUISES 75 % OFF".

He started checking out their web site and as Ian started filling out some of the information at the web site, He remembered that a few years back, he had inquired about teaching art on cruises. So Bishop decided to pursue that dream.

Ian Douglas Bishop has always been a peculiar person, but since he "retired" he has been busier than ever before. He says that he will not own anything that doesn't have wheels or isn't wireless. He doesn't want to be tied down with wires or anything else. Ian is as free as the wind.

His life was built on a firm foundation. Through the years, many roots had been planted and there was great growth because of that, but this was the time for him to pull up those earthly roots and only remain rooted to the spiritual side of life. Bishop would be quick to tell you "The Spiritual side of life is more real, than the physical side. You see there is much freedom in that line of thought, because it frees you to explore and experience adventures that you would not even think about earlier in life. Before that kind of freedom you were tied down to responsibilities and maybe more concerned about your personal safety."

It's not that Ian Bishop is not a careful man. It's just that he is now willing to take a few more chances to pursue his dreams. When ever he begins a new chess game, he intends to win.

So, Ian picked up his cell phone and called the corporate headquarters of the cruise line in Seattle, Washington. "Hello, this is Ian Bishop. May I speak to your art director, please."

The operator said;

"Sir, you will need to phone Global Arts in Miami, Florida. We don't personally handle the art work on our cruises any more." and gave Ian the number. Now at least he knew why they had not contacted him before. They had been in a state of flux and change.

"Nothing ventured, nothing gained."

Using that new number, "Hello, this is Ian Douglas Bishop. I was in touch with one of the cruise lines that you now represent. A few years ago, I left my information with their art department. You should be able to find samples of my work in your files. I was told that you were going to call me when you had an opening for an artist to demonstrate his work on one of your cruises." Ian stated.

The art director didn't remember the name. However he responded, "I'm so glad that you called. I just now found out that we had an artist cancel on us at the last minute because of illness." Ian heard a rustling of papers as though the director was going through files and then the clickedy click sounds of a computer keyboard. "Yes, I have your file. I am very impressed with your work. Nevertheless, the only opening I have is for a month long cruise departing from Rome, Italy, only two weeks from now."

Ian asked; "Where does the cruise go?"

The art director said "Ahh, Let me see . . Rome to Livorno, Italy over to Barcelona, Spain, Carnes, France, Lisbon, Portugal, then Trans Atlantic to the Azores, to Bermuda.

There is a stop in Port Everglades, Florida and then across the Gulf of Mexico to Galveston, Texas. Does that sound like something you would be interested in?"

Ian was really excited about being on a long cruise, but answered "I might be interested in doing a cruise like that for you, but how is the pay?"

Of course Ian Bishop would have been willing to pay them for a cruise like that anyway, but he was "cool".

The man from Global Art said "You will have to set this up through your art agent. We don't normally work directly with artists any longer, like we used to."

So, Ian told him "You can put me down as the artist in residence for that cruise and I will have my agent get right back to you."

Bishop did not have an agent that did that kind of work for him. Ian Bishop being in the art business for many years, had many different agents selling his work to different art markets, but nothing like this before. He talked with some other artist friends about a free lance art agent and was given a name and number.

"Yes? This is Max, 'Representing you to the max.' How may I help you today?" That was his way of answering the phone.

"This is Ian Bishop in Eureka Springs. Lamar Rowberry, an artist friend of mine from Santa Barbara gave me your number. I need for you to represent me."

Max came back "I am sorry Mr. Bitsop"

"That's B I S H O P" Ian interrupted.

"Yes, well that does not matter, my stable is full of artists right now looking for work."

"Max," Bishop said "I already have all the work I can handle. What I need for you to do is negotiate a contract for me with Global Arts out of Miami. I have the deal all wrapped up. All you have to do is call the man."

"Well then, that's a horse of a different color. I can handle that for you." Max said.

Ian gave Max all the details and hung up. "Representing me to the Max. What a joke! Probably what he should say is 'I will charge you to the max'."

When Max, the art agent got back to Ian, he said "The cruise line will pay you $3000. for three weeks of demonstrations on board the ship during the cruise."

Ian thought that sounded pretty good until Max continued "My commission will be $800. And, by the way, You have to book your own tour."

Well what could Ian say, but "Go ahead, set it up".

Bishop would have been willing to pay a discounted price for the cruise anyway, which he actually did, because the artist had to book the tour . If an artist did this for a living, he better be independently wealthy, because you could go broke real fast at that rate.

The reservations were all made through Yahoo.com and along with all the information Ian noticed, "Your passport can not expire within six months <u>after</u> your tour ends."

Ian's passport was going to expire only three months after the cruise was over. "Oh no, some new ruling through 'Home Land Security'!"

He only had a week and a half to get his passport renewed.

Once before Mr. Bishop had to have his passport renewed at the last minute. When you are a spontaneous kind of guy, you have to expect this sort of thing and you just roll with the punches. His passport still had the folder from the company that walked his passport through before. "VIP Services".

Back to the cell phone, he called the number and ordered their 24 hour service. A week later the passport had not come in. Ian called "Why have I not received my passport?"

They replied “Sir, we are working on it and will send it out to you today by Fed Ex Express. Since we did not get your passport walked through in 24 hours, we will not charge you for the twenty-four hour service.”

Mr. Bishop didn’t even respond to that ridiculous statement.

Ian Bishop waited the whole next day for his passport. He even paced up and down in his drive way, but that didn’t help it to arrive any sooner.

One time he saw a Fed Ex Truck drive right on by his place. Ian jumped into his car and chased the driver down for about five miles. The Fed Ex truck pulled into a parking lot, and Ian pulled in right after him.

Ian approached the driver, “Do you have a package for me? The name is Bishop.”

“No sir, you are not on my manifest. What kind of package was it?”

Bishop told him “Actually, it is a U.S. Passport. It was to be sent ‘overnight’.”

“Ohhh, Sir, that would have been sent Fed Ex Express, not Fed Ex Ground.” the driver said.

“Thank you” Ian said as he turned back to his car, dejectedly.

Three hours later, the package still had not arrived and Ian had only been away from home while on that quick chase after Fed Ex Ground.

Bishop spent the last half of that day on the phone to Fed Ex.

Right before closing time a supervisor called back and said “Your package has been delivered.”

"Where was it delivered? I have been waiting all day!" Ian responded.

The supervisor put the deliveryman on the phone "Sir, There was not anybody home, so I put the package inside the screen door."

Ian replied to that "Where did you deliver it? Not to my house! I was home all day."

The driver described where he had delivered the passport. Ian knew the area very well and was able to visualize where the man was talking about.

The deliveryman had left his package about a mile short of Ian's place.

Ian Bishop got into his car and drove to the place that the deliveryman described and found his passport inside the screen door of a vacant house with the same house number, but on a different road.

Ian Bishop now had his passport, twenty-four hours before he really needed it.

Plenty of time to spare.

☙

# CHAPTER 3

It was the end of the Play Season in Eureka Springs, Arkansas. Ian Bishop was playing the role of "Ciaphas the High Priest." How 'bout that, a Bishop, playing a High Priest.

After the final curtain, the actors made their final bows. Ian went down front to encounter some of the theater patrons. He met a couple of visitors from Houston, Texas. The Houstonians could not say enough nice things about the stage production.

Ian asked "How is the best way to get to South Texas from here?" The people started to tell him, when Bishop broke in, saying "I plan on going the scenic route. By way of Chicago, Frankfurt, Rome, the Mediterranean, Trans Atlantic to the Azores, Bermuda, and across the Gulf of Mexico to Galveston, Texas."

They said; "That sounds like you have the **best way** from here to Texas." "A lot better than the way we came." the man's wife added, as she poked him in the ribs with her elbow, good naturedly.

Ian thought so too. And, he was also thinking that he could spend the rest of the winter in South Texas, with eighty degree weather. "Yes, that's the ticket!"

Next on Ian's schedule was the cast party and then his winter adventures. Full steam ahead!

Ian Bishop got on the Net and reserved a hotel room in Tulsa, Oklahoma for the following night.

Mr. B also sent Maggie an email that he would not be using her house keeping services till next March, however, he would like for her to pick up his mail and let him know if there was anything important. Maggie had his cell phone number and his email address.

Ian got up early the next morning, drove to Tulsa International Airport, (TUL). He spent the night at one of the airport hotels. Ian arose first thing the following morning. He got some breakfast, parked his car in an airport security parking lot and was off to the airport in one of their courtesy cars.

Tulsa to Chicago, to Frankfurt with only forty-five minutes between connections. Ian Bishop also had to clear customs and make it all the way across the Frankfurt Main Airport for his flight to Rome in only forty-five minutes.

Ian never liked checking luggage. Maggie had told Mr. B, "Lay everything out on your bed that you think you can not live without, for this trip. Then cut it in half, putting half your clothes back in your closet."

Ian did even better than that. He laid everything on his bed and then put two thirds of it back. He then had stuffed what was left into a back pack, and one hanging clothes bag.

Bishop also wore enough clothes in layers that would have filled another small suitcase.

☙

# CHAPTER 4

Mr. B arrived in Rome, Italy with just enough time to be corralled with a group of older, richer people arriving from all parts of the world for the month long cruise. Ian always traveled light, but this time he not only had a good size carry-on but a full size clothing bag which included his tuxedo for the formal nights on board the cruise ship. He had his art supplies shipped earlier, that he would need for his classes.

Ian layered his clothes on this excursion about four deep.

To see this ship for the first time was an awesome experience. It was the length of two football fields end to end and about 18 stories high. Ian's state room was located mid-ship, two floors below the main lobby.

The transportation from the airport arrived at the port about noon. The cruise was scheduled to leave at six pm.

Ian's luggage did not arrive at his stateroom door until five-thirty pm. At that point Ian had been awake for about twenty-four hours so he thought he would catch a couple of winks before the Captain's Party at eight pm. Bishop woke up at eleven. He had totally missed the Capitan's Party, so he went for a midnight dinner and then off to bed again. This was after all, suppose to be a restful trip, but, he didn't want to spend all his time in bed.

The next day, rested and ready to take the world on again, Ian traveled the length and breadth of the ship. He read about all the events of the day and talked with several strangers. Ian had always heard that single women out numbered the single men by at least two or three to one. Those are odds he felt like he could live with. And, boy were they true. The problem was, that the women all reminded him of his mother. That second night he went to a Singles Party in one of the twenty lounges. There was a few young couples around, and then there were the old ladies. He didn't feel like he really belonged in that group so he accepted an invitation to dance with one of the older ladies. Ian didn't want to be rude. After that dance, he left. Ian hoped to find greener pastures another day.

There are so many scheduled events, you could never get bored. Mostly the ship would come into port for a day of travel adventures and exploring on land (solid ground). And then sail around seven or eight pm for the next port. With all the delectable foods and different restaurants on the ship, you can plan on gaining at least thirty pounds during a cruise like this.

Ian Bishop opted for the eat anytime plan. Which means you can eat anytime and often.

All you have to do on the "Eat anytime plan" is show up at the restaurant door and they would say "Stateroom number, Sir? Would you like to share your table with others?"

Ian always flashed his "cruise card" and said "Yes, a table with some good looking single ladies if you please." The help would always bow gracefully, and say "Right this way, Sir."

"And, then they would take me to a table of older couples or more single guys." Ian would say.

Ian Bishop, the artist, would have a time on the ships schedule between ten am and eleven am., every other day, while on the open sea, for art demonstrations and lectures. Other than that, his time was his own. This ship had about two thousand guests so it was like a small town. It wasn't too long before you began to know the people who were around you. And it was always a pleasant surprise when people would stop Ian in the hallways and call him by name.

One thing that Ian Bishop had never done in his life was karaoke. In his youth he played in several music groups and sang. Music was always important to him and it was something he enjoyed. When the ship's daily newspaper announced a karaoke contest, he thought to himself, "Why not." He showed up that night in one of the smaller lounge theaters.

One of the cruise directors approached him, "Good evening Mr. Bishop. Would you like to join us and have some fun?"

He answered with a smile on his face "I sure would, Peggy." She was wearing a name tag, as a cruise director.

Peggy told him "Here is a book for you, just find the song you want to do. Fill out this card with the song number and I will give it to our sound engineer."

With a "Thank you very much". He sat down and started looking for something that looked familiar. Finding a song he liked, he filled out the card. Ian handed the card to Peggy and said "I hope they play this in my key."

Ian was one of twenty people who showed up for these auditions. The cruise directors called this contest the "Cruise Pop Star."

Ian Bishop was no stranger to performing in front of an audience. He had been on stage, television and radio programs before. But for some strange reason he was very nervous. Never the less, he reminded himself that this was fun and it was something that he wanted to do.

Bishop passed the audition with flying colors, and was invited back for the first session of "Pop Star" the following evening.

☙

After an appetite had been worked up, he headed for one of the dining rooms. He was seated with a very friendly group. There was a couple from California, two gay guys from Kansas, an older lady from France and a man of color from South Africa. The evening progressed and everyone became very well acquainted. Ian mentioned "I love lobster and I know I already ate two, but I sure would like another one." The French lady said "All you have to do is ask." And she motioned the waiter over to their table for Ian.

So he did, "Waiter, may I have one more lobster, please?" The waiter brought him two more. Ian rolled into the bed that night a very satisfied gentleman.

☙

The man from South Africa seemed to be very interested in Mr. Bishop. Ian thought, "I might be able to sell this man an original painting, before this cruise is over. He seems to be very cultured and well spoken." Bishop was trying to remember this man's name. He had never been good with names, but he was working on that problem. Ian made up his mind that he would make a mental note, next time and remember.

Livorno, Italy was their first port of call after departing Rome the evening before.

Ian walked all over the Italian city of Livorno. He went down the narrow streets, past the rows of bicycles and motor bikes almost parked up on the sidewalks, the quaint shops, and the fish market.

The fish market was the most interesting to watch as the fishermen came in to sell their catch of the day and the salesmen would deal with their local clientele.

There was this one octopus that kept trying to escape while the salesman was doing his best to sell today's catch, as well as continue to put the octopus back in his pan.

The fish salesman looked toward Ian who had been watching the drama unfolding intently;

"Octopus, Sir?" the fisherman asked.

Just what Ian needed, an octopus for a traveling companion or a pet to take care of.

Ian answered "No, thank you." It was getting late and time to return to his ship.

With Livorno now behind them, the ship sailed on to Barcelona, Spain.

Ian Bishop already had been a world traveler and had been to Barcelona before and was not interested in seeing it again, so he just stayed on board the ship that day.

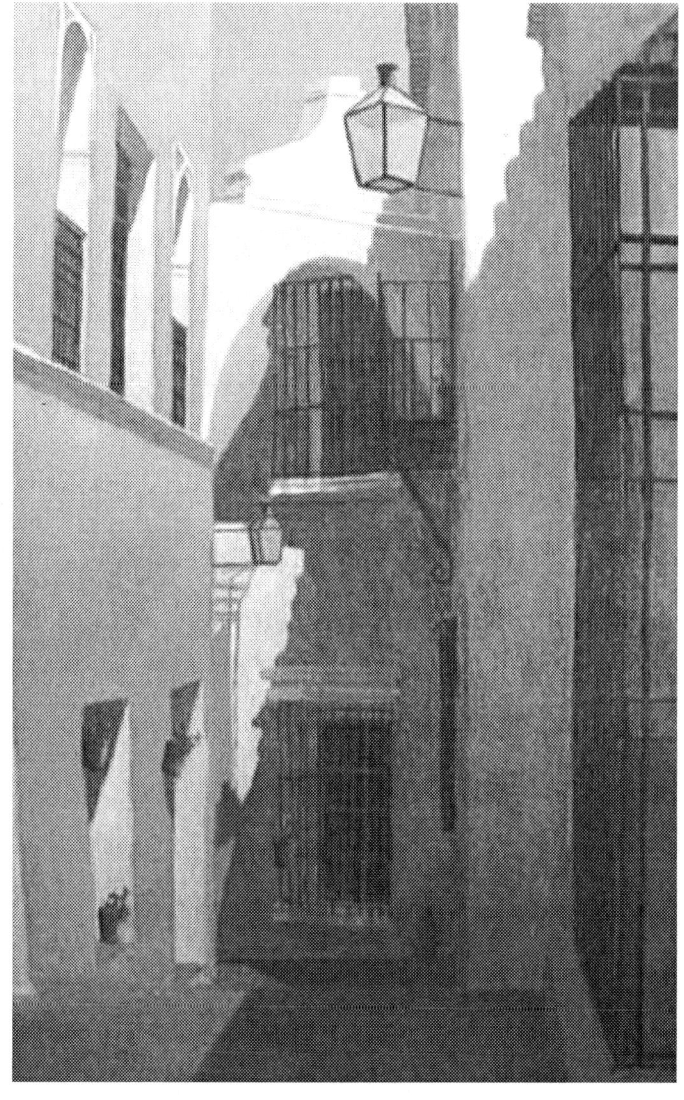

"Spanish Village" Original painting by Ian Bishop

Mr. Bishop did not usually like big cities and found them all to be alike in so many ways, the traffic, the noise, too many people and even pick pockets were everywhere.

He had spent some time here with his first wife, and would just as soon leave those good memories stored in his archives. Ian remembered briefly about the Spanish Village recreated for a World Fair there in Barcelona that they had visited together, as well as a colorful flower market where they had bought a large bouquet of beautiful paper flowers.

On board the ship that day, he ran into several people that knew him by name because of the dining arrangements, and the Pop Star Contest.

Several ladies mentioned "I just loved that song you sang the other night."

"Thank you" was all Ian could think of to say. Ian Bishop is not impressed easily by others. He tends to live pretty much in his own little world.

Also while in port that day, Ian went into the Ship's Spa, had a rub down and lounged in one of the hot tubs with a cool drink. This was a great place to people watch, one of Mr. B's favorite sports.

☙

# CHAPTER 5

At dinner that night on board the ship. Ian dined with a couple from England on one side and a young lady from Germany on his other side. The man he had met the other night from South Africa arrived a little late and sat on the other side of the table. Talk about an international night.

The dining room was elegant with crystal chandeliers and the kind of plush carpet that made you feel like you were sinking, as you walked. Ian was always amusing himself with his private little thoughts. He thought in passing; "One should never have a SINKING feeling while on a ship." There was also marble pillars and fancy archways from one area to another.

"Good evening, Ian" came from a couple from the U.K., as they saw Ian approaching.

"How are you?" was Ian's response.

They answered together, "Jolly good."

A young German girl, "Guten Abend, Herr Bishop", with a nod of her head, as the waiter pulled out Ian's chair and placed an open napkin in his lap.

The man with very dark skin said in the way of introduction; "My name is Alto. My mother was Spanish and my father South African. I am the youngest of eleven children.

They named me 'Stop' because they didn't want to have any

more children."

Ian added to the conversation "Actually, it was his mother that kept saying, 'Alto, Alto !' His father named him, Alto."

The other people at the table chuckled. That was a great ice breaker, and made everyone feel at ease.

Ian was thinking "the German girl's English was easier to understand than this English couple from the U.K." Bishop thought it was odd that the gentleman from South Africa was at his table again. Usually you always had different people every night with this style of dinning, but he thought no more about it. Ian was on vacation this time. This was not a "working trip" to solve a mystery. He was not here to resolve any crimes, but to follow his heart and rest his weary soul.

Ian headed for his stateroom early that evening, eleven pm. He wanted to get a good nights rest because Cannes, France was the Port of Call tomorrow morning. He had already arranged for a bus ride to one of France's most interesting of ancient walled cities; St. Paul Devince.

This was definitely the kind of place that Ian Bishop loved to capture on canvas.

The next morning at eight am, Ian came down the gangplank. There was at least ten buses lined up for different land tours. "Pardon me, Could you direct me to the bus that goes to St. Paul Devince?" Ian questioned the man at the bottom of the gang plank.

"Right over there Sir." as the man pointed to a big red bus. The purser had already delivered the ticket to Ian's Stateroom the night before.

As he presented his ticket to the woman standing outside the bus, Ian said, "Mademoiselle". He sat in the front seat so he could take photos along the mountainous route through

Cannes, and finally to the walled city on the top of a hill. The bus trip was very interesting and took about an hour.

Ian explored every alleyway and ventured down the cobble stone, winding streets to discover what was around the next bend. This was the kind of place that Ian lived to explore. In the background he heard some children laughing, as one ran by him saying something in French. A dog was barking in the distance and the smell of freshly baked sweet breads lingered in the air. There was a slight chill in the atmosphere as a mist filtered down through the narrow streets from an afternoon rain shower.

He had about five hours before catching the bus back to the ship. Up one narrow street and down the next, till the entire town had been covered.

Ian saw a couple of lovers walking hand in hand and a woman walking her dog, nodded to him as he passed. The dog was a “French Poodle”, believe it or not!

There was just enough time to stop at a side walk café and enjoy a French pastry with a cup of coffee. There, he met another person from the cruise ship.

“I am Pierre“, he said with a French accent. Please join me at my table Mr. Bishop.”

“Just call me Ian, please. I recognize you from my ship. Where are you from?”

Pierre said “I am from Quebec, Canada. And you?”

To that Ian had to answer, “I am a citizen of the world. Actually I was born in Pennsylvania, raised in Washington, D.C. and make myself at home, no matter where I am. What brings you on a cruise like this one?”

"I was just on a three month Pilgrimage, following the journeys of St. Paul across Spain and France. I have walked almost three thousand miles." Pierre said.

"You walked almost three thousand miles in three months? You must be tired!"

"Wee," Pierre answered, "that is why I am on our cruise. I am going to spend my winter in South Texas, before I head back up to Canada. That Pilgrimage, was the best time in my life."

Ian said "I intend to stay on Padre Island for part of this winter also. I will be in a fifth wheel trailer right on the beach at Port Aransas. Stop by and see me and we will break open a bottle of wine and reminisce about our journeys."

They had a good conversation, exchanged email addresses and cell phone numbers, before running to catch their bus back to port.

Ian had shot about twenty interesting scenes with his digital camera.

He would have liked more sunshine so he could have captured better "light and shadow" for his compositions. All in all a very good day, even though there had been a mid day rain shower.

❧

Back on board the ship that night, there were always parties to go to.

There was several different movie theaters with first run movies. Lounge acts of different varieties in some of the show rooms and of course the big Broadway Type Shows (mostly musicals). Ian liked to get front row center for the big shows.

One night a hypnotist was on stage and asked Ian Bishop to participate along with four other men and five women. He placed the volunteers, man - woman - man - woman. Ian Bishop had never really been hypnotized before. He thought he might enjoy the experience, but, alas, Mr. Bishop was too strong willed to be under any one else's control, even sub-consciously. The entertainer asked him to leave the stage.

Later, Ian was glad he had not stayed. The hypnotist made the suggestion to the women that stayed, that the men sitting next to them had pinched them on the bottom.

One young, good looking girl cried out in pain saying: "OUCH! He pinched me!" As she was rubbing her behind, she turned toward the man next to her and said, "That hurt. You do that one more time and you will be sorry."

The man looked at her in amazement and said "I didn't touch her" and then he looked out to the audience for his wife,

"Honest, Honey, I didn't touch her!"

Later in the same performance, the hypnotist suggested to this same girl that there was two people in the audience that was totally naked, her mother and her father. He had asked her earlier who she was traveling with and she had said her parents.

The hypnotist asked her parents to rise and tell everyone where they were from. When her parents stood up, the girl just about fell out of her chair and covered her eyes. It was so funny to watch.

&

The next day was a "sea day". Ian had an art demonstration on board the ship that morning. Bishop was explaining to his class that he had been painting out in a field. "Nature is the best teacher" He was telling them.

"A man came up to me and watched over my shoulder for a while. He was quiet for a few minutes as he looked out over my field of vision. Then quizzically, the man said; 'As I look out over the same field, I see what you are painting, but I don't see the colors of purple and violet and red, that you are laying down on your canvas.' I turned to face the man and said to him; But, don't you wish you could?"

Ian went on explaining to his students, "Art is an expression of emotion and feeling. Your task is to not only capture the picture but to express through color what you are feeling."

A student raised her hand, "Yes?" Ian questioned.

"How do you know the colors to use, in order to create the

depth of what you are feeling, in what you want to portray?"

"Excellent question, that shows that you are thinking." Ian told her.

Ian continued, "Different shades of red, usually give you a feeling of warmth, especially when mixed with yellows.

Red can also portray anger, or direct the eye to a particular point in the painting. Blues are cool colors and are sometimes related to happy feelings, such as blue skies. The full spectrum of everything in between will give you a blend and variety of different emotions. Dark shades for sadness and bright light with shadow for happy feelings."

As Ian was finishing his teaching for the day, he observed a very sophisticated lady come into the class. She was the kind of woman that turned the heads of gentlemen everywhere she went and the ladies pretended not to notice her.

She was wearing a bold yellow shorts set with short shorts that had up and down stripes. The stripes accented her long shapely legs and made Ian feel like her legs just went on forever. He was a "leg man". This woman had a tan and a smile that would put the great Mona Lisa to shame. She appeared to be very self assured, but maybe she was just compensating for a lack of confidence. One thing for sure was that the yellow accent framed her beautiful eyes and soft brown hair.

Bishop had remembered seeing her picture in the ship's photo gallery with an older man. Ian had made a mental note "Now there is a classic beauty. Too bad that youth is wasted on the man she was with." Of course Ian was just feeling a little jealous. He would never admit to that, however. Ian always had an eye for a beautiful woman.

"Our Port of Call tomorrow morning is Lisboa." Ian told his art class.

"It is one of the most interesting of the Mediterranean Ports. Be sure to visit the Alfama District of the old city and take your cameras and sketch books with you. You will find a master piece waiting for you around every corner."

Ian Bishop had been to Lisbon, Portugal before and had loved the food, and their "Fadu" music. The architecture was always worthy of many great paintings. Did he have enough time to walk all over the Alfama District, have a seven course meal, drink some of the Portuguese Port?

"No ! Not on this visit", but his thoughts wandered back to the time when he and his first wife had spent an evening in a Fadu Club. The voluptuous singer came over to Ian's table, kind of leaned over his table until he had a great view, and said in English "I SING FOR YOU."

Ian Bishop had said, "Boy, does she have a great set of lungs!"

"Well, she is a good singer", Ian added!

His wife had said "Yeah, right !" with a smile on her face.

Later Ian discovered that was the only English she knew, and she used it at every table she visited. But, she sure did know how to lean on those tables, and get the big tips. The singer also had a way of ignoring the fact that there was another woman at the table. After all, it was the men that gave her the gratuities.

"Lisbon is a very ancient port filled with mystery and romance", he was thinking, as he was walking down one street and up the next. Ian felt as though there was someone following him at a distance. Once he thought he caught a glimpse of a dark skinned man that ducked into a doorway, but he couldn't be sure. It was enough to make him feel uncomfortable. He spent half his time looking over his shoulder. Ian stopped into a grocery store and picked out six bottles of their best white wine and port.

Ian was wondering who that man was that ducked into the doorway. He looked a little like the South African man who sat at his dinner table on the cruise ship the other night, but he couldn't be sure. "How foolish of me." Ian thought "I am seeing mystery where none exists. It is probably just the fact of being in the Alfama District of Lisbon where sailors and rogues of old, used to hang out with the pirates."

Next Ian started looking for a music shop to buy a couple of Fadu C.D.s . If he did not have time for a Fadu Club on this trip, he would have a "Lisboa" evening after he got home. Ian Bishop always knew how to entertain himself. He just made it back to the ship before sailing time.

Alto had, actually been following Ian Bishop in Lisbon, Portugal. He went to the Ship's Library and got on the internet to South Africa. He needed to talk with his brother.

Alto sent him this email:

**"Bane, Bishop, is our man. I am sure of it. He spends money like he is made of the stuff. I saw him go into a store in Lisbon and come out with six bottles of fine wine all at one time.**

**The man has a lot of pride.**

**I am not sure that he has a lot on the ball, he thinks he is a comedian and has to keep everyone entertained. That all might work in our favor.**

**Regards, Alto"**

Two days later they were in the Azores and a few days after that in Bermuda. Ian rented a motor bike and rode from one end of Bermuda to the other. There was not much time to spend on the Island. The ship arrived a little late into port. Ian rode into Hamilton and dropped by a book store.

As Bishop went into the book store he was greeted by a young girl, "Good afternoon Sir. How may I direct you?" The young girl was talking with a guy, but didn't mind stopping to talk with Ian. She was very young as well as very flirty.

"Well, I am looking for a good mystery book. Which direction should I go?" Ian asked.

"Why, that's my favorite topic. Right this way." She said. "Was there a particular topic or author you are looking for?"

"I would love to find one of Ian Bishop's works in your shop ", he said.

"I believe I sold the last one we had of that author's works just last week. I will put more of his books on order for you if you would like."

"Yes, that would be wonderful of you to do that for me. Thank you so much for your time and your assistance." Bishop said as he left the shop and continued his bike ride.

"Well, that's one way to get them to reorder my books."

Once more, just making it back to the ship before they pulled anchor, dropped their lines and sailed for Port Everglades, Florida.

During the days at sea, for lack of something else to do, Ian would go play Bingo to see if he could win one of their thousand dollar pots. Peggy, the cruise director, was the caller, and she never seemed to call the right numbers for Ian, but she was full of personality and was fun to be around.

Ian Bishop also enjoyed the hot tubs on the ship.

At one time or another on this cruise Ian probably sampled each one of the twelve spas located in different areas of the ship. He could not believe that the weather had been so nice all across the Mediterranean and the Trans Atlantic passing was nice except for the time they had thirteen foot swells and had to shut down all four swimming pools on the ship.

The swimming pools would slosh back and forth and collide in the middle of the pool. The water would then shoot straight up, about fifteen feet into the air like a huge fountain.

There was a lot of people that became sea sick, especially those with staterooms located in the aft part of the ship. They had more up and down action back there. Fortunately Bishop's room was located mid-ship and he was fine.

That was only about a day and a half and the rest was smooth sailing.

# CHAPTER 6

One evening as Ian was looking over the third floor balcony of the ship down on the main saloon, he spotted a vision of loveliness, the kind of beauty that refreshed a man's soul, but she was sitting with an older man!

Then, Ian remembered "This was the girl that had wandered into his art class, wearing yellow shorts", earlier that week. When he had first seen her, she was wearing a matching shorts and top outfit that reminded him of youth and vitality. Now she was wearing a stylish black strapless evening gown that now spoke of elegance and clung to her figure in a way that would make any man wonder what wonderful mysteries lay beneath. Yet, she had a face that only spoke of innocence, and eyes that had also known sadness.

The older gentleman she was sitting next to was in his tuxedo. He looked like a man of the world, very distinguished and Ian supposed very rich. This was one of the formal nights on board the ship and everyone seemed as though they had just stepped out of a photo shoot on a Hollywood sound stage.

Ian thought, "Just my luck, she would have to be there with this older man." She was sitting near the grand piano in the main saloon enjoying the after dinner music. There happened to be an empty seat on her other side.

"Perhaps, that empty seat was an invitation from fate" Ian thought as he made his way down the winding staircase toward destiny.

The music filled the air with the promise of romance.

Ian headed straight for that empty chair before anyone else had a chance to claim it.

He asked "Is this seat taken?"

She looked up, Ian wondered what was going through her mind, as she answered "Why, no."

"Isn't this a great evening?" Actually more of a statement than a question.

"I am Ian, …Ian Bishop."

She responded by saying "Yes, I know. I saw you the other night in the talent contest and thought you were very good."

"Thank you so much for saying that. You are most kind. It is a delight to meet you." Ian told her.

The brown eyed beauty said, "My name is Jean. I also know that you are our artist on board this cruise. I watched you paint a canvas the other day, and saw some samples of your work. Most extraordinary, I must say." At this point she turned to the man seated on her other side and said "Dad, I would like to introduce you to Ian Bishop. He is an artist and an author."

"How sweet it is. There is a God in Heaven after all." Ian thought as he said "It is so nice to meet you Sir." He had seen her picture with her Dad, in the ship's photo gallery, and thought he was her "sugar daddy". And here he was just her DADDY.

Best news he had heard all day, actually the best news for the whole cruise. Bishop turned to Jean and asked "Would you like to go to the dance tonight?"

She said "I am so sorry, but my Dad is having a reception in the forward night club tonight and I promised him that I would help. The reception is a private party by invitation only."

Ian's heart sunk as he thought "Well, at least I tried. I should have known that this was too good to be true."

Jean continued ". . . But, if you would please come?

I will leave word at the door to let you in."

Just what he wanted to hear. Ian said "If you will excuse me for now, I will see you later. About nine okay?"

She replied "That will be great".

Later that evening she told Ian, "It makes me so upset when people think that my Dad is my date. He just asked me to go with him on this cruise because my husband died a year ago. I just have not been out of the house much since then. I go to work in the morning, for a financial firm in San Francisco and then I go home after work every night. One day seems just like another and they all run together."

Ian said "I know just what you mean, I lost my wife to cancer about five years ago."

Jean said "I came on this cruise to find myself."

Ian told her, "You don't really need to find yourself. You know who you are. You just need to figure out what it is that you want." She had a sophisticated air about her that one could never learn, it just came natural.

Jean thought for a moment and whispered in a sad tone, "**What I want, is what I had**", as she spoke these words, her head dropped down in repose.

That stabbed Ian right in the heart because he really understood where she was coming from. He had been there himself. Seeing her pain made Ian shed a tear, as he thought also of all the good times he had shared with his wife and the sorrow of loosing her. He had thought that he would never love again because the pain was too much to endure.

Bishop remembered the first night he had met Betty at a dance. He had asked her to dance. Actually he had gone up to the guy she was with and said "Are you going to ask this beautiful lady to dance, or am I going to take her away from you?" The guy was shocked !

Betty looked up and asked Ian, "Are you asking ME to dance?" Like, you need to ask me, not the guy I'm with.

"Yes", Ian said "Would you like to dance with me?"

She had said "Yes."

Ian became lost in his thoughts.

Ian reminisced how he was holding Betty in his arms, the music was soft and low, he had kissed her on the neck and said: "How 'bout we loose the guy you are with, find the back door to this place and go get some breakfast?"

Betty had responded to that by saying, "What do you mean?"

"It's almost midnight, and there is a place right across the street that starts serving breakfast at twelve. They are open all night." Ian said.

"Ohhh, Okay." Betty responded and they had been together every day since, that is until the day she had died.

☙

Coming back to the real world, Ian responded to Jean by saying, "What you need to do is figure out where you want to go from here, and not look back, except for the good memories." He was speaking as much to himself as he was to her.

They discovered that they shared many things of common interest and could relate to one another. A connection had been made.

She said, "I have enjoyed talking with you tonight. Could we meet again tomorrow. I will be in the Ping Pong Contest tomorrow morning at ten am. on the Sports Deck. Would you like to play?"

As Ian kissed her hand lightly and said, "I sure would. Till tomorrow." And he bid her farewell and "Good night."

The next morning Ian Bishop got out of bed with a new spring in his step and a glisten in his bright blue eyes that had not been there before. Oh sure he enjoyed playing Ping Pong, but that wasn't it. He was thrilled to finally find someone that he could enjoy some of the ship's events with.

Jean was also excited to have found someone whom she could enjoy and spend time with, other than her dad. Her dad had another companion that he wanted to spend time with, as well.

When Jean met Ian that morning she shyly said "Hi".

She had practiced many different things to say, some witty, some cute, and something even a little more somber to show her serious side. She had even practiced in the mirror different ways to say these things, but when she was face to face with Ian, "HI" was all that would come out.

"It's warm up time" she said, "Would you like to play me a game of ping pong?"

"I use to play, but it has been a long time." Ian mentioned "Be kind!"

Jean answered "All I try to do is return the ball when it hits my side."

After she zinged a couple of "slams" back in his direction. She just shrugged her shoulders with an angelic smile on her face.

Actually the score was not too bad: 21 to 18, her favor. Ian felt like she had designed that as well.

Ian played one of the other guys that morning, and had even won, one game.

After Jean had beat Ian at Ping Pong once more, they agreed to meet each other for the daily ice cream social at three pm.

Ian had mentioned to Jean the night before that he liked banana splits, as well as Banana Cream Pie.

Jean knew that the ice cream place didn't have bananas, so she had picked up a banana from the breakfast bar that morning and gave it to Ian when he met her at the ice cream social.

"How thoughtful of you to do that for me. I am not accustomed to that kind of care. Thank you." Ian said sincerely. She would not know how deeply that simple act had touched him. To him it was an act of kindness that showed that she cared. It also gave Ian some insight into her giving personality.

While they were sampling all the different ice creams, Jean asked "Would you like to go play Racket Ball with me this afternoon? I usually meet some new friends at the court about four-thirty"

Glad for the invitation Ian said "I have never played, but I am willing to learn."

They walked together up to the top level of the ship where the sports center was located. The first half hour of play turned out really well.

Ian surprised himself that he was really good at Racket Ball.

Then, one of the balls had been hit over toward his side of the court and trying to impress the girl, he tried for the ball with a flying leap and landed with his right hand bent backwards. "Ouch." His hand started to swell immediately.

Jean went for some ice and questioned Ian "Would you like for me to go with you to the ship's hospital?"

He said "I am more embarrassed than I am hurt. I apologize for ending the game like this."

"Don't even think about that. I am so sorry that you got hurt. It is your right hand. Are you a right handed artist?"

Ian said "Yes, but don't concern yourself with that. It's feeling better all ready." It wasn't really feeling better all ready, but he didn't think the injury would permanently hurt his painting hand and he did not want to distress Jean unduly.

Jean and her Dad did not have the "eat anytime time plan" but had the same table with the same guests every night for dinner.

Jean said "We have an empty seat at our dinner table. Would you please join us for dinner? We have a really interesting group of people and I am sure they would love to meet you."

Ian said, "I would be delighted. What time?"

"Which Restaurant?"

Jean replied "Nine pm. I will meet you in front of Michelangelo's."

Ian absentmindedly, totally forgot that this was Thanksgiving. And he just remembered the Pop Star Contest, was later that evening. Beautiful ladies always had that strange effect on him. He told her "I have to be at the Pop Star Contest at ten pm. Would you like to join me for that? You could take some photographs for me, when I get up on stage? Maybe your Dad would like to come also?"

Her dad said as he strolled up to the table, "I would love to come and I must tell you Ian, that I really admire you for getting up in front of a large audience like that to perform."

Jean said "That would be great then, and I will take some pictures for you. I'll look forward to it."

Ian handed her his camera. "It is a simple one. All you do is point and shoot."

He added, "Tonight is the finals. It's just like American Idol, with a panel to discuss what they think of your performance, the back stage interview on TV and the audience votes."

They all had a lovely traditional meal with pumpkin pie at the end. Ian excused himself early so he could go to the theater and report back stage.

Actually, Ian got involved in the Pop Star Contest, not because he ever thought he would win, but just because he had never done anything quite like that before.

The number had been narrowed down to two guys and two gals.

When he had found out that they were all professional

entertainers, he figured that he didn't really have a chance to win at all. Ian Bishop had just entered on the spur of the moment, as a lark.

Ian Bishop, Pop Star Contest

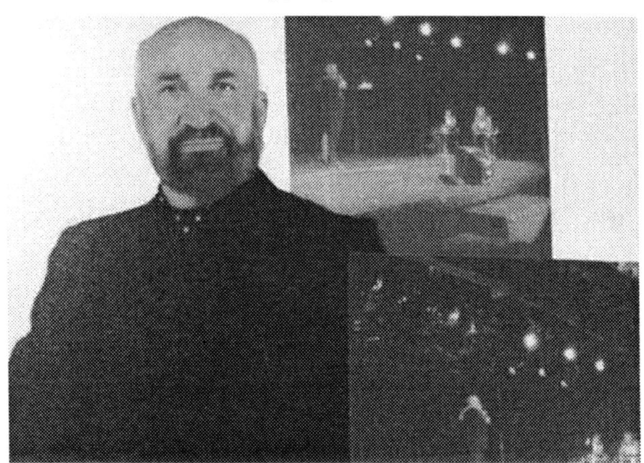

It was ten pm. Ian Bishop and four other contestants were back stage wondering what the order of appearance would be.

Jean and her Dad were out front. And, wouldn't you know it, Ian saw Peggy back stage and found out she was going to be one of the panel judges.

He asked her "Are you as good at judging as you are at Bingo Calling?"

Peggy said "I guess you will find out." with a smile on her face, or was that a smirk?

When Ian Bishop was introduced to the packed audience, Peggy told everyone "Ian said that I was not a good Bingo Caller. Is that any way to treat a judge?"

Ian quickly responded to that by saying "I didn't say anything negative to Peggy. I just asked her if she was as good at judging as she was at Bingo calling." There was laughter in the audience as well as agreement with Ian, about her calling. She had not called their numbers either. So Ian Bishop didn't think that would hurt his chances of winning.

Ian Bishop gave it all he had that night. He stepped forward in his black tux, black shirt and ascot and gave the audience what they came to see . . ."When I fall in love, it will be forever..." he sang as the flash bulbs went off from all over the show room.

When Ian was finished with his song, the panel said "Ian kind of reminded me of Dean Martin with his suave approach and his hand in his pocket totally relaxed, made everyone feel very comfortable and at ease for him."

Another panel member had said; "Quite enjoyable and easy to listen to."

The judges made the announcement that the voting was, oh so very close.

The audience voted one of the girls as the winner.

She was a professional lounge act at a club on South Padre Island, Texas. She was really very good.

That evening Jean and Ian walked the deck of their grand ship, toward the outdoor theater under the stars. There was a balmy breeze blowing through Jean's hair and the full moon added a golden glow to her face. She turned to Ian, and said, "You were wonderful tonight. I adored the way you performed your song. I really believed that you were looking to fall in love."

"I've been looking for love in all the wrong places. But, I have discovered that love does not come unless you stop looking for it. You can not make it happen.

It just happens!" Ian exclaimed.

Two ladies passed Ian and Jean as they were leaning against the rail, over looking the sea. They said, "Not to interrupt you, but I just wanted you to know that I voted for you tonight in that contest."

The other lady added, "Ian, your song has been playing in my head all evening and I can't get it out of my mind."

"And the moment that I feel that, you feel that way too, is when I fall in love with you." The song continued to rattle around in his head also. Ian's mind was always over-active, but tonight, Jean had sent his world spinning with thoughts of love. "Is it really possible to experience love at first sight, at my age?" Bishop didn't trust his own feelings. "Maybe, I am just in love with love." He had a tendency to do that too. Then again, it could be this place, this time, this ship and a beautiful lady so close to him, he could feel her warmth.

It must have just been the fairy tale atmosphere weaving it's magic on both Jean and Ian. They both felt it, It was as though love was in the air.

After the movie, Ian and Jean went to one of the shipboard clubs where they danced the night away.

The music was slow and romantic. A soft blue light filled the room and a crystal ball was hanging over the dance floor that cast sparkles of light, reflecting like facets of a diamond. The dancing light shimmered in Jean's eyes and glittered around the room. Ian was thinking "Her eyes danced with a radiance, with every word she spoke." He was entranced.

Jean intently looked into Ian's blue eyes as if she was trying to see what lay beneath the surface of who this man really was. Could it be that he was really as nice as she thought he was. In some ways, he reminded her of her late husband, whom she truly missed.

Jean's thoughts had taken her back to a time when she and her husband did not have much money. It was her birthday and he couldn't buy her a present. He had wrapped a special gift for her and tied it with a beautiful ribbon. The package was light in weight, but heavy with love. She carefully took off the ribbon and opened the box to find a very special gift.

"I have nothing to give you, but my love,

So this idea flew to me as a dove.

Jean, you have had no middle name,

Mine will fit you like a glove,

I give it to you, our middle names will be the same."

He had given to her his middle name and it would remain close to her for the rest of her life.

Ian had said "A penny for your thoughts?"

At first she did not even hear Ian. It was like she had to come back from a distant place, another dimension where our spirits can only visit, but we have to return.

"Oh, my thoughts are worth much more than that!" Jean replied. But, she didn't offer any further explanation. For the time being she would just remain a mystery to Ian.

This was the final night of the cruise. The time was late, Ian escorted Jean back to her stateroom which was located just down the same hallway from his own.

“How could this be? She had been so close, just down the same hall, for that whole month and they had not met till the end of this cruise. Sometimes fate can be cruel” Ian thought.

Jean had given him her room key earlier in the evening. Ian had thought at the time, that she had given it to him because she had no place to put it, but he was always a little naïve about such things.

He returned the key to her and she placed the keycard in it’s slot and turned the door handle, slightly . . .

She slowly, almost pensively turned to face Ian. “I had a wonderful time with you.” she said with a slight blush on her cheeks. They gazed deep into each other’s eyes. Within Ian’s deep blue iris she saw, cryptic signs of romance. Ian was transfixed as he stared into her beautiful dark brown eyes filled with longing. He sensed a flame of passion deep within Jean, as he looked onto the blush that filled her face with a glow of promise.

He leaned down to kiss her warm moist lips pressing her lightly against the wall. The kiss was like tossing gasoline upon an open flame of passion, and that flame flared.

They almost stumbled through the opening door, and into her beautiful stateroom with a balcony over looking the ocean. As the ocean slowly passed by, Ian realized that his heart was racing as fast as their time together was fleeting.

They walked over to the balcony as if in a trance, holding hands, opened the sliding glass doors without even speaking. They stood there for a moment, over looking a full moon reflecting in the waves of the Gulf of Mexico. Their minds were rushing, no words would come, but they were communicating at a much deeper level. There was the sound of the ship cutting through the waves and the scent of the sea foam laying heavily on the air, and a faint smell of the fresh cut flowers in her state room. Or, maybe that flowery scent was emanating from Jean. Once more they were caught up in each other's gaze. It seemed like forever, but it was only a moment before they found each other in an embrace.

A kiss filled with passion and need, passed between them.

Even while they were thinking that they were from two different worlds, they became lost in the heat of the moment.

They were suspended in time and nothing else mattered but each other. Ian and Jean wondered why they had not met sooner in the cruise instead of right at the end. Their time together had been so very short and yet so meaningful.

The two, had become one, if only for a magical moment. Perhaps a seed had been planted within both of their hearts that would grow into something even more beautiful and lasting. The Gulf of Mexico is a mystical place in the moonlight and has a way of weaving a spell into lover's hearts that can never be untangled again.

☙

# CHAPTER 7

The month of November was now over, but Ian and Jean had spent Thanksgiving together. It was a special time but now the cruise was over, and it was time to come back to reality. A cruise ship is sort of like a fantasy world. It was a welcome break from their normal work days back home, but now it was time to say goodbye.

Ian had always hated goodbyes, specially since his wife had died five years earlier. He would not say goodbye to Jean. They left each other knowing that their paths would cross again. They had already been through ten different time zones and seven different countries on this trip alone.

Now, Ian Bishop had the whole winter ahead of him and he was able to do what ever he wanted. He felt freshly renewed and empowered. It was him against the world, and he knew he would win.

The rain was pouring in Galveston, Texas, coming down in sheets. Everyone was coming out of the ship and down the gangplank. Well, not everyone. The cruise was going to continue down the coast of Mexico to points south for the winter. Some had cars waiting for them. Some people were waiting for buses to the Houston Airport. There were others trying to hail cabs.

Ian also noticed out of the corner of his eye, that the man from Africa had exited the ship in Galveston.

Bishop thought it strange, that the African had also exited in

Galveston, but dismissed the thought almost as soon as it had flashed through his mind.

Jean and her dad decided they wanted to go to the Johnson Space Center outside of Houston before heading back to California.

And, Ian was on his way to Central Texas to visit his sister.

Last winter Ian and his sister had spent a week together at the South Texas Beach, catching up with old times. They had not spent this amount of time together since their youth. Both had lost their mates and both were alone, but they discovered that they both had a few other things in common as well. It was good to renew the old kinship. So Ian Bishop set aside some time for his sister again this winter.

"How's your love life Sis?" Ian had asked when he saw her.

She looked at him, as if to say, "Are you crazy, love is reserved for the young and the foolish." But she had a little twinkle in her eye as she thought of a long lost love in her life. Just the thought of what she had and lost, gave her a new vitality and added to her countenance.

She smiled and said to Ian, "You know, my old love of fifty years ago called me on the phone this past week?"

"How wonderful is that?" Ian said as he was wondering about a lost love of his own.

Ian Bishop told his sister all about the cruise and his life as an actor this past year. She loved hearing about all of his adventures.

While in New Braunfels, Texas, Ian decided he wanted a new fifth wheel travel trailer. So he bought one and headed down to South Texas where the temperatures promised to be in the eighties most of the winter. He could park right on the beach and be a beach bum for the next couple of months.

At least that was his plan. As you know, plans do not always unfold the way you envision.

Ian Bishop's New Living Room on the Gulf of Mexico.

# CHAPTER 8

December was here and Ian was beginning to wonder what he was going to do for Christmas. He actually had done all of his Christmas shopping and gift wrapping last October. He is not usually that well organized, but this year he knew that he was going to be on that month long cruise. It had been many years since he really had that "holiday spirit". It was at this time of year that he missed not having a family at home and kids to open presents. Although, his kids often enjoyed playing with the boxes more than what came in the boxes.

The Christmas music which he had enjoyed in the past, just became background sounds to the thoughts of old fashioned family Christmases of years past.

Ian's phone rang . . . "Hello?" He was grateful for the interruption of his thoughts.

And on the other end, "Hi, Ian, this is Cindy." Ian was delighted to hear from her. He had met her this past year at the Play where he was working a summer season in Eureka Springs. Actually they were introduced by mutual friends and fellow cast members. She was a school teacher in Germany as well as best friends with Laura.

Laura was the wife of Ian's best friend, Leonard.

Bishop, surprised to hear from her, thinking she was still in Germany. asked "Where are you?"

Cindy replied "I am in Houston, Texas. My son and his family live here and we are going to have a good ol' fashioned family Christmas. I knew that you were headed for Texas this winter, so I thought that I would ask you to join with us for our Christmas Dinner. Would you come? P L E A S E ?"

Ian told her, "I am so pleased that you thought to ask me. I will be glad to come and join in the festivities." Ian was thinking, YES, now maybe I will be able to relive a few minutes of those memories of Christmases gone by. It wasn't that he often lived in the past, because he believed that one should be living for the future. He was missing the good family times together. People tend to do that, this time of year, especially when you live alone.

Cindy said, "Call me on my cell phone when you get to Houston and I will give you directions. I will be on the south side of Houston near Friendswood and Clear Lake."

Ian Bishop knew the general area because he had lived in Houston about twenty years ago. Ian's drive to Houston was a good one. He came the night before and rented a hotel suite for a couple of nights on the south side of town, near Hobby Airport. As soon as he arrived, he called Cindy and received further directions for the next day.

Ian arose early, went to get some breakfast and headed toward Cindy's son's address. Houston roads do not make square blocks and it is easy to get lost if you don't know exactly where you are going.

He called Cindy's cell phone again for more directions and in the middle of the conversation her cell phone died.

Her battery was dead and needed charging. "So much for directions!" Ian mumbled to himself.

It was a 20 minute drive from his hotel to Cindy's son's house. Ian Bishop arrived two hours later, after asking for directions from strangers many times. The road he was looking for, was one of those roads that stops and starts in different places. He brought a bottle of wine from Europe for the hostess, and lady of the house and a Christmas gift for Cindy.

Dinner was about three hours later. Ian had time to play with Cindy's grandkids and get to know her family, while she was fixing the dinner. "Cindy likes to cook." Her family told Ian, as he thought to himself. "She did seem to know her way around the kitchen."

In his years, alone, Ian had learned to cook and take care of himself. But, he was not really very good in the kitchen department. Cindy actually looked like she was enjoying herself and she loved having her family all around her. Ian Bishop was amazed that she still found time for him, even in the midst of cooking, loving on her family members and playing with grandkids. Ian was thinking, "She seemed to have her priorities straight. Could it be that a husband would come first in her life? That of course is very important. Ian desired to be number one in a woman's life. But, here again, that remained to be proved, and only time would prove that supposition.

Her son had a glass of Iced Tea that wasn't sweet enough for him and someone had poured some 7up in it.

He gave it to his mother, "Mom, taste this. Someone put 7up in my tea to sweeten it."

Cindy said "Ummmm, not bad!"

Ian said "Let me taste it." And Cindy passed the glass over to Ian and then Ian passed it around to the other ten people sitting at the table. By the time it got back to her son, there was nothing left. That was the last time that day that he offered to let anyone sample anything of his.

After a wonderful and filling Christmas Dinner, some of the

family played a rousing, wild game of "Spoons" around the kitchen table. Others that were not game oriented, went into the living room and turned on the television. Teenage girls reached for their cell phones and the boys ran out of the house to play with the family dog who was barking joyously. The children were playing with new toys and even a trace of Christmas music could be heard under the rest of the din.

Cherry pie was served later in the evening because everyone was too full after dinner. Cindy knew that Ian liked cherry pie so she made one just for him. "Ice cream?" she asked?, as she put a dollop on the top.

So this was the family Christmas that he had been day dreaming about? Ian Bishop was glad for the opportunity to get to know Cindy's family as well as drawing closer to her.

However, he didn't know if he was interested in pursuing a closer loving relationship with anyone at this point. He was enjoying a new found freedom having sent his son, and final child off to a university in Arizona just this past fall.

He kissed Cindy lightly and headed off for his hotel suite. Ian Bishop had always felt that long distance relationships are just too difficult to deal with.

But here he was with a lady in California and now a woman in Germany. Talk about long distance relationships.

Ian and Cindy exchanged email addresses and vowed they would stay in touch. He was also thinking . . .this woman was a little too "straight laced" for him but she had something different, an inner beauty and intelligence that went beyond the norm. One thing Ian knew beyond any shadow of a doubt was that a fun time was had by all. And, like everything else in his life, he would follow this road to see where it went. Ian Bishop always wanted to know what was on the other side of the mountain. It seemed like long distance relationships was all that he had lately. Well, it is true that it is difficult to get yourself into too much trouble, long distance, or was it?

The next morning he went up to Tomball, Texas, just north of Houston. There, he shared Christmas with one of his daughters and her family. Ian had spent time with his other daughter and her family in San Antonio. And, his son was back home in Texas from college and visited with his dad in New Braunfels, Texas. Any more Kids? No, that's the extent of Ian Bishop's brood, as far as he knew!

With a wonderful Thanksgiving in the middle of the Atlantic Ocean and a glorious Christmas with family under his belt, Ian Bishop loosened the belt to his pants a couple of notches and fastened up his new fifth wheel travel trailer and headed for one of the beaches on the Gulf of Mexico.

With every reason to expect a restful winter, he headed south, as his newly found friend returned to Germany.

Restful ??? That was the plan. Remember? Always dream the dreams and then go after that dream. Ian always did that, but what came next was not part of his plan.

Ian did not like living all the way down next to the Mexican border. It was too congested and too many Winter Texans. It was warmer down there, but Bishop figured that seventies and eighties was plenty warm enough for him. He did not like crowds, waiting in lines and RV Parks with trailers all in a row for as far as you could see.

Ian liked the idea of deserted beaches and some time alone. He didn't need people to keep him entertained. He had all the entertainment he needed within himself and his new trailer.

Living on a deserted beach, watching the beautiful sunsets over the Gulf of Mexico and soaking up the warmth of the sunshine had been Ian's winter dream for a lot of years.

Ian Bishop had thought of days like this even as far back as elementary school as he would walk to school on cold mornings in the snow. Bishop knew how to live "high on the hog" even on a low budget. He knew how to relax in the company of kings or lounge in the presence of peasants.

Ian Bishop was at peace, once more.

# CHAPTER 9

There would be no better time to write a new book. It had been about twenty years since he had done any serious literary works and those books were all sold out and now out of print.

Ian felt compelled to write a book on Spirituality and Quantum Physics. His mind had been working on this subject ever since he saw a special program on television about String Theory during this past year.

Talk about "strange bed fellows". "I know you are thinking how can you bring those two subjects together on the same page? But this was to be a book of contrasts and opposites in this universe that repel one another and bring balance to God's creation". Ian Bishop is a very deep individual. "You know that still waters run deep".

Ian came up with the title: "Light and Shadow", an artistic term that has duel significance.

"You see, we are living in the Shadow of God's Light". Ian Bishop was really tuned into the spiritual side of this life.

There is a lot of "duplicity" in this universe. If this was not enough work to keep him busy, he began to paint fresh new canvases from his "Ports of Call" in November. One of those original paintings was to became the cover to his new book.

This original painting was of a fountain from the Alfama District of Lisbon, Portugal.

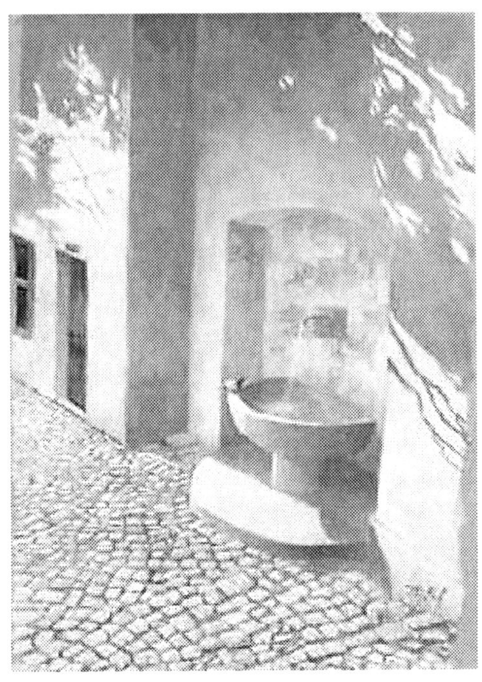

Bishop was thinking "Why is it, when ever I think that I am going to have nothing to do, I end up with more to do, than I think I can handle?" Ian Bishop was famous for biting off more than he could chew, or jumping in, over his head.

The strangest thing happened the later part of January. Ian Bishop began to receive very unusual phone calls from what seemed like different men, making odd inquires. By the end of January, Ian had determined that these men with unfamiliar accents, could be the beginning of another grand adventure.

Already Ian was filled with a feeling of trepidation or expectation. Right now he could not figure out which, but he could smell something in the air.

Cindy had also been calling from Germany on a regular

basis. She had a special deal, only two cents a minute for Trans Atlantic phone calls. So she and Ian had spent hours talking on the phone about his new book ideas as well as the unusual phone calls he had been getting from who knows where.

Cindy said "What kind of an accent was it?" In reference to the phone calls that Ian had been receiving.

Ian hadn't really thought too much about that, but said "I don't know. Normally I have a knack for figuring out what part of the world an accent was from, but this time it just eludes me." Ian had been a world traveler for a lot of years and it only took him a few days in a foreign country to pick up the essential language of that country in order to find a hotel, a W.C. (a rest room) and how to order food so he would not starve.

It wasn't until he had finished the conversation with Cindy that evening, which was early morning for Cindy in Germany, that he realized, "IT WAS SOUTH AFRICAN !" Ian had not been to South Africa before, but he had spent some time in northern Africa.

Talking with Cindy was always a delight. It was kind of hard to grasp the concept that as he was going to bed, she was just getting up to face a new day. A day that he could only dream about for now, she was beginning to live.

The following day Ian's phone rang "Hello." He knew as soon as the man spoke on the other end of the line, "Yes, it was South African."

The man on the other end of the bad connection said, "My name is Ruben Chizea. I have been in touch with a detective and a lawyer. We have been attempting to trace you. There is a matter, I wish to discuss with you. What is your email address? I will write to you in greater detail, and I will need to phone you some more."

Ian responded "Who are you?"

The mysterious man with the strange accent said, "I am a branch manager of a bank in South Africa".

Ian Bishop felt strange about the phone call from a banker in South Africa. His gut instinct told him,

*"Beware!"*

He had been in many strange and unusual circumstances in his life and some that were even dangerous as well.

*But this for some strange reason made the hair on the back of his neck, stand up, as a shiver ran down his spine in spite of the eighty degree weather in South Texas.*

*It was like that spirit of prophecy coming over him again, to help guide him through a difficult situation.*

Strange and unique events always brought out the best in Ian. He never accepted the word, "Beware" or danger to mean anything to him other than, this could be another extraordinary adventure in his life. Something that needed to be followed to the end. Never say "die". A real mystery to be solved. "Defeat" was not a word in Ian's vocabulary. Warning Ian Bishop of impending danger is like saying "Sick em'!", to a junk yard dog. An open door has to be entered, an opportunity that has to be followed.

Here again, that still small voice in Ian's head was saying:

"Another time and another place to be explored."

Sometimes it felt like another force was leading him to do things that others would not even consider. There was a special calling on his life. That force was impulsive and compulsive.

All he knew was that he had to follow this path to see where it went.

*His Protector would be there to guide him.*

*"You are not alone."*

There were several more phone calls after that.

On one occasion the South African said; "We would like for you to work with us on this, in secrecy, because this involves a great deal of money. The South African Government would like to lay claim to this money because it has been unclaimed. We feel that you are the legal beneficiary of a Will made out by John Cuthbertson. Did you know this man?"

Ian tried to think, he couldn't readily remember "I don't know if I did or not."

Ruben said "When moving large sums of money out of a country like South Africa, there has to be great secrecy. Don't tell anyone about our conversation. I will be back in touch with you."

After he put down the phone, he didn't know if he understood what the man from South Africa was really saying. The accent was hard to understand and the phone connection always seemed to be bad. "Wow! Did he really say that this involved a LARGE sum of money? John Cuthbertson? Did I ever know that man?" Ian had a million questions running through his mind all at one time.

Over the years, Ian had people that seemed to come out of

the wood work, with letters and emails about work, he had done years before. They would say how his books and paintings had been so important to them and had influenced their lives over the years.

Ian had always been willing to listen to other people and help them through rough times in their lives.

Ian was a "talker", but he also knew how to listen.

"That was it!" Ian thought "One time in Cairo, Egypt I met a friend of a friend that lived in South Africa."

Ian Bishop had a friend who was an oil man that lived in Houston. He hadn't thought about that man in years.

"That friend of my friend's name might have been John. I talked to him about several of my self help books in the lobby of the Cairo Hilton right next to the Nile River one evening, oh so many years ago."

But, that was so many years ago, Ian could barely remember. "Could it have been, that meeting, had meant so much to John Cuthbertson that he would name me in his Will?" That was a question, Ian could not answer.

He would call the man in Houston and find out about this mutual acquaintance.

It had been so long ago in his past, Ian could not remember that friend's name, in Houston either. But he could remember the name of a fellow author friend, "Richard", who also knew the oil man.

Bishop looked up his author friend on the Net. Yes, his old friend had a web site. There was information about his old friend's institute as well as a run down on all the books his friend had written over the years.

Ian sent an email to Richard and his wife.

Ian asked about that old friendship they had shared, with the oil man who was at that time, seeking a large oil field from the "foot of Asher" in Israel. And, did they remember his name? An email response came from Richard, the next day

**"Dear Ian, Yes, how are you doing?**

**It is so good to hear from you again after such a long time.**

**That man's name was Andy Sorrell, but he passed on, a few years back.**

**Your Friend, Richard"**

Ian thanked his old friends for this information and began to think, "Now I will never know how John Cuthbertson knew that I was in Cairo, Egypt that time so long ago."

☙

# CHAPTER 10

Ian decided to send his well-known author friend, Richard, in Houston, a rough draft copy of the new book,

"Light and Shadow". Richard had only known Ian as a professional artist, not an author. Ian valued Richard's opinion highly, as a professional.

A couple of weeks later Ian received an email from Richard about his new book:

**"Ian:**

**Enjoyed reading your book. Thanks for giving me the opportunity. I must say it was different.**

**It will be interesting to see what the folks at the Publishers have to say.**

**I can see the book as a hardbound special issue. I believe people who buy your art would want to buy your book as it tells your story.**

**Once again, thank you for the honor of reading it.**

**Keep in touch.**

**Your friend, Richard"**

Meanwhile, Ian spent his days working on his new book, painting scenes from France and Portugal, and exploring around South Texas. Ian enjoyed riding his motorcycle up and down the beach and into the tropical island town of Port Aransas.

One of Bishop's favorite haunts was a Ti Ki Bar Restaurant called Moby Dick's. Ian would usually order the coconut shrimp for lunch.

One time the Ti Ki Bar even had a free buffet to welcome all the new island winter residents. Who said "The day of the free lunch is gone?" They were wrong, why there was even live music for the patrons. The singer fashioned himself after Willie Nelson and sang "Of all the girls I've known before, the ones that came in and out my door."

"Ahhhh, what a life." Ian spoke to himself as he settled back in his lounge chair on the beach and sighed again. Closing his eyes to the bright sun, he soaked in the warmth of this winter's day and dozed off on the beach.

From time to time Ian received emails from Jean in San Francisco. It was always good to hear from her. It brought back memories of days well spent and even a very special evening. He would always secretly value that fond memory, but he was thinking that was all it was now. It was like a wild fantasy that never happened, and yet, it had happened and she had left an impression on his life.

Ian Bishop had also begun to look forward to the weekends, because that was when Cindy would call from Germany. Cindy had email at the school where she worked and Ian had a WiFi wireless computer with him all the time. He could connect to the World Wide Web no matter where he was. So Cindy and Ian would be in touch on most days.

Ian had just found out that Cindy was a Physics Teacher. Well, that was interesting because Ian was writing a book having to do with Quantum Physics in relationship to the spiritual world as well as the physical world.

Cindy had said in one of her emails "I thought you were trying to impress me with your knowledge of physics."

Ian told her "I didn't even know that you taught physics, I thought that you were just a science teacher." Now Ian knew that he could talk to Cindy more about the technical points that he was making in his new book. Someone with whom he could collaborate, even on a deeper level. "Wow, beautiful and smart. That could be a winning combination."

Her emails and phone calls began to etch themselves in Ian's memory banks. On days when he would feel a little down or lonely, he would make a withdrawal from that memory bank.

Ian Bishop was not one to think much of being lonely because he kept much too busy for self pity. He had noticed that Cindy's calls and emails had become an important part of his life and that she had become a valued friend and rather indispensable.

Ian Bishop only had a National Plan on his phone so it was Cindy who called him on the weekends because he had 3,000 minutes he could use on nights and weekends. Ian really did not usually like talking on the phone. He never even came close to using those nights and weekend minutes, but now Cindy and Ian were coming close to using them all.

Sometimes Cindy would get up at four in the morning (Germany time) so she could talk with Ian before he went to bed the night before.

It was Sunday afternoon in Texas and in Germany it was bed time for Cindy.

Ian's phone rang "Hello,"

"Hi, this is Cindy. How are you doing today?"

Ian replied "I am doing GREAT." Well, he was, now that she was on the other end of the phone line. He went on, "I had a wonderful day at the beach and a great lunch at my Ti Ki place and even got some writing done. A good day, and now I am talking with you."

"Oh, you are so sweet! Ahhhh, …Would you excuse me for a minute? I just noticed that I didn't get all the clothes I wanted out of my dryer."

"I am up stairs in my bedroom getting dressed for bed and I noticed that I didn't get all of my pajamas. I have to go down to the basement and get the other half of my pajamas."

Ian said "Which half did you forget? Maybe you don't have to go all the way down to your basement."

He could actually hear her blush over the phone, as she said. "You don't want to know!"

"Sure I do" Ian spoke into the phone, prolonging her discomfort. But, she had left for her clothes dryer in the basement of her three story house.

She got back on the phone out of breath. "Hello, are you still there?"

"I'm still here and still wondering if you are going to just wear your tops or bottoms?"

She ignored Ian's comment and continued "I usually wear a gown, but since there is no man around here, I wear pajamas."

That made Ian think and he said, "Actually, I don't like clothes to bind me at night. I am a very active sleeper, so I wear "Polo" or nothing at all."

Cindy ignored that statement as well.

It was now the first of March and the winter was winding down. What a great way to spend the winter.

The first part of November Ian was on a Mediterranean Cruise, giving art demonstrations on the high seas. Then, there was Thanksgiving in the middle of the Atlantic Ocean with new friends. And, after that, December with his family, and Christmas with Cindy and her family in Houston.

Then January and February in a brand new fifth wheel travel trailer on the beach in South Texas, it was like spending time on a tropical island.

A wonderful place to relax, write and paint.

And then, the mystery and intrigue of this contact from South Africa of all places.

A deal cloaked in secrecy, and high finance.

Life was good. Ian had everything. He had his health and energy to do the things he wanted to do. He had romance in his life and not a problem in the world. And, now, even the promise of wealth.

☙

# CHAPTER 11

Cindy was very concerned for Ian Bishop's safety, if he got involved with "people like that" she would say, or Cindy would also mention more than once, "If this deal was not on the up and up," Etc., Etc., Etc.

"If. If. If." Ian Bishop did not like to look at all of the ifs.

Ian of course realized the danger and began to document everything as it occurred. Ian looked at this opportunity as an open door, a new chess game with a formidable opponent. How could he get hurt? If he was very careful not to give these people money, he could not get hurt financially. But, then again, they had not asked him for any money. Ian Bishop also realized that there was a certain amount of danger involved, but he would never mention that to Cindy. He didn't want her to worry.

Bishop also saw the opportunity to begin writing another new book. This would be a true life novel. Fiction, of course, but based on his true life experiences." A year in the life of Ian Bishop." He liked the sound of that! This could be a mystery story with adventure, and romance. Ian could always make room for another new project in his life, after all he didn't have "chores" to do, or "Honey do" lists to perform. His time was his own! Ian decided "YES, that's what I will do. I will begin another new book while the past few months of details is still fresh in my mind. I will call this new book:

"Bequeath the Wind" and I will write it as I live it.

On the other hand he knew that people had been murdered for less than moving large sums of money across international boundaries and he had better be very careful.

Cindy said "Maybe these people are drug lords trying to move dirty money out of the country and launder that money."

Ian told her "That would be unlikely out of South Africa. That might be true if this deal was coming out of South America."

That didn't make Cindy feel any better. Ian said to Cindy, "I will be careful". He did sort of expect a scam, but hope springs eternal. Maybe it was for real. Good things do happen to good people, sometimes. It seemed like the adventure was worthy of his time. He felt that he would be safe as long as he did not front any money. Ian Bishop did not actually think that he might be in mortal danger if he pursued this escapade.

He would however find out later that people really have been killed before, over a lot less money than this deal offered.

Ruben Chizea had made several phone calls to Ian from South Africa the last of February and the beginning of March, explaining "our deal".

Ruben explained "This is a deal, Mr. Bishop so you need to not bring anyone else in on this. This deal must be our secret. When you move large sums of cash money, there are those that would go to any lengths to get their hands on it."

"Where do I fit into this? What do I have to do?" Ian asked.

"All you have to do is follow proper protocol in this matter in order to receive your inheritance." Ruben continued, "I have personally invested a lot of money through lawyers and detectives to find you, Mr. Bishop. If this money went unclaimed, nobody would get anything because the

Government of South Africa would confiscate the funds."

Ian said "I understand all that, but why have you worked so long and hard to put this deal together?"

"Good question, Mr. Bishop. I like the way you think. I would want you to share these funds with me and my associates who are involved in this venture." Chizea answered.

After the phone call was finished, Ian was thinking about all that was said:

"In other words, it sounded like this", to Bishop; "Ruben needed to move this money out of Africa, legally or illegally to Holland, Switzerland or the United Kingdom", where Ian would collect these funds and share them with Ruben Chizea and his friends. Ian liked to put things in their simplest concept.

This was all sounding really strange, but Ian assumed that things were different in the world of high finance and third world governments where everyone had their hands out for a big pay off. Ian could understand the need for secrecy when it came to moving large sums of money around the world.

You can wire funds from one bank to another but ultimately, the actual cash money had to be shipped and physically moved.

There were more phone calls from South Africa and then this email arrived on March 11th.

**"Dear Ian Douglas Bishop,**

**Further to our correspondence and your further information, I am hereby sending you copies of the following documents.**

**a) My ID card.**

**b) My International Passport.**

**As you can see, my real name is MR. BANE MALEKE as indicated in my ID.**

**The dead man is Mr. John Cuthbertson but for security reasons, I do not want my real name mentioned in this transaction. My real name is for you only. I want to be referred to as Ruben Chizea and my email sent to my private email address as usual. The reason for concealing such information is also for my own security. I have decided to reveal all this information to you because I have seen your seriousness in this transaction.**

**I believe that you will keep all this information very confidential.**

**I hope that these documents will help you in making a decision about participating fully in this transaction.**

**I am hereby assuring you that you will have no cause to regret your involvement in this transaction. I wish to let you know that the key factor in this transaction is trust and confidentiality.**

**If you need any other document in order to assure yourself that you are doing a genuine transaction, just let me know and I will be ready**

**to make that available to you.**

**On the other hand, if I need any document that will re-assure me that you will not make away with my share of the money, I will demand it from you and I trust that you will oblige me with such a document or documents.**

**I have already forwarded your address to the attorney, who will now go ahead to process the WILL, which will name you as the beneficiary to the estate of Mr. John Cuthbertson.**

**With this WILL processed and notarized in your favor, we shall now employ the services of another attorney to process the letter of probate.**

**This will authorize you as the beneficiary to the WILL, to write to our bank for the transfer of the money to your account.**

**The letter of probate is the legal bedrock of this transaction.**

**Once that has been obtained, it will mean that you can act according to the instructions on the WILL.**

**I assure you that this transaction will only take 10 working days to conclude.**

**I am waiting for your urgent reply via my email, that you have received these documents and we will discuss further.**

**Very truly yours,**

**Bane Maleke"**

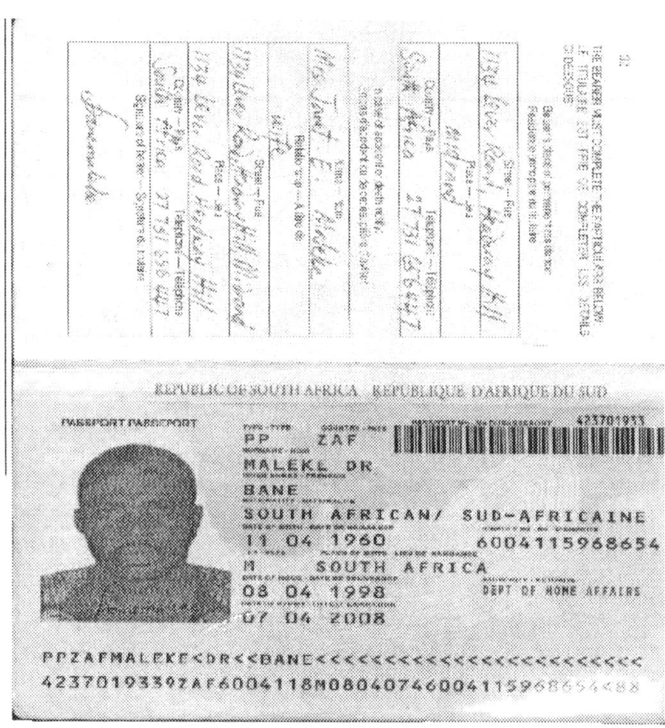


Ruben Chizea had been an alias to protect Bane Maleke at

the bank where he worked.

When Bane felt like he could trust Ian Bishop with this transaction and the forwarding of funds out of the country, he disclosed his true identity. Those inheritance funds were to be shared by all. His bank and the Government of South Africa would have frowned on such an arrangement.

Bane Maleke, according to the Bank I.D. card, that he had sent Ian proved that he was indeed a branch manager of The Development Bank of South Africa. Ian Bishop checked out the bank on the Net. And sure enough, it was a very large established bank. Bane had even sent Ian a copy of his passport . Which showed that he was married and his home address. He seemed to be exactly who he said he was.

Bane had asked Ian Bishop to email a copy of his US Passport and a copy of his driver's license to prove who he was to the bank so they could proceed with the legal paper work at the Development Bank of South Africa.

Ian Bishop figured that as long as he documented everything all the way down the line in this "deal" and shared it with a few very close friends that he would be safe. Ian Bishop was also recording all this information for the newest book that he was also writing.

The spirit within Ian spoke to him:

"D*anger is around the corner. You will have to step out of your cocoon of safety and face the real world of high finance on an international level with characters who are unscrupulous as well as dangerous.*

Ian Bishop realized that eventually he would have to meet with these people face to face.

Who would protect him then?

This new venture was occupying a lot of time and soon Ian Bishop had to return to his theater work in the Ozarks by the middle of March. He already had a phone call come in from the director of the Play, asking him "Are you planning on returning for the new season?" Ian told the director "I wouldn't miss it." He did miss his friends and fellow actors.

View from Ian's living room window on to the Gulf of Mexico

Ian Bishop decided to phone the Development Bank of South Africa. Bane Maleke had given him the number.

"Good Day" was the response that came over the phone to Ian.

"Yes, this is Ian Bishop calling from the United States. Is Bane Maleke at his desk, please. I would like to speak to him."

"Just one moment Sir, I will check." she said

"This is Bane, what may I do for you today, Mr. Bishop?"

"I have been wondering about how you plan on moving my inheritance out of Africa and when this will all come down? Where will I have to go to collect these funds? It has already been almost ten days since I have talked to you and my work will tie up my schedule before long." Ian said, concerned!

"Not to worry, Bishop. We will handle everything shortly and I will keep you informed of every detail. The consignment of money will be shipped out of Africa by diplomatic courier and we have not picked a courier yet. That will determine where the money will be shipped for you."

☙

# CHAPTER 12

Ian Bishop's winter was over. Spring was around the corner. And, as we all know "In the Spring a young man's fancy, turns to love." But Ian was not a young man and his fancy was leading him back to the Ozark Mountain Theater in Eureka. He still had to get his book, "Light and Shadow" published and marketed as well as continue to work on his novel, "Bequeath the Wind". Bishop was pursuing and very much looking forward to receiving a huge inheritance. That in itself required a great deal of thought and maybe even setting up a foundation with a board of directors to handle the monetary funds. He was already thinking about some worthy projects that he would like to finance.

It was now March 20th. He was back at his place of humble abode, Eureka Springs in the Ozarks. Ian's place was snuggled back in the woods, secluded and quiet. A good place to write, paint and read. A great place to relax on his off hours, away from the theater. Maybe, he would be safer if he wasn't secluded back in the woods, but he liked the solitude.

Then all of the sudden he found himself, under attack. Never before had he ever experienced anything like this. It was one of his days off and he was trying to take a nap. Unexpectedly, without warning there was a large BANG against one window in his living room and then again at another window. Ian Bishop awoke with a start, tempted to pull his 38 Magnum out of a drawer and challenge his intruder, when he realized another hard bump against the window beside him.

He jumped around to face the window and saw a young, very upset Cardinal..

Now this was not a Cardinal as meaning a Priest, but a Red Bird! A young male out to protect his domain. He was extremely territorial and didn't like Ian Bishop invading his home in the forest with "Mirrored Windows" that looked like another Cardinal just like himself. This male cardinal continued to attack Ian Bishop's home for eight more days before relenting that he could not scare off this trespasser.

Ian Bishop brought his best friend and fellow confidant into what had become the "South African Connection" on the QT of course. You would never want anyone to know that you were going to come into a very large amount of money.

Leonard and Laura Landerfeld was the couple that had first introduced Ian to their best friend, Cindy. A year had passed since then. And, that friendship was blooming. Even though she was still in Germany, their emails and phone calls were becoming intimate. Email has a way of making you feel like you are right next door. Ian's friendship had also grown with his fellow actors in the Play.

Ian asked "Leonard, would you consider being on my board of directors to handle all this money when it comes in? We will need to be very responsible with these assets and assess the needs, where this money will be spent."

Leonard said "I would be honored." His wife wanted to know if they would get a large expense account to go with the responsibility of overseeing the new foundation.

Laura of course was just kidding. At least Ian thought that she was just having some fun with him.

Then on Thursday, March 23rd. another email arrived from South Africa. . .

**"My Dear Ian Bishop,**

**I am happy to inform you that I have concluded with the WILL. I am hereby sending you a copy of the duly signed and Notarized WILL, which makes you the beneficiary / sole executor to the estate of Mr. John Cuthbertson.**

**With this WILL in your name, all we need now is for the second Attorney to process the letter of probate which will empower you as the beneficiary of the WILL to act according to the instructions in the WILL.**

**I have paid the first Attorney that processed the WILL a total of U.S. $6,700. I have also forwarded the original copy of the WILL to the bank and presented you as a client who needs their service.**

**The bank will contact you regarding your letter of probate. Note that the bank does not know that this is a deal. So do not discuss the other aspect of the transaction with them.**

**If the bank calls you, you may tell them to send you an email or fax message to avoid talking to them so that they may not ask you any question, which you cannot conveniently answer."**

PAGE # 1 OF WILL:

# THIS IS THE LAST WILL AND TESTAMENT OF MR. JOHN CUTHBERTSON, A CONTRACTOR/BUSINESSMAN OF No. 84 NORTH STREET, SANDTON JOHANNESBURG, SOUTH AFRICA.

I hereby revoke all previous testamentary dispositions made by me. I hereby appoint my Close-Friend **JAN DOUGLAS BISH** of **SHEPHEREDS INN, EUREKA SPRINGS ARKANSAS 72632 U.S.A** to be the sole executor/trustee and next of kin of this my will.

1. I declare that I made a deposit in cash in the sum of **$25,600,000 (Twenty Five Million, Six Hundred Thousand United States dollars)** with Development Bank of Southern Africa (DBSA) 1258 Lever Road, Headway Hill Midrand, 1685 South Africa.

I give the benefit of my time deposit Account in the sum of **25,600,000 (Twenty Five Million, Six Hundred Thousand United States dollars)** to my Close-Friend by name **JAN DOUGLAS BISH** absolutely.

2. I direct that my family home at No. 84 North Street, Sandston Johannesburg, South Africa be sold and the proceeds be donated to **Pacelli School for the Blind** in Johannesburg, South Africa absolutely.

3. I direct that all my cars, and personal effects be sold and the proceeds be donated by my executor to the **Pacelli School for the Blind** in Johannesburg, South Africa.

4. I forgive and release completely all debts whether secured or not which may be owning me at the date of my death by any person (but not by any body corporate, Government department, Local authority, firm or association of persons).

5. I declare that my inheritance is free from any indebtedness to any party, whether individual persons or body corporate, Government Department, local authority, firm or association of persons and therefore, upon acceptance, my heir will be fully entitled to benefit from the above mentioned assets in their entirety, with no legal necessity to correspond any funds to any third party.

**IN WITNESS WHERE OF** I the said **MR. JONH CUTHBERTSON** has put my hand and seal

this ....13th.... Day of ....January.... 2000

**SIGNED and SEALED** by the said **John Cuthbertson**
**AS FOR HIS LAST WILL** in the presence
Of us two who at his request in his
Presence and in the presence of each other
Have subscribed their names as witnesses.

CERTIFIED TRUE COPY

**MR. JOHN CUTHBERTSON**

PAGE # 2 OF WILL:

**Witness**

Name: Slim George

Address: TEXACO OVERSEAS

Signature: S.G.

Occupation: ENGINEER

**Witness**

Name: Richard Gross

Address: Gulf Oil

Signature: RGross

Occupation: Chemical Engineer

**BEFORE ME**

FREDRICK MGBUTU

Notary Public, Republic of South Africa

DECLARED AT THE NOTARY PUBLIC OFFICE

This 14th day of January 2000

**"My dear friend, this stage of the transaction is very important and you have to handle it with all carefulness.**

**It's all in your hands now. Remember to still keep the transaction confidential.**

**The processing of the letter of probate will take about 2 days after your conversation with the attorney. At this juncture, you will have to write a letter of instruction to the bank requesting for the transfer of the inheritance to your bank.**

**The letter should be written as below:**

The Regional manager,
Development Bank of Southern Africa.
258 Leter Road, Head Hill
Midrand, 1685
South Africa

Dear Sir,

Request for a Transfer of the sum of US $25,600,000.00 being payment of my inheritance. Also this letter is my authorization to close this account.

I humbly wish to apply for the transfer of my inheritance in the sum above lying in account number 0444012226 in your bank. My account details are as stated below.

I have attached a herein a copy of the WILL which stipulates my role in the estate of Mr. John Cuthbertson and my beneficiary status and also a copy of my International passport and Drivers License. My attorney is already processing the letter of probate and it will be ready soon.

I will therefore ask that you commence the necessary transfer procedures pending the receipt of my letter of probate, which I will send to you in the next few days. I am looking forward to your response.

Thank you.

Signed, Yours faithfully,

**This letter should be typed and signed with your address on top left side of the paper and sent to my email for necessary action. Please do this urgently and call me as soon you send the fax message.**

**Thanks. Very truly yours, Mr. Bane Maleke."**

"Can you possibly imagine what it looks like and how you would feel to see your name on an official document along with the figure of twenty five million dollars? Why It is almost enough to take your breath away." Ian just sat there staring at this email. He figured at this point that the money had to be real. If it was a scam they would have been asking for money. At the same time, Ian figured if it was a scam, it was Bane Maleke scamming the South African Government and that he, himself was innocent of any wrong doing.

"Okay," Ian told himself, "Don't get carried away. Let's not put the cart before the horse." That's an old Texas saying.

He read the email again. To Ian, it looked like he had to hire an attorney at his end and have his attorney to draw up a "Letter of Probate" and he had to make up a letter and send it to the Development Bank of South Africa. "Simple enough, I can do that."

He told himself as he called an attorney, "This is a BREEZE."

"Hello" Ian said "This is Mr. Bishop, I would like to make

an appointment with one of your attorneys. I understand that probate issues are your specialty?"

The secretary on the other end of the line answer "Yes, it is. Just a minute and I will check our calendar to see what dates we have open. . . .How 'bout next Thursday, at eleven am. Would that work out for you?"

"That's fine with me. I will see you then. Thanks." He figured that he should talk to an attorney about this thing anyway. Ian was interested in protecting himself.

Ian began working on the letter to the bank for the transfer of funds. "Let me see." Ian spoke to himself often, as he reread the letter to get the instructions correct. . . *"The processing of the letter of probate will take about 2 days after your conversation with the attorney. At this juncture, you will have to write a letter of instruction to the bank requesting for the transfer of the inheritance to your bank."*

Ian figured that the appointment with his attorney was next Thursday, March 30th. It would take about a week to mail the letter of probate to the Development Bank of South Africa. So this whole thing could be taken care of before the middle of April. Ian Bishop had further checked out the bank in South Africa and found them to be a very reputable organization.

Ian did not have a fax machine so he emailed Bane, a copy of the letter, he had mailed to Development Bank. He explained to Bane Maleke that he did not have a fax machine.

On Friday, March 24th.

Ian received a phone call from Bane. "I am very upset with you. You need to closely follow my instructions in this deal. You mailed the letter of transfer to my bank, but I need to have this in my possession now, not a week from now.

Also you hired your own attorney to draw up the letter of probate and he has no jurisdiction over here. We have to take care of that here at this bank."

Ian explained "I am sorry, I thought that I was suppose to send a signed copy to the bank, and it sounded like you wanted me to hire an attorney at this end."

On Monday, Ian Bishop's attorney called, "There is no such thing as a "letter of probate" in this country. A Will is probated, which is to say; verified that it is legally certified as genuine."

Ian told him 'I misunderstood that I needed to probate a Will in my name. The South African Bank told me that their attorney will do that." And Bishop canceled his up coming appointment while he had the attorney on the phone.

It was now, Saturday, March 25th. Another email from

South Africa arrived in Ian's Computer;

**"Dear Ian Bishop,**

**Thanks for your mail and your willingness to assist me with this transaction. What I want you to do is to re-write the letter of transfer I sent to you, sign it with your signature and scan it.**

**Send it via email attachment to me. I need to put all this information in your file so that approvals can be given for payment.**

**I have received a copy of your U.S. Passport and driver's license. I would need you to also send full details of your bank information, where you want the money to be sent.**

**We would need the following:**

**A] Bank Name**

**B] Account Name**

**C] Account number**

**D] Bank Address and any other information.**

**However, I would not want you to send documents to me from public fax or call me from public phones. I will do the phone calls and please do not send any document to my bank again.**

**My brother, you know what we are doing is a deal so please keep it very confidential and please no third party should know about it. I do not want any blackmail.**

**Regards,**

**Bane Maleke."**

Ian Bishop rewrote the letter with all the information that was needed, signed it and shot it with his digital camera so he could send it by email to Bane Maleke at the bank in South Africa.

It was now Monday, March 27th. And the days just seemed to be dragging on. Ian wanted to be done with this, but he realized that he has always been impatient, so he told himself "Just take one day at a time. Do what you can do, and don't worry about the rest. Everything is going to be fine. I am a happy man."

Ian Bishop's phone rang to snap him out of his reverie. It was Cindy calling from Germany. That was a welcome relief.

"H e l l o !" Ian said to her as soon as he recognized her voice. Cindy and Ian had become very good friends with all the emails and phone calls they had exchanged over the past year. They had even exchanged some intimate details about their lives. She was a very interesting person. Maybe those thoughts just blew in like a spring breeze, with April just around the corner.

Cindy was very concerned about Ian's safety.

She had no idea what the South African Banker was involved with.

Cindy said "Ian, what if Bane Maleke is involved in money laundering, or drugs or maybe even something even more dangerous?"

"Don't worry Sweetie, I am a big boy, and I know how to take care of myself. Don't worry about me." This was a macho thing to Bishop. He was intent on playing this game all the way through to the end. No matter which way the wind was to blow.

Cindy would continue to email and phone from Germany and every now and then Ian would also get a sweet email from his friend, Jean in San Francisco.

The Play was now in rehearsal and there were also staff meetings that had to be attended at the theater, as well as orientations. There were classes teaching new cast members where they needed to be, and when, on stage, this responsibility also fell partially on Bishop's shoulders. He was good at what he did. The director was always asking him to do things like that.

Ian's birthday was also just around the corner, March 28th. There was three other people in the cast that all had their birthday on the same day, so they decided to celebrate their birthdays together at a nice restaurant in town on that evening. Ian was looking forward to some fun with his friends.

The inheritance thing was getting kind of heavy, and he needed a reprieve. Ian had to think about other things. That was difficult when $ 25,600,000. USD was hanging over his head.

Ian was wondering once more about how he was going to manage a large sum of money. "What would the taxes be? How much would be left", once he shared it with the banker in South Africa, and everyone else that seemed to have their hands out for a payoff ?

Ian thought, "I am retired. This sounds like a full time job to me. I will have to allocate some of this responsibility to people whom I trust, like Leonard and Laura."

Ian Bishop phoned his good friend and fellow actor, Leonard.

"Leonard, I think we should definitely form a foundation with these funds and figure out the best way to distribute the money to worthy projects. I was serious when I asked you to be on my Board of Directors. Since the man's name was John Cuthbertson who left me the millions, I think we should call it, The J.C. Foundation. What do you think?"

"The J.C. Foundation sounds good to me. I think you should draw up a logo and contact an attorney and a C.P.A. to set this thing up." Leonard said. "Laura wants to know what Cindy thinks about all of this?"

"Leonard, just tell her that Cindy is for, what ever makes me happy. Actually, she is very apprehensive, but there is no need to worry Laura about that."

"Okay, Chairman of the Board, my man! I will see you in the Play tonight." Leonard said,

"Later !"

&

# CHAPTER 13

Ian Bishop received another email from out of Africa.

**"Dear Ian Bishop,**

**Thanks for your mail. I would want to know when you would be able to travel between now and next week, Friday. Once the LETTER OF PROBATE is received in your name and the final approvals are given, I would move the funds through diplomatic means to the United Kingdom where you will collect and sign for the funds. Please, this information is very important for this transaction.**

**Regards, Bane Maleke."**

Ian wrote back to Bane Maleke;

**"I will be able to take a trip to London next Friday. My time is your time until April 15$^{th}$."**

Ian Bishop had a contractual agreement with the production company in Eureka and had to be finished with all this, so he could get on with his life and concentrate on the Play for the new upcoming season. He also figured that he wanted to be fresh and alert in order to face a big deal like this wind fall of money, so he had planed to get to London a few days early so he could get over the jet lag.

As long as he was going to make a trip to London. He might as well also enjoy being there in the spring time and see some sights. "After all, this is your day, Birthday Boy!"It was now March 28th. And this email was waiting for Ian when he got up that morning.

**"Dear Bishop,**

**Thanks for your mail and your assistance. I am still a waiting the Letter Of Probate from the bank attorney. As soon as I have it, I will forward a copy to you via email attachment.**

**Once I have this in my possession, approval for the transfer will be given. Please prepare your mind for next week.**

**Regards, Bane Maleke"**

Ian Bishop had a wonderful birthday party with his friends that night.

The restaurant brought three birthday cakes to our table. This was not the kind of place that sang the birthday song. This was a subdued, quiet, reserved restaurant.

Ian suggested, "I don't think they are going to sing Happy Birthday to us. Perhaps we should sing it to ourselves?"

Matt and Betty, the other birthday people said "I agree. You first, Ian."

So Ian started and the rest joined in as the whole restaurant looked on. . . . "Happy birthday to us, Happy birthday to us!"

You know the rest of that song. They all said "Of course Ian was the ring leader".

"I usually am." Ian added.

On April 2nd. There was another email from Bane, the banker from South Africa.

**"Hi Bishop,**

**How are you today? Sorry I have not been able to contact you for some days now, I was out of town for some official business. Hopefully the LETTER OF PROBATE will be out for the close of work tomorrow.**

**I will keep you informed about every step I make.**

**Regards, Bane Maleke"**

Ian felt like he was in the midst of a daily "Soap Opera", like "The Daze of our Lives". His days were becoming hectic. Preparing for the new theater season, taking care of his art business and writing books was more than a full time job.

Then, there was his email friends to write. Keeping up with the banker in South Africa was no easy task because Bishop knew that he had to stay a couple of moves ahead or he could end up loosing more than just a chess game this time.

Time was getting close for the trip to London to pick up the consignment of funds, a bequeathal of $25,600,000.00.

That's enough circles to make your head spin. Especially when you see your name right beside a figure like that. "Unbelievable!"

Wednesday, April 5, another email from Development Bank of South Africa.

At last, the long awaited "Letter of Probate". The final approval and legal probate to authorize payment to Ian Bishop.

**IN THE HIGH COURT OF PRETORIA, REPUBLIC OF SOUTH AFRICA**

**PROBATE REGISTRY**

**<u>LETTER OF PROBATE</u>**

**<u>(Where there is Will)</u>**

**Probate** is hereby granted to **JAN DOUGLAS BISH** of P. O. BOX 986, **BERRYVILLE, AR. 72616 USA** as Beneficiary/Executor/Trustee in the Last Will of **MR. JOHN CUTHBERTSON** dated the 13th day of January, 2000 deceased of No. 84 North Street, Sandston Johannesburg, South Africa and who has accepted to act, and accordingly is hereby given power by this letter of Probate to carry out, execute and exercise all powers, acts, functions and duties contained in the said Will of **MR. JOHN CUTHBERTSON** deceased who died in an air crash on the 31st day of January, 2000 particularly as it concerns the following:-

(i) The sum of US$25,600,000 (Twenty Five Million, Six Hundred Thousand Dollars)plus Interest in Account No. 0444012226 DBSA (Development Bank of Southern Africa), 1258 Lever Road, HeadWay Hill Midrand, South Africa.

(ii) Property lying and situate at No. 84 North Street, Sandton, Johannesburg, South Africa.

This letter is issued in accordance with the provisions of the Administration of Estates Law of South Africa, 1994 as amended in 1999.

Dated this 5th day of APRIL 2006

F.C BEKO
Probate Registrar

Mark Hans & Co.
Notary Public, Republic of South Africa

**"My Dear Ian,**

**I am happy to inform you that the WILL has been PROBATED in your name. The final verification on the amount has been done also today.**

**Please, I would want you to start making arrangements to travel next week.**

**Once the funds are moved I will let you know.**

**Bane"**

Friday, April 7th. An email arrived from Bane Maleke to Ian Bishop . . . . .

**"My Dear Friend,**

**Greetings to you and your family. I am very happy with the way and manner you are handling this transaction. At the same time, I want to assure you that everything is under control.**

**Upon the final approval from the Development Bank of South Africa(DBSA), I quickly commenced the processes of the Discount of the cash and I am happy to inform you that it has been completed and the funds are being moved to London.**

**The funds are being transported by diplomatic courier and they are scheduled to arrive in London by Wednesday, the 12th of April.**

**The name of the person you will contact in London is MR. JOHN TEGI. He is the Administrative Head in the affiliate organization in London. His telephone number is 44 207 060 0057. You should therefore call this gentleman by tomorrow morning, London time. The purpose of**

**the call is to confirm that the consignments have arrived safely and to confirm to him your date of arrival for the delivery of the consignment and deposit in the bank. You should also ask him the convenient hotel to stay.**

**This process of transport of cash money is very classified and it is only accorded to GOLD CARD members of the ADB organization and this GOLD CARD members includes Heads of States in Africa, Ministers and very top Government officials.**

**Through my contact in the organization, I have fronted you as a GOLD CARD member.**

**You should therefore present yourself as a Gold Card member. Your pass code is: KK11WT.**

**You must mention this code to MR. JOHN TEGI, when you call him before he can give you any information regarding the consignments.**

**And then you inform him that you are expecting some consignments from South Africa and that you wish to confirm if they have arrived.**

**You must not let MR. JOHN TEGI know that you are NOT a Gold card member.**

**Upon your arrival in London, and you are asked for the GOLD CARD, just quote the pass code and tell them that you forgot the card at home."**

GOVERNMENT FREIGHT AGENCY
(Federal Government Diplomatic Baggage Carriers)

NON-NEGOTIABLE

Shipper

Reference No: BS/CP/RSA04 Airway Bill No: 3764060796

**AIRWAY BILL**

ADB ORGANISATION
AFRICA

RECEIVED in apparent external good order and condition except as otherwise noted the total number of packages or units enumerated below (*) for shipment from the place of Receipt to the place of Delivery subject to the terms hereof. One of the original Airway bill must be surrendered duly endorsed in exchange for the Goods of Delivery Order unless otherwise provided herein.

In accepting this Airway bill the Merchant expressly accepts and agrees to all its terms whether printed, stamped or written or otherwise incorporated, notwithstanding the non-signing of this Airway bill by the Merchant.

IN WITNESS whereof the number of original Airway Bill stated below have been signed, one of which being accomplished, the other (s) to be void.

(Terms of Airway Bill continued on the back here of)

Shipper's Declared Value .......... US$ subject to clause 8 (2) overleaf.
If no value declared, liability limits applies as per clause 5 (2) (C), or 29 as applicable

Consignee

JOHN TEGI
LONDON, UNITED KINGDOM
TEL: 44 207 060 0057

Notify Party
JAN DOUGLAS BISH
P O BOX 986, BERRYVILLE
AR 72616, USA.
TEL: 479 981 1567

| Pre-carriage by | Place of receipt PRETORIA |
|---|---|
| Government Freight Agency DIPLOMATIC BAGGAGE CARRIERS | Port Loading PRETORIA |
| Port of discharge London, UK | Place of delivery London, UK |

Also Notify (For Merchant's reference only)

Final destination for the Merchant's reference

| Transaction/Diplomatic Code | No. of baggages | Description of goods | Gross Weight | |
|---|---|---|---|---|
| FSA/FMV- FGN 045/WR-KD/200 | TWO (2) | FREIGHT PREPAID - PRECIOUS STONES | 11563 | |

Total number of Containers or other Packages of Units received by the Carrier (in words) TWO BAGGAGES.

| Code | Tariff Item | Basis | Freighted as | Curr | Rate | Per | prepaid | Balance |
|---|---|---|---|---|---|---|---|---|
| | | | | | | | £ 22,700 | 68,500 |

AS ARRANGED

| No of Originals | Place and date of Airway Bill issue | Total Freight charge £ 29,300 | £ 22,700 | 68,500 |
|---|---|---|---|---|
| TWO | PRETORIA April 07, 2008 | | | |

Government Freight Agency

Date: April 07, 2008

COPY

Signature: GOVERNMENT FREIGHT AGENCY

CF 0747

Government Freight Agency
By ____________
As Agents.

Bane continued with his email to Bishop;

**"Like I already explained to you, the cost of**

**moving this consignment is £6,500 and you are required to come with it on your arrival to London.**

**After the payment, the consignment will be released from the vault and once delivery of the consignment has taken place, you will be accompanied by MR. JOHN TEGI to the bank for opening of account and lodgments of the funds into the account you shall open in London.**

**Upon the completion of this process, you will then issue instructions for the bank to wire to your bank in any part of the world.**

**Please take note of all these instructions. If you have any question, please do not hesitate to contact me.**

**Very truly yours,**

**Mr. Bane Maleke."**

The instructions were a bit complicated, but should not be any problem. All you had to tell Ian Bishop was that the funds were there and he would be there, sign for the funds and be on his way.

Ian liked to handle things the easy way. Keep it simple!

He had handled business on an international scale before, so the task was not overwhelming for him. He was also looking forward to his trip to London in the spring. The last time Ian spent anytime there was in the fall and it was raining and cold.

# CHAPTER 14

Mike Crowe of the Government Freight Agency had introduced James Jimytyme to Bane Maleke and collected the front money of 22,700 British Pounds Sterling for the delivery of the consignment to London, U.K.. Mike went his own way and James picked up the consignment from Bane Maleke at the Development Bank of South Africa located in the village of Midrand on April 7$^{th}$., ten am.

All the arrangements had been made for a safe journey. James was ready to climb into the front passenger seat of the armored vehicle, that was parked curbside, next to the bank.

"Excuse me Sir, I am Alto Maleke, Bane's brother and head of security for Development Bank of South Africa. I just want you to know that we are here to assist you with any problems that might arise while you are in South Africa."

"That is most kind of you, I am sure, but we have rather high security already arranged and in place for a shipment of this nature."

"I am sure you do, however you will notice our vehicles along your route to the airport in Johannesburg. I just wanted to make you aware of our presence and also let you know that there are no facilities between here and Johannesburg, so midway on your route we have arranged for a rest stop for you and your team of men. You will see a large DBSA truck parked next to a motor home that also says DBSA on the side.

There will be high security all around the perimeter. You and your men, and our shipment will be safe, if you care to take a break and have something cool to drink. Then, you can continue your journey fresh and renewed. I know how grueling high security trips can be. I have been there done that."

"Well, thank you very much. My men and I will take advantage of your hospitality. Show me your position on this map."

Alto said, "Right here", as he pointed to a small intersection half way to Johannesburg.

James waved "Bye" to Alto as Alto headed off to his car.

After Alto got in his car and started up the air conditioning, he got on his two way radio. "We are all set. I will check the line."

Alto headed on down the street ahead of the GFA armored vehicle. He pulled out way ahead of them and as he had planned, he saw the trucks with DBSA printed on their side, parked every ten miles along the route. Each truck had someone sitting in the driver's side in uniform that waved a friendly "Hello".

As Alto drove down the road he got on his radio and said "Lookin' good guys. Remember as soon as GFA drives past you fall in line behind." As he was driving down the road Alto was thinking about his brother, Bane. Bane thought he was just too good to ever get caught.

Alto was even remembering when Bane had told him, "I feel like I have lost control of this situation." Alto was going to save all their skins. He would stop his money from leaving Africa, share a portion of it with his friend over at the Department of Finance, and they would all be better off. He resented the fact that Bane was gambling with his money, as well as the other guys in this organization.

Driving up to the main check point, Alto saw his men in smart uniforms with automatic weapons, at the ready, standing around the bank trucks and the new motor home. Alto thought, “That ought to make the Government Freight Agency feel very comfortable.”

Alto Maleke parked his car around behind the motor home, got himself a nice cool drink and came around to greet his men and their soon to arrive, guests.

“Gentlemen, you look sharp. Our guests will be arriving shortly. When they pull up, be at the ready. They have two men in the back and one main man in the front with a driver. After they drive up, station four men at the rear of their vehicle and stand at attention with your rifles in the up position. The rest of you, stay at your present positions, but make sure that you will have a good line of fire after the men get out of the front.”

“Sir, when will we take out the men in the back?”

“As soon as they step out and head for the motor home. Do not put any holes in my new motor home!” Alto demanded, as an after thought. “I will drop my glass as the signal.”

A couple of minutes later the armored truck pulled in and parked right where Alto had figured they would. The men got out of the front and looked around, satisfied that the perimeter had been protected. They saw Alto with a cool drink. Boy, did that look good.

Alto had waved the two men forward of the truck with his cool drink held in the air.

James got on his radio and summoned his men. “It’s okay men. Come on out.”

WR and KD stepped out, stretched and said "That was a rough, dusty ride." They turned to go toward the motor home, the guns blazed as Alto dropped his glass, which was the prearranged signal. That was the last words they would ever say.

At the same moment the driver and James Jimytyme were cut down where they stood in front of their truck.

"Well, done men. They didn't even have a chance to go for their weapons. Take the lock boxes out of the armored vehicle and put them in the number one truck, drive the armored truck up into the back of truck number two. Clean up this mess like it never happened."

Alto barely got those words out of his mouth when he noticed out of his peripheral vision, three attack helicopters coming in fast. As, he was running for his car he saw GFA on the side of the copters. He arrived at his car and jumped in just in time to see his new motor home go up in flames. The concussion made his car jump sideways and blew out his back windows as he sped away.

It was like all Hell broke loose at the same time.

As Alto rushed away from the scene, he remembered the words of James Jimytyme; "We have rather high security already arranged and in place for a shipment of this nature." He had never expected judgment and fire raining down from the sky.

The three Government Freight Agency Attack Copters landed on site after firing at everything that moved. They decide to let the old car go. It probably would not go far after that concussion blast. The Agency men found the armored vehicle still in good shape. The DBSA trucks were set on fire, that is the ones that had not already been blasted. The Agency men loaded their dead into one of the copters and the men from that copter took their place with the armored vehicle.

They looked at the consignment, opened it up and checked the lock boxes against the Airway bill, and found out that this was not "PRECIOUS STONES" but cash money U.S. currency, and a lot of it. They sealed the lock boxes again and vowed they would get to the bottom of this and tell John Tegi in London that Bane Maleke had lied about the shipment from Development Bank of South Africa. There would be a price to pay. You don't mess around with Agency men and get away with it. They continued on their way to the airport in Johannesburg, just like nothing had happened. All in a days work.

This was all in a days work for these paid mercenaries, but they had missed the scheduled flight out of South Africa to London. They would now have to make other arrangements and the shipment would be late arriving in London.

❧

# CHAPTER 15

This was the day that Ian was dreading. It had been four months, from the beginning of this deal and they are finally asking him for money.

"Bane Maleke had asked him for money!"

"But then again, why wouldn't he? Bane had already told me about the money that he had personally spent on this project. Wasn't it only fair, for me to share some of this expense. I was going to inherit a lot of money. I could afford that. I had the bill from the Diplomatic Courier in my hands and I could clearly see that there was a balance due on the other end, before shipment would be released."

Ian Bishop went to his bank the next day, Saturday April 8th. and withdrew $12,000. USD for his up coming trip. He was surprised to find out that 6,500. Pounds Sterling was the equivalent of $10,000.00 United States Dollars. "Still, when you come to think about it, pretty cheap, when you will come out with twenty five million dollars."

Also, on Saturday, April 8th. Ian receives this email from Cindy (the school teacher in Germany) She was on Spring Break and trying to figure out how she and Ian could spend some time together.

Ian also wanted to spend some time with Cindy in Germany. He longed to spend some time on German soil.

Cindy wrote:

**"See if you can get to somewhere and call me by Monday, April tenth, before I leave Germany. I will fly into Rome Airport, arriving at 21:40 on the tenth. I fly out of Rome on Wednesday the 12th at six-fifty am to Venice, Treviso airport.**

**My flight is out of Venice, Treviso at 17:15 to Frankfurt Hahn on Sunday, April 16th. I sure hope that I will be able to see you while you are in Europe.**

**Love, Cindy"**

Cindy continued on with her email giving Ian, the hotel names and dates along with their phone numbers and email addresses.

Right away Ian got on the internet and lined up his round trip flight to London on British Airways. He had to find out where he was going to be and when. He had to get up at three on Monday morning to call John Tegi at the beginning of his London work day for an appointment to pick up the consignment of cash. Ian also had to get back to Cindy and let her know what his schedule was going to be before she left Frankfurt on her Spring Break to Venice, Italy.

AT one-thirty Monday morning Ian was woke out of a sound sleep. RING, RING, RING !

It was the banker from South Africa. "Mr. Bishop, did you make an appointment with John Tegi yet?"

Ian, just barely awake, "No, I had my alarm set for three am to call him. I am to fly out of Arkansas this afternoon for London."

Maleke said "Make sure that you do call him and pay very

close attention to details and do exactly what he tells you to do, so we will be able to complete our deal."

After that phone conversation, there was no way for Ian Bishop to get back to sleep so he made himself a hot cup of tea and tried to organize his thinking.

It was now two-thirty am and he thought he would try Mr Tegi's number in London. All Ian heard was a recording that said, "The number you have dialed is for sale, please phone such and such a number for inquiries." British English at times is very hard to understand, especially at two-thirty in the morning.

This really concerned Ian so he called South Africa back and said "Mr. Maleke, I just tried Tegi's number in London and got a recording." He said "Try it again, maybe you dialed a wrong digit."

"Actually" Ian said "That could be a possibility, I had to dial so many numbers to get through internationally using my calling card."

Ian Bishop phoned John Tegi at three am Central time which was nine am in London.

"Mr. John Tegi, please, Yes, well I am Ian Douglas Bishop. I am calling to confirm that there has been a shipment sent to me from South Africa. My Gold Card membership number is KK11WT."

"Just a moment Mr. Bishop. I will check on your Gold Card Membership and be right back with you."

"Yes I have a record that shows that there was a consignment that left South Africa for London. It has your name on it. That shipment is suppose to arrive on Wednesday, April 12th.

There will be a balance of 6,500. Pounds Sterling to be paid so they will release the shipment."

Ian said "Thank you very much, South Africa just told me that there would be a balance due on the shipping fees. I will be arriving in London, at ten am on Tuesday, April 11th. On flight number 298 from Chicago to Heathrow." Bishop was willing to pay the shipping fees in order to receive a consignment worth Twenty Five Million Dollars.

Then, John Tegi said. "Mr. Bishop you will also be required to pay my administrative fees as well as the balance due on your shipment."

Ian said "That should be no problem." Not wanting to ruin the whole deal.

After Ian had talked to the London connection, a call came in from South Africa.

Bane wanted to know what transpired. "Well Bane, I made contact with Tegi. In London and gave him my flight information."

He told me that I had to be very careful to follow the complete protocol and all his instructions."

Bane responded to that by saying "Did you make an appointment with him to pick up the consignment?"

"Well, no, but I figured that I could do that as soon as I arrived in London."

Bane said "You should call him back and make the appointment now."

So Ian got on the phone again to call London. . . . .RING, RING, RING. No Answer.

"That's strange Ian thought. "It had to be at least eleven am in London and the security company should be open." It was now five am Central Time in the U.S. and eleven am in London.

Ian tried once more, . . . "Hello ?", "Yes !, This is Ian Bishop again. I need to go ahead and set up an appointment with you either for Tuesday afternoon, the $11^{th}$. or Wednesday, April $12^{th}$. In order to pick up my consignment."

Tegi said "We better wait until we know that the consignment has arrived".

Ian said "Fine, I will phone you as soon as I land in London. I will be staying at the Hotel 82 on Gloucester Place. A block off Baker Street, downtown London."

On the other end of the line there was a pause, "Now, Mr. Bishop, you know that you are not following protocol."

"I instructed you to fly into London, and then phone us.

Make sure that no one knows of our business together. This is for your safety as well as ours. When you are dealing with large sums of money and the movement of these funds, it can be very dangerous.

We will meet you, arrange for your hotel and supply transportation to the hotel. We will take care of your ground connections and appointments. All you have to do is show up with the proper documentation and the balance that is due on the cost of handling these funds for you. The holding company will want their money before they release the consignment. Do you understand?"

Ian replied "Understood." But, he did not like the man's tone on the other end of the line, before he hung up.

Ian was accustomed to being in charge and did not like being told what he needed to do. Besides that, Ian always liked to arrange where he would be staying. He liked the convenience of staying somewhere that had their own restaurant and he liked being right in the heart of things. Bishop also wanted a hotel that offered free WiFi Internet, so he could stay in contact with his friends.

Bishop was used to taking care of financial matters and already understood proper protocol. Ian knew the proper way to take care of his business matters in a legal and organized way.

If things did not match his way of doing things, which had served him well, it always sent up red flags.

Bishop knew that this was a high stakes game they were playing and when you lived in a realm of high finance the rules changed accordingly, so he decided that he would go with their plan, but only up to a point.

After all, maybe the London connection was a man just like himself, that had a need to be "in-charge". Maybe, there was a personality clash here.

*There was a strong feeling of "Impending danger!" That inner voice continued to talk to Ian, just enough to keep him on his toes.*

"Boy did that business shoot a good night's sleep" he thought to himself. Ian was tired but had no time to go back to bed and too keyed up to be able to sleep anyway. He was going to leave from Northwest Arkansas Regional Airport, XNA to ORD, Chicago at five pm on Monday, April 10.

Ian Bishop was no stranger to XNA. He had even waited on more than a couple of occasions for Air Force One to take off before the Secret Service would allow him on the airport grounds, back in the Clinton Daze.

Ian also knew that this was going to be a very hard trip.

He was going to be prepared for anything ! When you go big game hunting you go "loaded for bear". When you play a high stakes chess game, you better be ready for what ever move they throw at you. You better think fast on your feet and know a counter move. This might very well be the most perilous game he had ever played.

It was back on the phone to the banker in South Africa.

"Bane, this is Ian Bishop again, I forgot to mention that the London Connection wants another 5,000. Pounds for administrative fees besides the balance due on the diplomatic courier charges, and I don't have that kind of money to spend. If you want to split this money with me, you will have to come up with that front money."

Bane Maleke said "I will sell some family property to a friend of mine and wire the money to London."

Ian said "That ought to work."

The following message was waiting for Bishop on his computer, from London.

**"Dear Mr. Douglas Bishop,**

**Following our telephone conversation today, I wish to reconfirm to you that your appointment date for delivery of the consignment shall be on 18th day of April.**

**Upon your arrival to London, we shall send our protocol officer to pick you up from the airport and take you to the hotel that shall be reserved for you.**

**Like I explained to you on the phone, you will be required to pay the total sum of 11, 500 pounds sterling. That being payment for freight charges of 6,500 pounds and 5,000 pounds for the administrative charges."**

**"The sum of 6,500 pounds which is equivalent of US $11,333.65 shall be paid to our offshore agency account below:**

SOCIETE GENERALE BANK.

ST. DENIS, FRANCE.

SWIFT CODE: SOGEFRPP

IBAN: FR7630003040250002030206013

ACCOUNT NAME: SOXIMEX LTD.

ADDRESS: 31, RUE PLEYEL. ST. DENIS. 93200

BENEFICIARY: ADB.

**Upon the payment of the sum, please send the receipt of payment by email attachment or to our fax number 44 207 060 0189.**

**The sum of 5,000 pounds should be with you in cash and you will pay it upon your arrival in our office before the consignment will be delivered to you. Our organization will assist you in opening an account in the United Kingdom where the money will be deposited for final transfer to your country.**

**Please, in virtue of the foregoing, I would advice you to cancel your reservation to travel today pending your accomplishment of the required items mentioned above, as a Gold card Member.**

**Please acknowledge receipt of this email.**

**Thank you. Mr. John Tegi"**

Was this whole thing turning really complicated or was Ian just so tired he could not think straight? There was no way that he was going to cancel his reservations now, at the last minute.

Ian was so tired, he had no concept of time anymore. He was tempted to just turn this whole deal over to Scotland Yard to straighten out. At the same time, Ian really didn't want to get involved with Scotland Yard and get tied down with details and depositions and loose his freedom of movement to leave the country. He did after all want to go over to Germany and spend time with Cindy as well as take care of the inheritance business in London.

Monday, April 10 in an email to South Africa, Ian wrote:

**"Dear Bane,**

**Well, I didn't get any sleep last night.**

**The next time you transfer money, I would think that you should go through a discreet, established business place. As you know, banks can be very discreet, and I would trust that kind of transaction.**

**As I told you before, I am not a greedy man.**

**Neither am I a rich man. I will not lay out, U.S. $20,000.00 to bring about a deal like this, even if I could afford it.**

**I am still going on my trip to London. If you want this deal to go through, you figure out how to make it happen. I have inherited money before but never had to go through "Cloak and Dagger" things to get it, or had to lay out "front money".**

**This is turning out to be a bequeathal of the wind.**

**Too many words, not enough action.**

**If our deal is 'legal, and true' then work it out where I can go in and pick up the money. I will cover the 5,000 Pounds for "Handling".**

**You can tell John that you are representing me, in wiring the other funds.**

**You will also have to get back in touch with me on email. I will continue to be on line, while I travel.**

**My phone is only good in the U.S. and I am leaving at eleven am. That's little more than five hours from now."**

REPLY FROM SOUTH AFRICA on Monday, APRIL 10:

**"Dear Bishop,**

**Thanks for your mail and also your willingness**

**to assist me with this transaction.**

**I am also very sorry for keeping you awake t five am. I want you to know that this is not bank to bank transaction. You know that thi transaction is "a deal" and we have to cover up all the tracks. This is why I decided that the money be moved out via diplomatic courier in order to avoid any trace to you or me in the near future.**

**My dear friend, it is very important that you understand that this transaction is built on trust and without that trust, we cannot achieve success.**

**It is therefore very disheartening for you to make statements which shows that you do not trust the transaction.**

**I have constantly made it clear to you, there will be expenses in this transaction both from my part and your part. I have had quite a lot of expense from the beginning of this transaction to date and I have constantly given you information on all my expenses."**

**"Even in the Airway bill attached, I have also paid a part payment of 22,700 pounds sterling for the courier of the baggage, leaving a balance of 6,500 pounds which is what is being demanded by the organization.**

**I have exhausted my resources in this transaction**

**and I need your assistance as my partner. I will therefore plead with you to make sure that you take care of this transaction as a partner.**

**Note that this ADB organization believes that you are a gold card member and you know the rules.**

**Please do not give them any reason to doubt your membership.**

**Please make sure that you abide by their instructions.**

**You must note that the consignment was shipped as precious stones, and as such only Mr. John Tegi is aware at this point, the content of the consignment.**

**Mr. Ian Bishop, I know you are a smart man and that is why I am doing this transaction with you.**

**However, I will strongly advise, that you do not allow your smartness to become foolishness on your part.**

**As far as I'm concerned, your smartness lies in your ability to conclude this transaction with all carefulness by following Mr. Tegi's instructions.**

**Mr. John Tegi is a representative of the organization in London.**

**It is not a one man affair.**

**This is a big organization, whose primary function is to move funds in cash for very top government officials in Africa like heads of state and ministers.**

**Please get back to me urgently with all the information as to your date of arrival in London.**

**Bane Maleke."**

# CHAPTER 16

Leonard and his wife, Laura volunteered to drive Ian to the airport. On the way, Ian suggested that they stop for an early dinner in Springdale, on him. He wanted to do something nice for them.

They chose a Chinese Restaurant. The food was good and the fellowship even better. When the fortune cookies came around, Ian gave his to Laura. She opened it and said, "This one belongs to you, Ian."

Ian read it out loud,

"**You are about to inherit a large sum of money.**"

"That is what it said. I would not lie to you."

Then, they were off to the airport. Leonard pulled the car right up to the front door and let Bishop out.

Leonard said, "You be careful when you get to London, my man. It's a jungle out there!"

"Give Cindy a hug for me." Laura requested, "And, watch your back."

With all the goodbyes spoken, Ian said, "I will see you on Friday, April 21$^{st}$. At eleven pm. They had also offered to pick Ian up on the other end of his trip. Well, why not? He was the Chairman of the Board of the new foundation.

April 21$^{st}$. had to be the end of this fanciful journey because the theater opened their doors in Eureka for another rehearsal on Monday, April 24th. And, Bishop would need a couple of days to get over the jet lag when he got back home, a much richer man!

The flight left XNA (Northwest Arkansas) and was right on time for Chicago (ORD). It was one of those smaller executive jets with the soft leather seats and a male flight attendant. He had found his stage with a captive audience, so to speak. The flight attendant had a great sense of humor. That made the trip seem a little easier. Ian arrived at ORD two hours before the international flight to London Heathrow.

Once onboard the British Air 747, Ian Bishop discovered that he had an "inside seat" and knew that he was in for trouble. There was a family seated around him. One mother and three kids, ages three years to eight years old. During the flight Ian tried to ignore the hyper activity and the changing of seats between the six year old girl and the eight year old boy. They climbed over the back of the seats to the mother behind him.

Ian tried to watch three different movies on the tele in front of him, thinking that watching the movies would make him sleep better. He did not get any sleep the night before, with all the phone calls and emails.

Ian Bishop even took a sleeping pill hoping it would just knock him out on this flight but that was wishful thinking.

Bishop was not going to get any sleep on this trip.

The eight year old boy who was in the seat beside him and on the floor under his feet, slept like a helicopter, with arms and legs flying in every direction.

IF, Ian dozed off at all, it was interrupted by an arm in his face or a swift kick to his shins.

It was actually a relief to get off the plane in London and go through customs, even with two nights of no sleep behind him. Ian headed for the super train that would take him to downtown London in only fifteen minutes.

IT WAS NOW ELEVEN O'CLOCK London Time at Paddington Station. TUESDAY, APRIL 11

Ian Bishop had made reservations at the Hotel 82, because they had advertised that they had free High Speed WiFi Internet Service in their rooms.

The advertisement on the Net had also said and I quote "A brand new refurbished property right in the centre of town, minutes walk from Baker Street of Marble Arch. Paddington Station, with the Heathrow Express just around the corner. Rooms are fully equipped with all mod-cons for travelers." Ian wasn't sure what "mod-cons" were, but liked the idea of the hotel being around the corner from the Heathrow Express Train. Later, Ian discovered the hard way, that "just around the corner" was even in a different zip code, all the way from W2 to W1. It only took him an hour to walk around that corner.

Fortunately, Ian met a very nice “Bobbie” who was with the Metropolitan Police of London, along the way.

“Good day Sir, You look a little lost?” he had said, “May I direct you somewhere?”

“Yes, you certainly may” Ian responded “I am looking for a hotel on Gloucester Place“. Ian showed the man the ‘print out’ from his computer printer.

“Oh, Sir, that’s way over in W1 and we are in W2. That’s a different section of London.” the Bobbie said.

“I was beginning to discover that” he told the Bobbie while the policeman waved down a cab, to ask the cabbie, directions.

The Cabbie answered, “That’s way over in that direction Captain, about twenty blocks.” He waved off in another direction. The light changed and the cab was off and running.

Bishop thanked the Policeman and was on his way again.

Well, at least he got to see a whole lot more of London.

Ian arrived at his hotel just after noon, which turned out okay because they would not “let” the room to him until one pm.

Ian asked the desk clerk, “Is there an internet café in the area?” Bishop walked another five blocks for lunch with his computer. This was the only outside connection that Ian had to the real world, and to the world of his friends.

AT THE INTERNET CAFÉ, Ian sent an email to the banker in South Africa:

**“Dear Bane,**

**I am in London. This makes my second night without sleep. Being on the air plane gave me more time to think. You know the answer is very simple, and everybody wins.**

**The London contact doesn't mind bending the rules (He even has an off shore banking account.) You could call him, as my agent as well as being from the bank that shipped the consignment.**

**You tell him that he has your permission and mine to open the consignment with me, and he can have all of the money that he is asking for plus we give him a bonus.**

**That still leaves plenty of cash funds for you and for me.**

**Everybody gets their money. You can not loose and everyone is happy. It probably is not the first time he has made a 'special deal'.**

**After you do that, email me and I will meet with him to finish our deal. There is no reason why that would not satisfy everyone, because we would all get what we want.**

**Actually, the only reason that would not work would be if he was scamming us, and there is no money in the box.**

**This is a good idea, and would not hurt anyone.**

**Signed; Ian Bishop"**

After Ian Bishop had mailed this email to South Africa, he happened to think that this was probably too logical for the banker to wrap his head around. They just did not seem to do business like Ian Bishop did business.

&

The banker in South Africa and the administrator in London probably thought that Bishop was either extremely intelligent or a complete idiot to think of such a plan.

At one-thirty, Tuesday afternoon,

Ian Bishop checked into his London hotel room and phoned John Tegi to set up an appointment. He was anxious to collect the inheritance and be on his merry ol' way, in "bloody ol' England".

"John, this is Ian Douglas Bishop. Gold Card Member KK11WT, I am in London to collect the consignment of funds from South Africa. Your fees have been wired to your account in France, as you requested."

Ian continued on the phone; "Also as you instructed, I have the cash according to our agreement for the balance due the courier service, in order to release the funds from the security company. Tomorrow, Wednesday, April 12,would be good for me or Thursday, April 13, if that would work out better for you."

John said "Actually with the long Easter Holiday ahead of us it would work out much better if we could meet after Easter, Say, maybe on April the 18th? That way we will be sure that the consignment will be ready, for delivery to you. We could then handle the transfer of funds to your bank in the U.S." John Tegi did not want to tell Bishop that there had been some sort of hold-up on the delivery.

Ian said "That will work out for me. I have business in Germany and will return to London to finish our business together."

"I will notify you by email as to the date and time of my arrival back in London. Thank you for your time." and, Ian Bishop hung up the phone from talking with John Tegi.

TUESDAY, APRIL 11, Ian wrote an email to South Africa,

**"Bane,**

**You may act on my behalf to wire required funds to offshore account in France. I have already told John Tegi the funds have been paid.**

**You know the money is real, I do not. For all I know, this is all just a bunch of wind.**

**After you have complied with John's demands, please email me. I have made the appointment for around April 18th. Those funds can be taken out of my share of the inheritance, when we have completed our deal.**

**Personally, Bane, I like you. All seemed to be good information until you started asking for money (up front), and THEN the contact in London almost doubled that amount. All of this without any guarantees or established place of business here in London.**

**And on top of that, you are not dealing with an established business."**

**"They don't seem to have secretaries, or workers. As far as I know they don't even have their own established place of business. I have not been given any of the information I had asked for. There is no need for that kind of secrecy.**

**In the past I have dealt with some people involved with high finance and they deal with reputable banks, security companies and couriers. Everything goes according to plan without last minute charges and unexpected fees.**

**I don't trust the way this has been set up. I will not be taken advantage of, and pay money up front for a product that I have no proof exists.**

**Show me the money. I will pay what ever is owed, and we should all be happy. I am not playing around. I know that you have worked hard and deserve to be paid. The courier deserves to be paid. Let us pay all that is owed out of the money that is to be delivered.**

**If we can not take care of this business properly on Wednesday, as previously discussed, I am flying out of London on Thursday.**

**If John thinks I can be taken advantage of, he is mistaken." Ian continued his email with Bane.**

**"If you want this deal to take place. There is no reason why I would have to go "out on a limb" and front MORE MONEY, when we already**

**have a box that contains $25 million.**

**If you take care of this matter by tomorrow morning. The London connection can pick me up at MY hotel and we can complete this deal and EVERYONE will have their money.**

**The BALL is in YOUR COURT now. Let's finish this deal.**

**Sincerely, IAN BISHOP"**

*Bane Maleke @yahoo.com>* wrote: Tuesday, April 11th.

**"Dear Bishop.**

**Thanks for your mail. I must let you know that I am not happy with the way you are handling this transaction.**

**This consignment was sent in your name, and I asked you if you where able to travel before I sent it, and you told me, yes.**

**Now you are coming up with your own ideas.**

**Please Bishop, this is not a joke.**

**I want you to know the consignment will arrive tomorrow as planned.**

**If you can not raise the 6,500.00 pounds please let me know what you can raise.**

**I am waiting your urgent reply,**

**Bane Maleke."**

Weds. April 12th. EMAIL TO BANE FROM IAN,

**"I am not joking either!**

**We can handle this matter "private arrangement" quietly.**

**Yes, I am concerned about my well being at the moment.**

**You call John Tegi in London and tell him that I have arrived in London and that as my banker, you guarantee that all fees will be paid during transfer of funds, as soon as Silver Box has been opened to verify that all the funds are there.**

**He should understand that such a large amount has to be verified.**

**I do not want to play around. Let us get this thing done. I am here like I said I would be.**

**I figured that we were dealing with an established business when I agreed to pay fee up front, but under these circumstances, there is no reason why all funds can not be paid out of proceeds on the premises.**

**You may tell John Tegi that he can verify these arrangements through emailing me and make arrangements to pick me up at my hotel today. Thank you. Let us take care of this now."**

***Bane Maleke @yahoo.com*>** wrote:

**"Dear Bishop,**

**Thanks for your mail and I hope you are doing fine? I told you that this was a private arrangement in getting the money to the United Kingdom. This organization helps government officials move money out of Africa. The money you are paying up front is for administrative charges.**

**So please call Mr. John Tegi and let him know exactly where you are in London.**

**I would also want you to send your telephone number so that I can call you.**

**However, I would want you to know that there is no need to be afraid of anything.**

**Regards, Bane Maleke."**

Ian Bishop has always known that when ever someone had a need to say, "There is no reason to be afraid" that there is every reason in this world to be afraid, and he better watch his back. That was exactly what Ian Bishop was going to do. He didn't trust John Tegi and his organization in London.

Ian thought to himself, "I am not going to let John know EXACTLY where I am."

Ian Bishop emailed back to BANE MALEKE, the banker in South Africa . . .

**"If our deal does not take place today or this**

**evening, You will have until next Tuesday (April 18) to pull this off. John had said he could meet with me on the 18th. Either you come up with the front money or arrange for the advance money to come out of the consignment. It does seem very strange to have to pay front money for a shipment of cash money, doesn't it?!**

**Being a bank officer you càn guarantee the funds, as representing me. Figure it out!**

**I will be in Germany till April 20. If you want this deal finished, email me and I will rearrange my plans to be back in London again on the morning of April 19 . Other wise I will be back on my way to the U.S. on the April 20th. Out of Gatwick Airport, London."**

Ian Bishop was a logical thinker and would not do a deal when it did not make sense to him. Why should he have to pay "front money"? Why not just open up the consignment?

---

Ian Bishop was not flying out of Gatwick Airport, London. But he was not about to let them know that. Who did they think they were dealing with?

Ian was thinking, "I am not a pawn that they can just move around the board at their own discretion, a pawn that could be easily sacrificed."

Another email arrived for Bishop from Bane Maleke in South Africa,

**"This transaction belongs to both of us and we**

**should handle it as men. Mr. John Tegi has told you he can meet with you on the 18th of April, so please communicate with him on the protocol involved."**

Ian Bishop had already come to understand the term "protocol" in the context of how these people were using it. They were really saying,

"You have to do things our way or not at all." Ian Bishop was actually beginning to hate the word;

"PROTOCOL".

Ian had read that book and it ain't necessarily so.

Bane continued with his email to Bishop:

**"However, on my side I am making arrangement to sell family land to raise some money before Friday. Could you assist with half of it? You know I did not make plans for this up front payment myself, so please let's help ourselves, so that you can get this money out for us.**

**That I am a Bank Manager, does not mean I have access to cash.**

**The consignment should be in London today. So please write Mr. John Tegi an email explaining your situation to him, that you are trying to raise the money and he should make arrangements to pick you up from the airport as he has promised.**

**Mr. Bishop I also want you to know that this is not a hoax.**

**Regards, Bane Maleke"**

Ian had already made up his mind that he would pick up the money in London, if Bane Maleke set it up from South Africa. Ian made it known that he would pay ten thousand dollars in cash if the deal looked good to him. Any other up front funds would have to be paid out of South Africa. If the deal did not go down this way, by next Wednesday or Thursday, Bishop would be on his way back home on Friday.

Email sent to London Contact, John Tegi, from Ian Bishop Weds, April 12

**"The rest of your money should be shipped to off-shore account by this Friday and I will be flying into London airport from Germany on Weds. April 19$^{th}$.**

**I will have U.S. $10,000. cash to pay you, when I pick up the consignment.**

**I am waiting for you to confirm that consignment has arrived and that the above date will work for you, as far as having me picked up at the airport, and taking me to a hotel. I will then sign for the consignment.**

**I also trust that U.S. $10,000. cash will be okay when I sign and pickup consignment. The other funds sent to your account will be sent from South Africa.**

**Ian Bishop"**

Ian Bishop had never been so tired of dealing with another person in his life. Of course he had never dealt with anyone over twenty-five million dollars before either. Ian just did not like this person named "John Tegi". That in itself was strange because he had pretty much been like the old comedian / diplomat who once said "I never met a man I didn't like." That man had probably never met John Tegi.

Maybe after a week in Germany he could come back to London refreshed and able to finish this deal.

Right now he just wanted to be another tourist in London, on holiday.

Ian Bishop wanted to follow the road to Germany and see if that path would lead him to a fate filled journey into the future, or back to his past ancestry.

Ian Bishop always wanted to know what was around the next bend in the road, across the next river, or through the woods to the house of Little Red Riding Hood. He was going to leave the big bad wolf behind in London.

# CHAPTER 17

With all the emails sent and answered, Ian felt like he needed a diversion. He decided to just take what was left of the day and walk all over London Towne. It was a beautiful day and the spring flowers were in full bloom. Ian began his walk down Gloucester Place and discovered only a few doors down from his hotel, a plaque on a door that read: "Major General Benedict Arnold, AMERICAN PATRIOT resided here at 60 Gloucester Place, 1796 till his death, June 14, 1801" Ian thought "I guess he was a patriot to the British. It's all in how you wanted to look at it."

Ian's walk took him past the famous Wax Museum of London with a line going all the way around the block.

This was interesting in light of all the detective work that he found his way into the middle of, a statue of Sherlock Holmes at 221 B, Baker Street, the address of the very famous Sherlock and the original address of Abbey National.

If he was involved in the investigation that had Ian Bishop entwined at the moment, Holmes probably would have said;

"It is elementary my dear Watson." But it was not so elementary to Bishop. This probe had taken Ian from South Africa to London and may have even begun on the Mediterranean Sea last November and followed him to South Texas for the winter.

Before Mr. Bishop was finished with this case, it would probably also end up at the New Scotland Yard, London.

His inheritance was becoming more involved by the moment.

But, this afternoon was meant to be a diversion, a little side trip. Ian could not help thinking about it all, over and over again.

This was one game he had to win.

Maybe, this was not the time to be thinking about all the red tape that enveloped him.

"Then again maybe this was the best time to think about it" he thought as he headed across Queen Mary's Park in the heart of London. That evening with a clearer mind and a fresh new outlook on things Ian stopped at a British Pub for "Steak and Mash".

Ian Bishop had continued to keep his special friend, Cindy in Germany well apprised of his situation as well as Leonard and Laura Landerfeld, who were on the Board of Directors of the J.C. Foundation back in the States. If Bishop found himself in mortal danger, he would want his pursuers to know that he was not the only one with access to his complete files.

Ian had even added a special code word to all of his correspondence with Leonard.

With this special code in every email, Leonard would absolutely know that it was from Ian, and not from someone who had abducted Bishop and stole his computer.

Ian Bishop knew that in this High Stakes Game of Finance that he had to keep his opponents guessing as to what he would do next and never actually let them know precisely where he was. This time Ian decided to fly out of Stansted Airport, London to Frankfurt, Hahn in Germany.

Stansted Airport is a little known airport a long way out of London. It is known by local travelers throughout Europe, but not generally known by International and trans continental travelers like Bishop.

That's why he felt like he would be safe exiting the country that way. He also hired a private car for the trip to the airport, rather than public transportation where he could have easily been followed.

The private car cost him 85.0 Pounds Sterling but he felt like his safety was worth that. Besides, Ian was tired from his ordeal during this past week in London. This ride through the U.K. countryside was beautiful as well as interesting.

He could now put this part of his journey on hold for a few days and look forward to his personal time with Cindy in Germany.

❧

# CHAPTER 18

Ian Bishop's ancestors came from Germany in the year of 1860, on both sides of his family and settled in Pennsylvania, USA.

He had only been to Frankfurt, Main airport on one occasion to make another connection to Rome, Italy, and yes, there was one other time as a refueling stop on his way to Israel, if you wanted to count that one.

Bishop had never spent more than forty-five minutes on German soil before and was really looking forward to this visit. Even beyond that was the expectation of seeing his friend, Cindy and spending some time with her. Ian needed a break from the dangerous game of intrigue that had brought him to London, and he needed to place himself beyond the reach of the people in London for the time being so he would be safe. He could now let down his guard for a while and just enjoy himself.

Cindy was due into Frankfurt, Hahn Airport on Sunday afternoon, April 16, from Venice, Italy where she was spending Spring Break with her daughter, who was a Missionary from Budapest. She had not seen this daughter for several years.

Ian Bishop now had a couple of days to relax and enjoy his Mother Land.

He had made reservations at a small hotel near the airport in Lautzenhausen, Germany. This part of Germany probably had not changed since before World War Two. The only blazon difference was the new cars parked around the little village.

There were lots of underground bunkers, like aircraft hangers with big steel doors all over the woods that surrounded the airport where the Nazis kept their fighter planes during the war.

The landscape mixed with the rolling hills was beautiful. Ian knew that this was going to be a very special time.

Ian always enjoyed thinking good thoughts. It was nourishment for his soul.

Then the emails started again on Friday morning. At least Ian Bishop was out of their reach in Germany, but he had to tend to business.

Friday morning, April 14,

**"Dear Bishop,**

**Thanks for all your mails. I have been out of office all day trying to raise this money for the administrative charges.**

**I have been able to get a friend who lives in London to buy the family land.**

**But All I can get for the land is about $5500.00 USD and he would pay from his bank in London once we finalize the paper work by tomorrow.**

**Please help with the balance by paying $5500.00 USD also, and tell Mr John Tegi that you would be coming to London with $5000.00 USD when you arrive on the 18th of April. We have to make the payment by tomorrow.**

**Waiting your urgent reply. Bane"**

**FRIDAY, April 14 Ian answered the email from Bane;**

**"I already told John that I would be coming into London with U.S. $10,000.**

**I have already told you that if you want this deal to work, you will figure out how to make it work. I have helped you get this money out of Africa. If you want to split the funds, Make it work !**

**Signed, Ian Bishop"**

Friday, April 14 from Ian Bishop,

**"Dear John Tegi,**

**I have a partner in South Africa who is taking care of the payment that you want sent to your account in France. He is arranging for those funds right now and will email you a receipt and/or arrangements for payment.**

**I have the $10,000. USD in cash to pay you for the consignment in London.**

**As soon as I hear from you, I will make arrangements to fly into London on Wednesday, April 19, at which time you may pick me up at the airport. We can either take care of our business late on Wednesday, April 19, or on Thursday morning, April 20.**

**Please confirm our appointment now, so my plane reservation can be made.**

**I need to know that all is arranged by Monday evening. After You confirm our appointment, I will send you the details, so you will know exactly when to have me picked up at the airport. I am looking forward to the swift completion of our business.**

**Thank you.**

**Ian Bishop"**

☙

# CHAPTER 19

THIRD FLOOR WALK-UP FLAT, LET BY JOHN TEGI OF THE ADB ORGANIZATION IN LONDON

Meanwhile, in London, John Tegi was fuming. He had never been so upset in his life.

Two of his thugs were standing there listening to John rant and rave . First they would stand on one leg and then the other. It always made them nervous when Mr. Tegi was like this.

Well, yes he had actually been this mad before.

John recalled; "The last time I was this angry, a deal had gone wrong and it was up to me to make the problem disappear. That man was just like Bishop! He just would not follow proper protocol! I sent you guys after him. I told you that he had ten thousand dollars in cash, but you killed him before you got your hands on the money. You made me look bad in front of the organization. THAT WAS REAL SMART !"

John Tegi yelled at them sarcastically.

"But, Mr. Tegi, It wasn't our fault. That man was going to go to Scotland Yard. We had to stop him." alleged the larger thug that looked like he could have been a pro wrestler.

"There were other ways to stop him. Don't you ever do that again, unless I tell you. If he didn't have the money on him, we could have at least held him for ransom!

Now, about Bishop. He slipped right past you at Gatwick Airport this week and has ended up in Germany. He probably had the $10,000.00 on him and you let him get away.

What Ian Bishop is doing in Germany, I don't know, but he will be coming back for the inheritance money this next week. We have a sweet deal here," John confirmed,

"Let's not ruin it."

"But Mr. Tegi we had all the departing flights covered at Gatwick!" repeated the other man."

Tegi said, "I don't want to hear any excuses. So far we have managed to stay under everyone's radar."

"The Diplomatic Courier Service out of Africa gets a cut of our take. We get paid our administrative charges, and the man that Bane Maleke sent to us will get everything that he has coming to him." chuckled Tegi with no mirth.

"When Ian Bishop returns to London this next week, he is

suppose to tell us which airport he will be coming in to. We will send a driver to pick him up, but not until we have all our men in place to follow him. I want to know where he is at all times. Nothing better go wrong. We will even have the hotel covered and his room bugged. We will know who he talks to and where he is. Do you understand?"

"Yes Sir" both of his men said at the same time.

There was also a stunning lady sitting on a divan with sagging cushions in this third floor, walk-up Flat. The divan was over in one corner of the room. This office was obviously 'Let' by the month. On the frosted glass window in the door facing a long hall and an old staircase there were Stick-on Letters; "ADB".

Lynnette Robinson was too classy a lady to belong in a place like this, but she was considered John's lady. She was a real looker. She wasn't hanging around John Tegi because he was one of the "beautiful people". John Tegi was a reprehensible man, but he was very shrewd. Everyone knew that he was extremely dogmatic about his protocols.

It must have been that she was following the money. John had a face that even a mother would have trouble loving.

Lynnette knew her place. Her place was to be a quiet, beautiful decoration and do what ever she was told.

John Tegi, as ugly as he was, liked beautiful things, and fine art, of collectable value. He even had a few of his original paintings hanging in this workplace. But, it would take more than that to make this place look better.

Most of his collectables were in his up town apartment in a fashionable section of London.

Everyone around Tegi knew to be silent unless they were spoken to, especially when he was in a rotten mood like he was now. He did not like to be made a fool of.

He planned on laying a trap for Ian Bishop. This time Bishop would not slip through his fingers. John Tegi would insist that Bishop follow his protocol. He would have Heathrow and Gatwick Airports staked out and catch Ian Bishop before he could leave on his own. This time Bishop was not going to get away from him.

"Sweet Cakes, My Queen." John said, "You can help also. I will want you to meet Ian Bishop at the hotel and pick up a package for me, from Bishop. When he sees you, he won't be able to think about anything else. He will be so distracted, he will do exactly what I want him to do. Take him down Babe."

Lynnette knew what that meant, and she was willling to do whatever John Tegi wanted. Tegi was the "King Pin" of this organization and she was his Queen. She was a pro and she was in it for the big haul. That could be right around the corner. She had heard them talking and knew that there was over twenty five million tied up in this deal.

They would be ready for Ian Bishop's return to London next week. They all wanted a piece of this pie.

The scene was now ready for Ian Bishop to set foot on stage.

The Queen was going to take this Bishop out of the game!

John Tegi was telling his people, "If Ian Bishop knows what's good for him, he will play by my rules this time."

☙

Email Letter to Bane Maleke in South Africa from Ian Bishop,

**"Dear Bane, April 14th.**

**I am ready to meet with Tegi and sign for the consignment on Thursday, April 20.**

**I would recommend that you contact him by phone and/or email and make arrangements to complete payment right away so he will meet me at the airport in London.**

**John Tegi is not an easy man to deal with.**

**If I am to go any further with this, you are going to have to answer my questions as to exactly how much cash is in the 'big silver box'? How are we going to divide the money? Where are we going to meet?**

**Time is running out. If this whole thing does not come together, where I can sign for, and receive the consignment on Thursday, April 20th, this whole thing just goes away. I have to fly back home on Friday morning April 21st**

**And, that will be the end of our deal.**

**Let's stop all the changes, make the appointment in London and be done with this now."**

Ian Bishop was getting confused by all the different numbers being tossed around by John Tegi and Bane Maleke. It was like they were involved in a high priced auction and everything was up for bids. They kept trying to get as much money out of him as they possibly could. It was difficult to keep up with all that was happening. Ian felt like the confusion was all part of their plan. He knew that he needed a clear mind to stay at least one move ahead.

***Bane Maleke <@yahoo.com>*** wrote:

**"Dear Bishop,**

**I will conclude the sell of the land in about an hours time and I will let you know the final payment. what is in the consignment box is cash, but when sending it I declared it as precious stones.**

**I would want us to work together to pull this transaction through. You said you had $10,000.00 cash. I will pay $5500.00 USD and you will pay $5000.00 USD to the same account Mr. John Tegi has PROVIDED. If this is okay with you I would tell the man that bought the land to make direct payment to that account in France.**

**I would advise you write Mr. John Tegi today telling him the situation that you are making arrangement to pay the 6,500.00 POUNDS and that you would be coming with $5000.00 USD.**

**Plead with Mr. John Tegi on this matter. I would also need your number in Germany so that I could call you to discuss this transaction.**

**Awaiting your urgent reply.**

**Bane Maleke."**

Ian said to himself once more "No way am I going to give

them Cindy's phone number or address. I am untraceable here in Germany and that's the way it's going to be". He was even moving around to find different "hot spots" where he could send out and receive email on his computer.

Ian Bishop could see that he was being 'played' by Tegi and by Bane. "That's fine" Ian thought. "Let them play their game."

*

# CHAPTER 20

Ian Bishop needed another short respite for a few days before all the intrigue continued. Tomorrow was Easter Sunday. (The traditional day of rest and resurrection.)

Cindy was flying in, to Hahn Airport from Venice. How wonderful it would be to find himself in her arms again and to experience more of her wit and charm, especially after dealing with the man in London.

Ian arose early that Sunday morning. What a great day this was going to be. A new day of resurrected spirits and a day of new beginnings. Ian decided that this was going to be the first day of the rest of his life!

The young girl behind the hotel desk welcomed Ian into their dining room for breakfast. This gave her a chance to practice her English, which was easier to understand for Ian, than the British, in London.

She was just learning English and was so proud to be able to speak it to Herr Bishop, and have him understand her.

Ian told her "Sehr gut!" which she accepted as high praise. He had to be careful when he spoke German. What little bit that he knew sounded pretty good and the other party would tear right in with their German.

Ian read the Sunday Newspaper before he left his breakfast table, at least the parts he could understand with what little German he could read. He had no problem at all understanding the pictures, and there was a lot of pictures in the Sunday Paper.

When Ian walked out the front door of the charming Inn, he noticed that the sky looked like rain, but he did not allow that to dampen his spirits.

He decided that he wanted to walk through the village before heading up the hill to the Hahn Airport. Ian loved to explore and it gave him a chance to think about Cindy, as well as clear his head of the ordeal that was waiting for him, back in London.

Ian never did like detail work and there was a lot of details to be worked out, in the inheritance of $25,600,000. U.S.D.

He didn't even mind sharing with everyone that already had their hands out for a piece of it.

Lautzenhausen town centre had an interesting old well which at one time was meant to be used as a public water supply. On the other side of the small plaza was a memorial to the fallen war dead.

He found an old bier garten near town centre where he had some lunch and then headed for the airport to meet Cindy.

Cindy's flight was fifteen minutes early. Ian caught sight of her as she was going through customs. She waved and said, "I just have to pick up my luggage and I'll be right there, Darlin'."

She was like a breath of fresh air that blew into Ian's life and drove away the worries of London. It was as though they shifted into slow motion and the rest of the world went into high gear, passing them by.

This is the kind of space in time that memories are made of.

She came rushing toward him, dropped her suitcase on the way, as she ran into his arms, a sweet embrace and the warmth of a long awaited kiss.

They headed off to her car that was parked in the long term parking lot with a cool rain and a dark sky covered with storm clouds. But being together, made it seem as though it was a beautiful day in mid summer. Just two days ago there was snow flurries in the air.

It was like in the old movies where the young couples in love rode off into the sunset. But there was no sunset, and actually it was cold and rainy. It was like "Singing in the Rain". But, this was the real world. Even though Ian has always been a romantic, he still had thoughts that pulled him back down to reality. Ian Bishop would prefer to live within his own little fantasies, like he did in elementary school, but he knew how to survive in the real world. That fact, has kept him going all these years.

They were driving south of Frankfurt, Germany on the auto baun at what seemed like a hundred miles an hour (actually it was more). Cindy mentioned that she lived about three hours south of the Frankfurt Hahn Airport. Ian had no idea it was that far from the airport to her house. She had spoken of it, like she drove up to the airport quite often and thought nothing of it.

They drove through Frankfurt and past the small village of Reichenberg and on to Wurzburg. Cindy knew of a really good German Food Restaurant that had been there forever. She parked and they walked hand in hand down the narrow street, through a misty rain on this cool evening.

Winter in Germany was not yet ready to pull back it's icy fingers and embrace the inevitable spring.

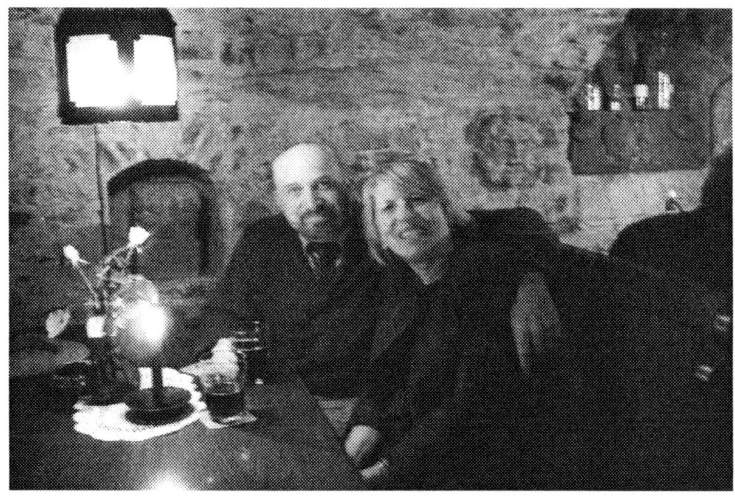

They huddled together for warmth. Ian and Cindy went up a hill and around the corner to the front door which was made out of ancient wood with old world hinges. The Bier Garten looked like they were closed. For the first time they realized the time. It was eleven pm, on Easter Sunday. But did they give up?

"No, we were hungered." Ian had said with a lilt in his voice.

Cindy saw some lights down in the basement level of the building and found another entrance.

The basement part of the restaurant was still open and several other couples were also having dinner. The basement was actually the old original section of the restaurant that dated back to the 1100s.

It was like eating in an old German Wine Cellar with rock walls, which is probably what it really was. Romantic soft music filled the air along with the wonderful scent of German cooking. Candle light and roses were at every table. Delectable food, vintage wine and the company of a beautiful lady.

Ian thought, "What more could a man want?" It was cold and wet outside that night, but they were seated by the hearth and they were feeling warm all over.

Cindy was thinking "Could this be true? Is he really here, and so close to me that I can reach out and touch him? This is so much better than email and phone calls. Ian is so handsome, debonair and charming. He is like a big teddy bear that I want to take home and hug."

Cindy and Ian didn't care that they were the last ones to leave the restaurant that night, they didn't even realize that they were. It was probably two am on Monday when they got back to Reichenberg and Cindy's Château. She lived in a nice three story house. There was no time to go sight seeing around the house. Both Cindy and Ian were totally worn out from their traveling and from the week before. They kissed a gentle loving kiss and said good night.

Cindy had to get up early the next day and go teach high school science at the U.S. Army Base in Wurzburg, Germany. Ian got up at his leisure and was going to do a "walk about" in the small village, when Cindy phoned and told Ian that she was on her way home to pick him up for lunch.

It was a delight to see her but, there was no time left for lunch, so she dropped Bishop off at the Base Library so he could do some emailing. The library had three rows of computers and all but a few seats were filled by service men and a couple of wives sending email to loved ones back home. Bishop signed in and checked his email. Then he walked over to look around the PX and eat lunch in the Food Court of the Post Exchange.

Cindy told him that she would pick him up at the PX after she got out of school at three-forty-five or four pm. He kept his eye on the door, waiting for her to arrive.

In, she stepped like a vision, in one of those ads on TV where they slow down the motion for emphases. She was ravishing in her tailored business suit, looking like a high paid attorney, the kind you would like to have on your side to impress the Judge and the Jury!

She had a way of filling a room with her presence.

"Hi Cindy" was all Ian could say. She said "HI" and gave him a slight hug. Well, there were people all around, and an army base is like a small town and it didn't take much for people to start talking. She was concerned about her reputation being a single gal in a straight laced society.

She said "What would you like to do this evening, Ian? Your wish is my command." Ian thought about that for a moment before answering.

"You mean as far as, where we should go eat this evening is concerned? Or, was that an all encompassing remark? "

Cindy said "I mean would you like Italian, German or Greek?"

Ian responded to that "Since we had German last night, I would like Greek. I love variation with my appetite, and I have a lot of appetite."

She ignored that statement. She knew exactly what he wanted. "Let's have Greek Food tonight, I know of an authentic Greek Restaurant. The food is magnificent." After an all evening dinner of many courses and wonderful conversation about everything under the sun. Cindy drove Ian around Wurzburg to help him become oriented.

Cindy would take Ian with her when she drove to school in the morning and drop him off in downtown Wurzburg. Then pick him up at "The Residence" a local castle, after school was out for the day.

After breakfast together the next morning, (Tuesday the $18^{th}$.) Cindy drove Ian to town centre and said "Have a lovely day, and I will see you about four pm.

Ian Bishop was in his element, here in Wurzburg, Germany

He loved new towns in foreign lands to explore, especially new towns that were as old as this one. And in Wurzburg, Germany he felt a strange pride.

Ian thought "It must be a feeling of ancestry, a feeling of belonging." It was so strong, as he gazed at the beauty all around him that he even had an urge to cry. Of course he didn't cry, but he wiped a tear away from the corner of one eye which he thought must have been the cold wind that made his eyes water.

It was as though some old ancestors had stepped across that spiritual dimension to greet him and welcome him home.

After canvassing the city, and taking photos at every turn, he found a great looking pastry shoppe and decided it was time for lunch and a WC. (water closet)

That afternoon Ian Bishop came across a small plaque on an ancient stone wall that was written in German, but he was able to understand. There was a very old solid metal gate in the center of that antiquated stone wall, that lead to a solitary austere court yard. The sign read that this was "the holding place of Jews, before they were deported, out of Wurzburg". Ian just stood there in silence, understanding what they meant by "deportation of the Juden"

Suddenly Ian felt the need to change his mood so he headed to the most colorful place he had seen earlier. He returned to the old world flower market. All the colors of the rainbow encircled him like the warmth of a hug, and returned his thoughts "To Life!"

Ian chose one of the living flower arrangements, with some different species and a splash of color, for Cindy. He carried it around the rest of the afternoon and found it to be heavy, but he didn't mind. He even dropped it once as he was trying to take a picture of something.

Ian picked up the plant and put it back together again as he was making his way back to "The Residence" where he would meet Cindy after school.

The yard out behind the castle type building of The Residence was beyond words. He meandered down the different paths among statues, tailored flower gardens and artistically trimmed trees.

This had to be the best time of year to be here. The flowers were just beginning to bloom, and the blossoms left their scent heavily in the air around him.

It was sweater weather and just cool enough for a most comfortable brisk walk all through the gardens and around the town.

Ian passed a statue of two praying cherubs in the garden that really struck him because he had remembered seeing a picture of Hitler at that very spot. The years of history, parade by many different people. The just and the unjust.

Ian was making and creating the present that would turn into his own history. "Living memories! Savor every moment! Don't allow any little detail to escape your attention."

"This is life, live it to the fullest. You may not travel this path again."

Cindy picked up Ian Bishop at The Residence in Wurzburg at four pm. She was right on time.

They decided to go straight home. The flower arrangement took the back seat. Cindy said that she would whip up some dinner at home. That was an understatement. Ian thought it was a real feast. He did not have much opportunity to eat "home cooking".

Ian and Cindy had discussed the fact that they would go to bed about eight pm because they had to get up at one am in order to get Ian to the airport, so he could make his early morning flight to London.

That evening they snuggled on the sofa as they watched a DVD; "Dinner with a Perfect Stranger". The visit had been much too short, but there would be other times.

Another day, another country, another time zone to look forward to. For now they had to go their separate ways but the future looked bright. Perhaps, around the next corner, they would find that pot of gold at the end of their rainbow.

At one am. Wednesday, April 19 they headed out of Wurzburg, through Frankfurt and other unknown German villages on their way to Hahn Airport at about 120 miles per hour in the dark.

Ian said to Cindy, "I don't like goodbyes. It seems like life is full of them. I know you have had more than your share as well." To lighten up the scene Ian decided that he would tell her what his son-in-law had told him in an email.

"Cindy, Mickey told me yesterday in an email, that I must have a hard time getting dates because I came seven thousand miles for this one."

Cindy smiled but her heart was breaking to think that they would be separated again.

That thought would have to sustain her, because they pulled up in front of the Frankfurt / Hahn Airport. With a kiss, they said "Till next time."

# CHAPTER 21

Wednesday, four am, April 19, at the Hahn Germany, Airport

***Email waiting for Bishop,***

***Bane Maleke <@yahoo.com>*** wrote:

**"Dear Bishop,**

**Thank you very much for your mail, I am very happy with the progress that we have made so far, as you can see from the telegraphic transfer copy that I have sent to you earlier today.**

**I have sent the money to the requested account in France. It was not easy for me to come up with that sum.**

**But I know we will all be smiling in a few days from now. I have given all my trust to you and I know very well in my heart that you will NOT disappoint me.**

**Do NOT feel confused in anyway, we are still in charge of our dealings and I assure you that nothing will go wrong.**

**Please as much as possible follow Mr. Tegi's**

**instructions to the letter.**

**These are the answers to all the questions you have asked :**

***1, The amount of money in the consignment is US$25.6M***

***2, The terminology "discount" is a banking term used for cash payment in favor of the requesting customer.***

***3, As soon as the funds are released to you I will make the necessary plans to come over to your* country *for the sharing and investing of my own share of the funds* with *your assistance.***

**I would like to call you in Germany, please if you have any number I can reach you with, please send it to me via email.**

**I also want to remind you that any monies that you have spent during the course of the transaction both your flight ticket and hotel will be refunded to you before the sharing.**

**I wait to hear from you. Best regards , Bane"**

Wednesday, four-fifteen am April 19,

FROM Ian Bishop to Dr. Maleke in South Africa;

**"Dear Bane,**

**I have been constantly on the move and no way**

**you could have called, but email has worked well because of my computer being "wireless" with built in WiFi Internet.**

**I will be in London by seven this morning. I will be in London all day today, and tomorrow, (Wednesday and Thursday) that should be enough time to sign for consignment and pay John Tegi."**

***John Tegi <@hotmail.com>*** wrote:

**"Dear Mr. Ian Bishop,**

**I received your emails and I wish to confirm to you that your appointment shall be Thursday, the 20th day of April.**

**I am looking forward to receiving the receipt of payment of US$5,500 for confirmation.**

**Please come along with the US $10,000. in cash.**

**Do not pay into the French account.**

**I will therefore await your flight confirmation for a pick up from the airport.**

**Thank you.**

**Yours faithfully,**

**Mr. John Tegi."**

Wednesday, April 19 in answer to John Tegi in London (four-thirty am)

**"I will be coming into London Stansted on flight 753 (today) Wednesday, April 19 at seven am.**

**I will wait in the International Arrival area to be picked up and transported to a hotel."**

When John Tegi read that email from Bishop, he went into another tirade. John noticed that it was already eight am in London and Bishop would have already landed at Stansted an hour ago.

He had his men staking out Heathrow and Gatwick. He had no idea that Ian Bishop even knew that there was another airport in London. Caught off guard again, John had to withdraw his people from Gatwick and Heathrow, and arrange for a driver to get over to Stansted.

That would take hours. He was so upset that he would spit as he spoke. His men tried to stand off at a distance as he spit out the orders. How could Bishop have thrown him another curve. It was his job to keep Ian Bishop off balance, and yet Bishop was keeping him off balance. John Tegi did not like the direction this venture was taking him. He had a bad feeling about this whole scam, but he was so caught up in it, that he had no choice but to ride this thing to the bitter end.

*He felt like he was riding the London Underground on a run-a-way train. His train kept going faster, there were no brakes and at the end of the line was a solid wall.*

John Tegi had his own demons whispering in his ear, full of despair and foreboding. He WAS just like Ian Bishop, but he was his opposite. Ian was Light and John was Darkness. This was like a battle between good and evil.

It would seem that all is well. Ian arrived at the Stansted Airport, London right on time. Seven am. He looked around, there were drivers lined up holding signs with Traveler's names. Ian did not see his name.

“That’s fine”he thought. “That will give me time to have some breakfast at the coffee shop right next to the International Arrivals Gate.”

He would have a moment to relax and still keep his eye open for a driver holding his name card. That would also give Ian Bishop an opportunity to figure out if he wanted to get into a car with a stranger, if that driver did not look trustworthy. Ian was good at sizing people up and that instinct had not failed him yet.

John Tegi sent Ian an email at nine a.m. telling him that he needed to phone John at his office for further instructions. He gave Ian two more phone numbers where he could be reached.

However, Ian Bishop was not here to mess around with any new information or further instructions. All Ian wanted to do was take care of the business at hand. Ian was not in a good mood. He was still at the airport waiting for his ride to a hotel where he could rest. Ian had just spent another sleepless night and the loss of sleep was getting him down. All Ian wanted to do right now was get to a hotel and go to sleep.

Ian Bishop was not going to be treated this way. After all, wasn’t he a dignitary, a V.I.P., a “head of State” here in London to complete a twenty-five million dollar deal? Where was his chauffeur? Ian did not like to be kept waiting.

Wednesday, two-thirty pm email to John Tegi from Ian Bishop

**“Why do you want to complicate our deal?**

**Let's just take care of our business. There is**

**nothing else to talk about. We should have covered all the details, and you will get all your money as soon as I verify contents.**

**I am very tired and I do not want to mess around any more. I am out of time and patience."**

Ian Bishop had been up since one o'clock this morning. Ian was getting more distraught by the minute. He was not use to being kept waiting.

Wednesday, two-fifty pm. letter to John Tegi,

Ian is still waiting at Stansted Airport, London

**"If you are not going to have me transported to a hotel where I can rest, I will have to get one myself.**

**It would seem better if you would do what you said, that way you can have me picked up in the morning and I can sign for the consignment, verify the contents, pay you and go to the bank for my transactions.**

**I wanted to get here early enough today to where there would be no problems or no delay, no more red tape. I told you last Saturday that I would be arriving on Weds morning. You should have had a driver on stand-by, waiting for me to arrive. I didn't even go to bed last night so I could travel from southern Germany up to Hahn to catch my plane on to London this morning.**

**So, you can see that I don't want to run around**

**making more phone calls, buying pre-paid phones or anything else new. I don't like change and I really don't have the time for it, or the energy.**

**Is this the way you treat V.I.P.s and "Heads of State", Gold Card Members? I would not think so.**

**One more time . . .I need to verify contents of consignment, pay you your money, go to the bank, and fly home.**

**That is simple enough, is it not?**

**I am not accustomed to being treated this way…..**

**Ian Bishop"**

# CHAPTER 22

This escapade had turned into a

Ten Hour, Three Act Play right in the middle of the Stansted, London Airport.

The stage was set, people roaming everywhere, Lights, Camera, Action ! The curtain was rising . . .

**Act 1:**

Bishop was overly tired from his journey, and of the run around that he had to endure.

Ian Bishop was very dismayed that anyone would let him wait at an airport for ten hours. He felt that a driver should have been there waiting for him upon his arrival from Germany. After all wasn't he suppose to be a Gold Card Member, a Head of State, a Very Important Person, here to collect twenty five million dollars?

Ian Bishop felt like he should be treated with respect. He definitely expected that he would be driven to a nice hotel where he could relax until the next morning. He would then be transported to the security company with John Tegi. He expected to pay $10,000.00 USD cash, for the balance of the shipping charges.

Ian wanted to sign for the consignment of his inheritance, make a deposit into Citibank London and have the funds wired to his bank account in the States. This is the way this was suppose to work. Ian felt like John Tegi was trying to keep him off balance on purpose. It was like John was trying to make this more difficult than it had to be. It was either that, or John Tegi did not know what he was doing.

Ian had a lot of time to think about all these things during his wait. Ian spent hours in the coffee shop, always watching for the driver that was suppose to pick him up. Ian spent so much time on his WiFi Computer that he was beginning to think his battery would die. It was a good thing his computer had Centrino (long lasting) Technology.

Ian Bishop had made up his mind if the driver did not look reputable that he would just ignore the driver and be on his merry way.

The voice within Ian was telling him . . . "Stay cool, relax. The pressure is on them. You took them by surprise again. They are trying to regroup, make new plans. Stay one step ahead, and watch your back."

*Bishop had a feeling of dread and trepidation.*

That usually meant extreme danger, so he was going to play out this game, very close to the cuff and he would have to make the wisest of last minute decisions.

That's what he needed, WISDOM, if he wanted to come through this high stakes game, alive.

Ian's driver finally arrived at the airport, Ian was in the coffee shop and eyed this black man up and down. Bishop decided that this man was alright. He had learned to trust his judgment.

*If he listened to that still small voice in his head, he would be fine.*

As Ian Bishop approached the driver, the man recognized him because he had told John Tegi in an email, that he was wearing a gray sport coat. Bishop knew that he could have just taken his sport coat off and make it through the crowd heading the other direction if he had to make a fast exit, just in case he didn't like the looks of the driver.

## Act 2:

John Tegi was even more distressed and frustrated than Bishop was. He had been playing both ends against the middle. Originally John had thought that there was precious gems in the shipment from South Africa because that is what Bane Maleke at Development Bank had first told him. When he found out from the Government Freight Agency that Bane had deceived him he was irate. John reassured the Agency they would be paid for their losses.

To begin with, John Tegi was just going to "play" Ian Bishop, the "dumb American" for the few extra dollars he could skim off the top.

Then he had found out that there was cash money in very large amounts in his keeping at the security company and was angry with Bane for not letting him in on the deal from the beginning.

At this point John Tegi decided that he was going to skim $600,000. right off the top of the consignment and also hit Bishop up for as much as he could get. Besides all that, he just did not like Ian Bishop. Mr. Bishop was as aggressive as **he** was, and he did not like that one bit.

Not only that, but this American was not playing by his rules and he did not like that either! Over and over Mr. Bishop had wanted to "verify the contents of the consignment", plan "his own schedule and itinerary" and come and go in and out of the country at his own will.

When Tegi was working a deal like this he wanted to know exactly where his "mark" was at all times. John was beginning to feel that he had lost control of this deal and he always wanted to stay in control. John needed to know exactly where Mr. Ian Bishop was, in case he had to deal personally with that man. And, when John Tegi "personally dealt" with someone, it was not a pleasant experience.

Chances were that if John had to deal with someone "personally", they would never be heard from ever again. John and his organization had always dealt with the consignments in his charge on the very edge of the law so it did not bother him when he had to step over that line on occasion.

Ian Bishop had made John's job very difficult.

He did not give John enough time to line up the proper people to take care of, and watch over Bishop while he was in London. Bishop had a way of letting him know at the last minute, and Tegi could not take care of the details of signing over the consignment without the advance planning.

That was one of the reasons he could not bring his plan to a close the first time Bishop was in London Towne. The other reason was that the shipment had been held up in South Africa.

John Tegi did not trust Ian, and he did not want to spook Bishop into running to Scotland Yard. He had once threatened Tegi with that very thing. John Tegi did not like to be threatened and felt like he had to keep Ian under close control as long as he was in London. John thought to himself "Ian Bishop does not know who he is dealing with!"

Then again, John Tegi did not know who he was dealing with either. Here we had two strong minded men butting heads like a couple of rams in the Spring time.

# Act 3:

Bane Maleke had put a lot of time in on "his deal" and he wanted paid for his trouble. A friend of his had told him about John Tegi in London. John had done some work for that friend on the sly. and their arrangements went smoothly as planned. Bane knew that if he could pull this deal off that he would be sitting pretty, and ready to retire.

Bane Maleke didn't plan on Ian Bishop being a free thinking, free spirit type of person. He also thought that he could trust John Tegi. Boy, was that a big mistake! Bane was thinking that as long as he could keep Bishop and Tegi working together, that he would come through alright in the end, no matter what the split would be. Bane did not know how dangerous John Tegi could be. Or, if he did know, he did not care. All he cared about was "his money".

Bane was out to safeguard his money so the South African government would not confiscate the proceeds from his last fifteen years of illegal hard labor.

Bane also had other people that he had to pay. He had been working on setting up this particular deal for over six months at least. His ultimate plan was to personally end up with all of his money again. He didn't care if Bishop gave up in the end or Tegi ended it for him. Either way Bane Maleke could reclaim the money for his bank and wire the funds someplace else.

The banker in South Africa had worked so hard to move this money out of Africa under the radar. He was deeply concerned that he was just going to loose everything that he had been working towards for so long, because Bishop would not play by the rules and he might just blow this deal out of the water for everyone concerned.

Also Bane was concerned about John Tegi's attitude and had

begun to realize that John Tegi might just abscond with all the front money, as well as Bane's savings.

Then there was the possibility that Ian Bishop would go to the authorities.

If that was the case, Bane Maleke would loose his position as well as do some jail time for moving over twenty five million U.S. Dollars illegally out of South Africa. It did not matter if he was guilty or not.

Then there was John Tegi. He seemed to be running scared and did not know what to do. He was head of administration for the security company in London.

Being the head administrator of ADB meant that he had been involved with illegal movements of high value consignments across international borders for quite some time.

Normally, when other people did what they were told and operated by his rules, things went well for John Tegi, but Bishop just might have to be eliminated from this game, he was creating too many waves.

He just didn't like Mr. "High and Mighty" Bishop.

Bishop was not a team player. He wanted to run the game. Bishop had already threatened to turn this matter over to Scotland Yard and that did not set well with John Tegi or with Bane.

Bane felt like he had done all that he could do. Not that Bane had been eliminated from the game, but the major moves were now left up to John and Ian, to see who was left standing in the end.

# CHAPTER 23

Email from John Tegi in London to Ian Bishop,

Wednesday, pm April 19

**"Dear Ian Bishop,**

**I wish to clarify this issue of verification of the contents of the consignment before payment.**

**Firstly, I made it clear to you that the total payments are 6,500 pounds sterling for the shipment of the consignment and 5,000 pounds sterling for the administrative must be paid.**

**I also made it clear to you that all these payments will have to be made <u>upfront before</u> the consignment will be delivered to you.**

**You said that you have paid US $5,500 to the account but I do not have the receipt yet.**

**Please note that you must pay the U.S. $10,000 in cash first before the delivery of the consignment.**

**The consignment is not in our custody and therefore the courier company cannot release it to us unless we pay for it."**

**"This is the procedure and we cannot change.**

**Please note this instruction and adhere to it strictly.**

**It is very important."**

Email from Bane Maleke to Ian Bishop:

**"Dear Bishop,**

**Weds. 3:30pm, April 19**

**I want to find out where you are at the moment and also to let you know that you have no cause to fear in this matter.**

**If you trust me to come all the way from the United States on this transaction, It would not be the payment of the balance of the shipment that would make us miss out on this.**

**I have done all the arrangement to make sure the money got to London. Just make the payment as I have told you and all the other processes will follow.**

**Please Bishop I want you to get back to me once you get to the hotel."**

When ever anyone says to Ian Bishop "You have no cause to fear" or "Trust me!" That always concerned Bishop. His guard was up and his game plan was operating. Ian was in close contact with Leonard Landerfeld on the Board of Directors back home. The prearranged password was in every correspondence from Ian to Leonard.

Then another email from John Tegi as follows:

**"Dear Ian Bishop,**

**Weds 3:45pm. London Stansted:**

**I received your email and the receipt for the payment of US $5,500. From South Africa.**

**You must adhere to our rules and that is final. I explained all these to you on phone before you left United States of America.**

**On the other hand, It is very unbelievable that you doubt our organization and this leaves us with doubts about your inheritance.**

**If you have doubts about the contents of the consignment, then your inheritance claim is not genuine and this gives us a cause to investigate your claim.**

**On that note, I would like you to send me a copy of the WILL and the Letter of probate for verification from Probate registry in South Africa before we can continue this process of payment.**

**Finally, have you seen the driver I sent to pick you up? Please confirm.**

**Thanks, John Tegi."**

If John thought they were going to alarm Bishop with the threat of investigating his claim, they were wrong again.

Ian Bishop just ignored that attempt at intimidation. Ian did have all the papers with him and all was in order.

All Ian wanted to do at this point was to check into the hotel, take a nap, eat a regular meal of some sort, and get a good night's rest.

❧

The driver did finally pick him up in a nice vehicle and was transporting him to a hotel. Stansted Airport is a long way out of town and the trip took about an hour.

Ian talked with the driver "Do you live here in London?" The driver's name was "Bo". Ian had noticed that from the driver's papers and license hanging up in a case off the visor.

He said "Yes, I have lived here for eighteen years."

"I am from Tanzania. That is a very poor country."

Ian asked Bo if he had a family.

"Yes, I have three children, two boys and a girl. We live in a terraced house, which means that we do not have a back yard. The kind of house with a back yard, cost a lot of money."

Then the driver added, "I am very hard on my daughter, she is thirteen and I want to bring her up right, but she does not like it."

Ian said "Daughters should probably be kept in the closet until they are twenty-one," with a laugh. Ian had raised three of his own, but he was only kidding with the driver.

The hotel was not as nice as he had hoped for, but all he cared about now was some rest. Ian Bishop knew that he would have to stay alert for his next encounter with John Tegi.

***An email arrived, Late Wednesday afternoon.***

***Bane Maleke <@yahoo.com>*** wrote:

**"Dear Bishop,**

**Thanks very much for your assistance. You have no cause to panic everything is under control. You would sign for consignment tomorrow and also open your new bank account.**

**I will start making my plans to meet with you in the United States.**

**Please keep me informed with every development.**

**Regards, Bane."**

Ian answered Bane's email:

**"I don't like the looks of this, Bane. This whole**

**thing is coming down like a drug deal.**

**I don't trust John any further than I could throw him. Actually, I don't even know if I could throw him at all because he has not crawled out of the wood work, long enough for me to see him.**

**All I know of him is a voice over the phone and emails."**

Bane's EMAIL REPLY to Ian Bishop:

**"Dear Bishop,**

**This is not a drug deal and**

**I want you to know that the problem was that you did not send them your traveling details yesterday.**

**If you had done that they would have picked you up today.**

**Please, you have to trust them because I arranged this business.**

**Please Bishop make this work for us, you have to trust me on this.**

**Please do not expose me to the world.**

**You know what we are doing is a deal so please follow what I have told you.**

**Make the balance of the payment and they will bring and open the box for you.**

**Bane"**

# CHAPTER 24

The phone rang in Ian's hotel room. He awoke with a start. What day is this? Where am I? Is it day or night? He was so tired ! RING, RING ! "OK, OK, I am coming." "Yes?"

"This is John Tegi, I would want you to know that we will meet tomorrow to handle the transfer on the consignment to you. I am sending an associate of mine over to your hotel to pick up the balance due for the courier services, so I can have the release all ready for you tomorrow morning.

There should be no more delays. She will be coming over to see you about eight pm."

"Well that's odd." Ian thought, but he didn't respond to that. To begin with he was still half asleep.

"Did you say that she would be coming over at eight pm?"

"Yes, eight pm. She will know your name and will tell you that John Tegi sent her. Her name is Lynnette Robinson. It would probably be a good idea if you met her out in the parking lot so she won't have to find her way to your hotel room. She knows that she will pick up a package for me, but she will not know that there is cash involved."

Ian looked at the clock. It was now seven-thirty pm. And it was still only Wednesday. Ian had just dozed for a couple of hours. He took the $10,000.00 cash that he had stored in a security belt and put it in a package.

Then he placed the money package in his inside sport coat pocket. He was hungry so he got cleaned up and headed for the hotel lobby. It was now just a couple of minutes before eight so he stepped out the front door.

It was a beautiful warm evening. The stars were out, although he could not see the moon.

Ian then began looking around the parking lot and saw an attractive young lady approaching him from around the corner. She said “Ian?” in the cutest English accent he had ever heard. He was totally taken aback with her beauty and demure personality. He almost forgot why he was there.

She spoke, bringing him back to earth from that place where he had momentarily traveled.

“Earth to Ian” she said.

“Oh, she has a sense of humor too,” he thought as he responded, “Yes, I was just caught up in my thoughts.”

She knew that she had that effect on men and enjoyed exercising that power. She said, “My name is Lynnette Robinson. John Tegi sent me to tell you that your appointment is set for nine in the morning. Do you want me to come up to your room with you?”

Ian quickly mentioned that he was famished, “Perhaps you would like to go get some dinner with me first and we could chat further.” He could not get enough of that cute accent. Also she really was a sight for sore eyes. “Eye Candy” Ian thought. And, how he loved candy. “She should have been named Candy instead of Lynnette.”

”Sure, I have nothing better to do tonight, than enjoy your company” she responded.

There was a restaurant right across the parking lot so they

walked over to the front door. "Boy did she know how to walk". Lynnette knew to walk just enough ahead of Ian to give him the best view, and that view was not wasted on him. He was an artist, he knew how to enjoy the finer things in this life to the fullest.

They walked into the restaurant and Ian felt every eye turn in their direction. They settled in, at a little table in the corner and the others turned back to eating, to their conversations and some to the national football contest on the tele.

England was winning by one point and everyone was in a good mood. There was even a man across the tavern that sent a glass of wine over to their table.

Ian had heard the man say to the waiter, "One for the Looker and one for the Yank."

Ian turned to the man and toasted him lightly and then turned back to the young lady who had already taken a drink from her glass. They ordered from the menu and exchanged some small talk for a while before the food came. The faire was not anything special but it was filling.

Bishop was wondering if this girl was just a pawn in the virtual chess game that he was playing, or if fate had smiled down on him with a very special gift. Just as Bishop was wondering if she was even of legal age . . .

That still small voice in Ian's head had to speak up and say "*Beware of special gifts. If it is too good to be true, chances are it isn't truth, but a snare to trip you up, a situation that is both alluring and dangerous.* Could be, she is not just an innocent pawn, but maybe a Queen. Beware!"

So Ian paid their bill and left the restaurant.

Lynnette thanked Ian for the meal and asked him. "Do you have something for me? Would you like for me to come up to your hotel room?"

Ian Bishop said "Yes, I have something for you. Please tell John Tegi that; nine in the morning will be fine for our appointment, and also say to him for me,

**Thanks, but no thanks**."

"He will know what I mean. I will give him the package he is expecting in the morning, right before we go to the holding company to pick up my consignment, together."

Ian continued, "You are most delightful. Maybe we should have met in a different place and time. Goodnight."

Ian kissed her hand and turned toward his hotel.

All he wanted now was bed, alone.

When Lynnette returned to John. He was not happy. Bishop was not playing by his rules again.

John Tegi was going to keep Bishop waiting in the morning,

just long enough to make him think that he had blown the deal by not paying the money, the night before.

John would also have his thugs watching from their car across the street from Bishop's hotel.

THE DAY OF TRUTH HAD ARRIVED.

Ian Douglas Bishop would either be filthy rich by the end of this day or no worse off than he was before.

It was now Thursday, April 20 at seven-thirty am

Ian Bishop was lost in his thoughts. . . .

"I am sitting in my 46. Pound Sterling, hotel room where I spent the night (Like a Motel 6). These people did not even have the refinement to put me up at a first class hotel."

When John Tegi told Ian, that he was sending his driver, what he should have said was that he was going to send a cab to pick him up at the airport. "Well, at least I had a nice talk with the cabbie from Tanzania, Africa." Bishop thought.

"I am waiting to be picked up one final time this morning and taken to pick up my inheritance. At first I thought they would not show up today at all. But, then I thought that they might show up and ask for even more money for some unforeseen charge or document that they needed."

Bishop had a thousand thoughts per second running through his head. His mind was running like a computer, but this line of thought was not paying off for him this time. Usually he could reason every thing out, but there were too many variables, to factor everything into the equation.

If Ian did not come up with the money, they would blame him, that the deal went sour.

No wonder Ian is not a lonely man. He always had himself to talk to.

Bishop continued to think on this subject, because he had to stay one step ahead of these people and just maybe his life depended on that.

"Last night, the way the transfer of money was suppose to go down was interesting. They always dealt through other people. John sent a young English woman to pick up the cash funds." Her name, had been given to Bishop by John over the phone about an hour before she showed up at his hotel.

So now it was time to go down and have breakfast from the breakfast bar and wait for the "pick up".

Ian told the desk clerk in the lobby of the hotel that he was going to be in the Breakfast Room in case there was any phone calls for him.

Bishop finished breakfast and checked back at the front desk. "Sorry Sir, no phone calls."

Ian said "I will be waiting here in the lobby for someone to pick me up this morning. Please let me know of any phone calls for Ian Bishop, or if anyone is looking for me. Thanks."

It was now nine am or a little after when Ian approached the desk again. "No Sir, no one has called or been looking for you. If they arrive, I will come to your room and let you know."

Ian said "Thanks, but I will just wait here in the lobby." Ian Bishop waited till ten a.m. and opened up his computer to check his email. "Nothing new," he mumbled to himself.

Bishop was actually relieved when it looked like Tegi was not going to show up. If he didn't show up, Ian would not have to deal with that man. If Teḡi had shown up, it probably would not have been good news, but danger.

Ian Bishop was beginning to thank God, that Tegi was not there. It might have even been a gift of providence, that kept him away from Bishop that morning.

Ian decided to write an email to Bane Maleke. The banker in South Africa.

**“Well, Bane we have followed this through to the end.**

**At first I thought that he just would not show up today, but maybe he will show up, and want more money.**

**That's the way it works, you know.**

**I will not pay him the money, of course, But he will say,**

**‘You are so close, surely there is some way you can raise it?!’**

**So you better be in a position to pay it yourself, if that is the deal.**

**Gee, now I can see into the future.**

**I will give John Tegi one more hour to show up, and then I am out of here.**

**Ian Douglas Bishop”**

&

# CHAPTER 25

Thursday noon, April 20$^{th}$.

Ian Bishop had a feeling of relief when neither John nor his driver showed up for the appointment. He had waited three hours and no show. Like it was mentioned earlier, Ian Bishop was not a man to be kept waiting. He always had things to do and places to go.

You would think that Ian was disappointed that he would not end up a Millionaire, but NO. Bishop felt like he had been given a reprieve, a stay of execution. He wanted to go do the town.

Speaking of that, Ian was going to fly home the next day. For the time being, Bishop had to be very careful. John had not shown up, but he might have sent one of his flunkies to corral Bishop before he could get to Scotland Yard.

John Tegi did not know that Bishop had decided not to turn the whole thing over to the Yard right now, because he did not want to be held as a material witness. He wanted to go home.

But, nonetheless, Tegi's goons were watching Ian from across the street.

Ian Bishop had a reservation with British Airways to fly out of Heathrow, London at noon on Friday, April 21$^{st}$. Ian decided that he would be safer if he stayed in busy places and kept on the move for the rest of today.

When John's men saw Ian Bishop go into the London Underground, one of the men jumped out of the car and followed him. The thug had a knife in one pocket and a gun in the other. This place was too crowded to use the gun and John's goon knew better than to stick it to Bishop without getting his money first.

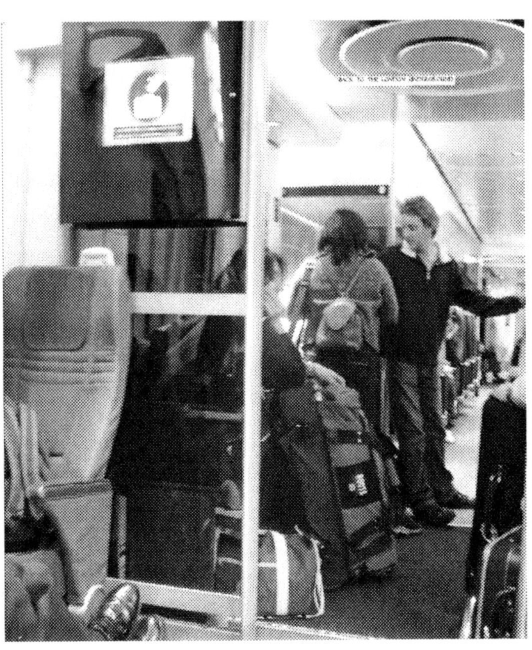

Ian decided to buy a "Day Travel Card" on the London Underground for 6. Pounds Sterling. He could get on and off as many times as he liked.

Bishop knew that this would be a great time to do some more sightseeing on his own. He traveled the full length of several different lines, not knowing that there was a man on his tail just two seats behind him.

Ian Bishop loved to listen in on the conversations of others and figure out who they were and what they did for a living. There was a couple of really nice looking ladies in one carriage. Naturally Ian would notice them. He soon figured out that the taller one with the long legs was a professional model. She had been pounding the pavement looking for a gig that day. She had her portfolio under one arm and "Headshots" under the other. She was talking with the other girl who was a friend.

The other girl wanted to be a model, and was asking for advice.

"I have some advice for that gal", said Ian Bishop to himself;

"Never ask professional advise from someone else who is out of work."

Ian got on and off the Underground several times that day, in order to go exploring above ground. It was a nice day, and he had nothing better to do.

Once Ian visited a London Flea Market in the streets and ate at a small kiosk right on the street.

Ian felt like someone was following him. As he stopped to look in a store window at their display, he was really looking at the reflection and saw a man watching him. Ian did not like the looks of that man, so he went quickly into the front door of that store, around the corner and straight out a back door he had noticed.

The Underground was right across the street. Ian ran for the stairway and darted into the first train he saw. The doors closed right behind him as he noticed the man just entering the stair well, looking around.

Bishop got off the train at the next stop and caught another train going in the opposite direction. Five minutes later Ian got off that train, looked around the area, feeling that all was clear. Bishop decided that he was tired, but he did not want to check into a hotel where his passport might be traced so he got back on the Underground again and headed for Heathrow.

Heathrow Airport is like a small city, nice restaurants, W.C.s and shops all over the place. He found a good place to eat, took out his computer and checked his email. No word from John Tegi or Bane Maleke. He figured that he had heard the last from them, and that was fine with him. There was a nice letter from Cindy. He was glad to hear from her. Now he did not feel so alone.

John Tegi was furious when he heard from his men that they had lost Ian Bishop again. He vowed that Ian Bishop was not going to come through this adventure alive.

John Tegi shouted at his men; “I don’t care if it takes you all night long. You will find out what hotel Ian Bishop is in. You will take all of his money and make sure that he is never seen or heard from again. I also want you to bring his computer back to me, as well as ALL of his stuff. If you do not succeed this time, I will have your heads stuffed and mounted, and hung over my fireplace.

DO YOU UNDERSTAND?”

His gangsters well understood, that John was indeed serious about having their heads. They said “Yes Sir.” and out the door they ran.

Ian Bishop felt safer by not getting a hotel room. Bishop knew that Tegi and his men would think that he would head for a first class hotel, because that's the kind of guy he was.

Ian began to scout around the airport for a good bench to spend the night. A lot of kids do that in Europe. Ian found a nice semi secluded place under one of the escalators on the top floor, with a good view so no one would be able to sneak up on him. There was a row of soft padded chairs without arms to interfere with stretching out and making yourself comfortable.

"Perfect." he thought "Well, maybe not really perfect, but it would do", and he would not have to try to figure out how to get to the airport in the morning for his flight. He was told that he could check in for his flight at ten a.m.

This time Ian managed an outside seat with an empty place beside him so he could stretch out and be comfortable for the long flight home.

What an ordeal this was! He was glad it was over and he could get back to his normal life. What ever normal was for him anyway.

Ian was so glad for the great time he had with Cindy in Germany. They had made a few memories together, that would last them for the rest of their lives.

Three movies, two meals and eight hours later the British Airways 747 touched down at ORD in Chicago, U.S.A. Ian spent a few hours at another nameless restaurant and checking WiFi email. He wrote a nice letter to Cindy and one to his friends in Eureka who were going to pick him up at eleven pm that very evening.

Ian's friends and fellow Board Members met Ian at the doors to the airport in Northwest Arkansas and He was in his own king size bed by one am. Saturday, April 22nd.

AHHHHHH. He was able to catch a few Zs!

As tired as he was Ian woke up and was wide awake on Saturday morning at three am. Jet lag at work!

Ian decided to have some breakfast, send an email to Bane Maleke at the Development Bank in South Africa. Ian Bishop felt like he needed to give Bane a complete report on his trip. If the money was real and actually sitting there in London, he didn't want to throw it away and thought the banker had a need to know what had happened.

Just maybe John Tegi was the problem and the reason this deal did not go through. If that was the case, then Bane Maleke had to straighten out the difficulty in London, take control of this situation and rectify it.

**"Dear Bane, Saturday, April 22nd.**

**I made the trip to London to sign for the consignment. The trip cost me $5,000. I expected to be treated well and with courtesy.**

**This deal also cost you the money that you invested up front.**

**I first arrived in London on Tuesday the 11th Of April. The first thing that I did was call John. I tried to take care of our business and make an appointment for Wednesday. The consignment was supposed to be there on that Wednesday.**

**John was angry because I got my own hotel room.**

**I had a phone and internet in the room, to make**

**it easy for me to be reached. He called me back and reported that with the Easter Holiday, he could not see me until at least the following Tuesday, April 18$^{th}$.**

**He said the holiday would be over then. He also mentioned that he was suppose to meet me at the airport and take me to a hotel that he had arranged for, and that the money had to be paid up front. John Tegi said that he had to be paid the money so he could pay the holding company, which I thought was strange because the shipment was suppose to be sent to him. (according to the bill of laden) It was also strange that there was no address for him on the shipment order, but it contained my full, complete address in the States.**

**I told him that I wanted to verify that the shipment was complete before I signed for it. That only makes good business sense. I also asked him if we could pay him all his money plus a bonus out of the proceeds. That way all we would have to pay was the balance of the cost of the shipment up front.**

**So, I had to spend another week in Europe. I have a friend in Germany so I went there. I kept in touch by email the whole time. And checked my email sometimes twice a day. I told John Tegi on Saturday, April 15$^{th}$. that I would be flying back into London on the morning of Wednesday the 19$^{th}$.**

**I also emailed John about four am on Friday morning to remind him that I would be in London so he could pick me up at Stansted and transport me to the hotel of his choice. I gave him all the details.**

**He should have known that I was going to be there on Wednesday at seven am.**

**I continued to email him every hour to find out what in the world was going on. I gave up another night's sleep so I could be there to meet him and he was not there. Nor did he, or his driver show up at the airport until ten hours later.**

**I watched people come and go all day long. People being met by drivers with signs showing names. I read every sign. Didn't even go to eat because I did not want to miss him. Finally he emailed me and said that he was "sending HIS DRIVER to pick me up.**

**I waited another hour. And when the man showed up, it wasn't "his driver", it was a cabbie that he hired. The cabbie took me to a second rate hotel (and I had to pay for it). John said that he was going to send someone to pick up my $10,000 cash.**

**He called again and said that he was sending a girl to pick up the money and that I was suppose to meet her in the parking lot of the hotel. I said**

**something about getting a receipt for the money to prove that I paid what was necessary.**

**He said that the girl would just say that he had sent her. She also told me that John Tegi would meet me at nine am on Thursday morning or have me picked up and taken for the transfer of funds.**

**Finally I was able to go to a restaurant and get something to eat, but it was about nine pm and that was the first real meal I had all day. I also had no sleep for over 24 hours again and I was not happy.**

**I get up at seven am on Thursday morning, a bit apprehensive about the way this deal was going down. I had breakfast at the hotel, checked out of my room. I told the front desk who I was and that I was expecting a phone call, or a driver to pick me up. And, I waited on a hard chair in the corner of what they called a lobby. I waited till eight am, and then till nine am.**

**I had checked out of my room so I got on my computer and tried to find out what happened.**

**I waited till ten am and then till after eleven am before I figured that he had skipped out.**

**I don't think he ever intended to meet me or take me to the holding company and pick up the cash. He probably wanted the cash for himself.**

**Naturally, I was angry, and yes I do have a complete file on everything from the beginning.**

**So if I do not get to finish the rest of this deal in an efficient and expedient manner, I will turn all my information over to Scotland Yard. That would be so easy with fax and net. I was going to do that on Thursday afternoon, but I got your email and decided to give YOU another chance to pull this off. John has been paid with your money. I need to get paid my inheritance and you need to receive remuneration.**

**Therefore I need for you to tell me exactly how soon it will take to wire the funds from the holding company that John was talking about to my account in Eureka.**

**You already have my signed letter with all the information you need, in order to make the wire transfer. Then all we will have to do, is for you and I to get together and split the funds.**

**So let me know right away, how long will this take? I know of course it only takes a couple of minutes for the wired funds to be sent out of London. What I need to know is how long will it take you to send my signed letter to make the transfer.**

**Let me hear from you right away on this.**

**Thanks, Ian Douglas Bishop"**

With that email done, Ian made up his mind to take a sleeping pill and go back to bed. He had to get over the jet lag before Monday because Monday he had a Play Rehearsal.

Ian Bishop did not see the light of day again till six pm Saturday. He fixed himself some scrambled eggs with catsup and a coke. He watched a little TV in proper English, took another sleeping pill and this time he slept till four am on Sunday morning.

Ian checked his email and found a letter from Bane.

***Bane Maleke <@yahoo.com>*** wrote:

**"Dear Bishop,**

**Thanks for your mail and I pray you had a safe trip back home. I would start the process of recalling the funds on Monday.**

**As soon as that is done and I confirm that it has been done, I will make the transfer from my bank with a different name.**

**I would want you to re-send your bank details where you want the funds to be wired to.**

**Regards, Bane"**

Ian sent Bane Maleke an email asking him how long before this deal would be finished.

On Sunday, April 23 Ian got out of bed long enough to make himself some supper and read this email:

**"Dear Bishop,**

**I am happy you have gotten home in good condition. I would let you know by money. Have a nice weekend.**

**Regards, Bane"**

Bishop read some from a Clive Cussler book he bought at a PX onboard the U.S. Military Base at Wurzburg, Germany. There is only one thing that is better than living through a real live adventure, and that's reading about one. Ian loved his adventures, but it was always so good to get back home and to peace and quiet.

He had started the Cussler book on his return flight home.

After only reading one more chapter he laid the book down and went back to sleep.

This time he slept in, till five am. on Monday before he got back up.

☙

# CHAPTER 26

It was now Monday, April 24. A rehearsal day at the Play. The full dress rehearsal did not begin until six pm that day but Ian had to check in with the director. The director had tried to get a hold of Ian and ask him if he would train some new people, but found out that Ian Bishop was in Europe. So Ian wanted to check in with his boss that morning to find out what kind of a schedule he would be running.

Ian was talking with his director "I heard that you were looking for me, while I was still in Germany. Leonard told me in an email."

"I sure was, I should have told you earlier that I needed for you to help me break some new people in with their parts. I know that you do such a wonderful acting job no matter what the role, you are asked to do."

"Yes" Ian said, "I remember when you phoned me at seven-thirty, one morning last season and asked me if I would do the role of Mary that day. I asked you, if I had to shave?"

"I remember that, I told you NO, but get in here and read over the script before you start. I knew that somehow you would pull it off."

Yeah, I did. I remember reading that script and changing it around so I could play it as a third person. Then I stepped into the role. You liked the way I did it so much that you left me in that role for a whole week."

And the director also told Ian, "Not only that, but it wasn't long after that, I asked you to do another female role and you pulled that off as well."

"I really don't want to work that hard this year. I love working for you, but I don't want a heavy schedule this season. It's time for me to slow down a little. I am not eighteen any more, you know." Ian said.

On Tuesday, April 25th. John Tegi phoned Bishop :

"Hello?" Bishop answered.

"This is John Tegi calling from London. I regret that I did not make our appointment. I got tied up with the Courier Service in getting the consignment released. I tried to phone you but the desk clerk had told me that you had already checked out."

Ian said "I waited for you for three hours before I checked out. But, anyway, Where do we go from here?" Not wanting to upset John any further for the moment, anyway.

Ian had come to know how John Tegi was, it had to have been hard for him to use the word "REGRET". That was probably the closest anyone had ever came to receiving an apology from Tegi. Bishop really was good at sizing people up, knowing what buttons to push and how far he could go, so he allowed Tegi to continue.

John replied, "I need for you to send me another letter, hand signed with the transfer information so I can wire the money to your account. I will be sending you a form for you to fill out so I can open the account for you at Citibank London."

John added, "I will then wire the money from this bank to your bank."

Ian replied, "As we say here in Arkansas,

LET"S GET R DONE!" His way of throwing some humor on John Tegi. He knew that no one else could get away with a statement like that. John was not in the mood for humor. Ian was just playing with him.

So, Ian sat down and sent this email to John Tegi in London;

Tuesday, April 25

**"Thank you for your phone call.**

**Here is the letter for the transfer of funds. I will work with you on this matter as long as you deal with me in an honest, straight forward manner.**

**I do have trouble hearing over the phone. I can only understand about half of what is said. That is why I prefer email.**

**However if you need more funds, you need to go through Bane Maleke in Africa.**

**It was you who did not make our appointment or try to come back to the hotel. I waited at the front desk of the hotel till after eleven am last Thursday morning.**

**Anyway, with this letter you should be able to wire the funds to my bank in the U.S. without further delay or problems.**

**You will have no problems with me as long as you complete our deal.**

**Thank you very much, Ian Douglas Bishop"**

At this point Ian Bishop just knew that this whole thing was a scam. He couldn't totally figure out why they wanted to continue playing this game with him. "Maybe they are just buying more time before I turn them over to the authorities", Ian was reasoning with Leonard, of the J.C. Foundation Board of Directors.

"You are right, my man. But, they are biding their time for another reason also. If you play this game for a little longer, you will find out what that is. Then you will be able to reveal their whole plan and bring their organization into the light, to expose them. It is also possible that the banker in Africa brought some kind of pressure against Tegi to force him to cooperate with you."

Ian retorted, "Yes, that is what I shall do. After all, I am the Bishop in this chess game and I have brought down kings before, with a little help from my friends. We are so close to discovering exactly what these people are up to and how they pull in their victims in deeper, and continue to drain their finances. They are like blood suckers, that drain the body of blood until there is no life left."

"It is a good thing that there are a few people like you, that put their own life on the line to expose people like that." Leonard said.

"Ahhh, you only say that because I am the Chairman of the Board."

"Yes, that's true! I mean that it's true that you are the Chairman of the Board."

Another email popped up on Ian's computer screen from South Africa. This time from the Manager of Internal Audit of the Development Bank of South Africa. This letter was in response to a correspondence sent to them earlier by Mr. Bishop in regards to Bane Maleke being a Regional Manager and the account where the twenty-five million dollars was hidden.

**"Dear Mr. Bishop, Weds, April 26**

**In reference to your letter to the Regional Manager of the Development Bank of Southern Africa regarding the transferring of your inheritance money.**

**Please note that this could be a Nigerian financial scam.**

**There is no such open account number at the Development Bank of Southern Africa at this time.**

**Please do not enter into any agreements with them.**

**Regards**

**Norman Weitz, Manager : Internal Audit."**

"This is exactly what I expected, but now I have more to go on", Ian was talking with Leonard on the phone.

"You need to be very careful, Ian. People like this can be very dangerous."

"Ahh, don't worry about me. I have been playing with bad guys most of my life. My momma didn't raise no fool." Ian was just fooling around with his friend. But only, to leave his friend in a lighter mood. Ian knew that he was flirting with danger.

FRIDAY, APRIL $28^{th}$

***Bane Maleke <@yahoo.com>*** wrote:

**"Dear Bishop,**

**I have contacted London and arrangement is on, to transfer your funds to you. I would advise you contact Mr. John Tegi on the transfer process."**

**We have made all payments for the consignment.**

**Please call him first thing tomorrow to find out what is keeping the funds.**

**Awaiting your reply,**

**Bane Maleke"**

Ian Bishop understood the ploy of "find out what is keeping the funds", so he ignored it. Ian replied:

**"I am ready to receive the transfer of the consignment of funds from my inheritance, and my bank in Eureka is waiting for the wired funds. My banker here assures me that there should be no problems with a transfer of this type, and all should go smoothly. All is arranged at this end.**

**Thank you, IAN"**

Ian Bishop also ignored "I would advise you to contact Mr. John Tegi on the transfer process". Ian knew that this was just a plan to get more money or more information out of him.

This was just one more way that they wanted to stay ahead

of Bishop and he was not going to allow that. They wanted to be in control of this game.

But, it was the Bishop who was one move ahead now.

April 29, Email sent to John Tegi from Ian Bishop:

**"We need to finish our dealings by the first of this next week.**

**John Tegi, you need to wire the consignment as promised or return my investment in this project, all the costs incurred by me for my London trip.**

**If not, I will turn my files over to Scotland Yard, Interpol and to the Development Bank of South Africa.**

**The Cab Driver in London has been identified. I have a copy of his credentials and Toyota Van Plate Numbers. That driver can be traced back to you because you hired him and paid him. He knows who you are.**

**You think you covered your tracks, but there are a lot of trails that lead right back to you.**

**You would be wise to wire the consignment of funds to my bank and into my account by close of business on Monday, May 1.**

**There are three people in on this, on my behalf and each one has a complete file of everything that has been said and done.**

**Wire the money to my bank in Eureka and you will never hear from us again.**

**Ignore this and you will have people seeking you out on three continents. IAN"**

⁂

John Tegi was really angry now, "Who does this Bishop think he is, to order me around?! He might think that he is one move ahead of us, but I will show him. I will never release this consignment to him. Ian Bishop thinks that he is smarter than me. He will never win this game that he is playing. I can not be played or threatened."

At the same time, Ian was thinking, "At last I have the upper hand and John Tegi's arm is not long enough to reach me here in the States." Bishop felt like he still knew which buttons to push and how far he could go when dealing with people like this.

Ian Bishop was becoming very weary of this game. It had been difficult and long. He was going to force an ending. All of this would end, one way or the other.

Saturday, April 29 from Ian Bishop to Bane Maleke,

**"I am tired of this game." Ian said.**

**"I have not said anything to Development Bank yet, but they have been in touch with me, because of the letter I sent to them originally, a couple of months ago. The bank told me that there was no such open account number at their bank.**

**You are the one to work with John Tegi. I do not**

**trust that man and I have more information on him than he even knows about.**

**I told you a while back that I am no dummy.**

**I have covered myself from every angle.**

**If you do not want people following you from three continents, I would advise, that you complete this deal by close of business on Monday. With today's technology, there is no reason why this can not happen. If all you were interested in was getting the $25 million out of Africa, then we can complete that right now.**

**Please see to this, Bane. I would not want to see this blow up in your face.**

**Sincerely, Ian Bishop"**

Ian Bishop knew that this would bring an immediate response from Bane Maleke.

Ian assumed that this would bring to the forefront any future plans and schemes that were yet to unfold.

Ian Bishop wanted to force their next move and put pressure on the London Organization and Bane so they would make the next move rashly and carelessly.

A hasty move is usually a bad move, in chess.

***Bane Maleke <@yahoo.com>*** in response wrote:

**"Dear Bishop, April 30**

**I am not happy with the tone of your mail.**

**Both of us are in this whole transaction together and we have to work hand in hand to make sure we pull it true.**

**You have started talking about the Scotland Yard again. This was the same thing you said that made Mr. John Tegi not to see you in London. What we are doing is a deal so we have to keep it very low, so no body knows about it. Mr. John Tegi is working on your matter right now as I am writing you this mail. So hopefully before the middle of this week everything will be okay.**

**There is no need for you to contact the Development Bank of Southern Africa.**

**This account is a coded account and no body will give you any information about an account that does not belong to you.**

**I am the only person that has the information to this account.**

**Bishop, I know you are not a dummy, So please stop talking about tracing the funds and people following me from three continents. We would complete this whole transaction this week.**

**Regards, Bane Maleke."**

Monday, May 1, Ian's REPLY to Bane Maleke:

**"Originally you told me that this whole thing**

**would take 10 days to complete. That was back in March.**

**Okay, I will hold off till the end of this week for the funds to be wired into my account.**

**I am not happy either.**

**John Tegi did not receive a threatening email from me until AFTER he stood me up in London.**

**I will send a copy of this email to John Tegi in London also.**

**Till the end of this week. Take care of this business and we will all be happy.**

**Signed; Ian"**

***Bane Maleke <@yahoo.com>*** Monday, May 1; wrote:

**"Dear Bishop,**

**Thanks for your mail. You have to call him to put pressure on him so that he can act fast. I want us to conclude this transaction as quickly as possible.**

**Regards, Bane Maleke."**

"You have to call him to put pressure on him", simply means that they wanted to put pressure in Bishop. He would not fall for that. Bane had even phoned Bishop to make sure that he was still involved in this deal and that he wasn't going to turn them in. He tried to encourage Bishop to continue dealing with John Tegi in London.

Ian emailed Bane telling him that he was apprehensive because of the way he had been treated in London, but he would assist Bane with the transfer of funds.

Ian Bishop had mentioned the "**inheritance scam from out of Nigeria**" to let Bane know that he knew more about all this, than Maleke thought he did. Just because Ian lived in the States and not in Africa, didn't mean that he did not know what was going on in other parts of the world.

Wednesday, May 3

Ian's phone rang. He had a feeling that it was from either London or South Africa. He almost did not even answer the call. Sure enough it was from London. The connection was not real good and Ian had trouble with Tegi's accent as well. It was hard for Ian to understand what Tegi wanted so he said "Send me the details in an email so there will not be any misunderstanding."

John Tegi had said something like "This is going to cost you money one way or an other. There are fees that have to be paid. Also there is one more document that has to be filled out, signed and sent back to me by email."

Ian said "I will look for your email." and hung up the phone. He had forced their hand and made them move before they were really ready. This was what he had been trying to do.

Ian Bishop wanted this game to be over, but at the same time he wanted to get to the bottom of things. He didn't really understand why they wanted to continue with the game.

Did they really think that they were going to get money out of him?

"Could they still be trying to pull what ever money they could still get out of me or was something else at play that I just don't understand yet?" Ian was thinking out loud.

Tegi had mentioned "This is going to cost you one way or the other."

"Was that a threat?" Ian pondered. But, he decided to ignore it.

Thursday May 4, Email from John Tegi in London, U.K.

**"Dear Sir,**

**Following our telephone conversation yesterday, I am hereby sending you the bank account opening forms for you to fill out, sign and send back to me via email attachment.**

**You will recall in our conversation yesterday that I requested for the drug clearance certificate in order to enable the bank to transfer the funds to your account. This document is very necessary and can only be obtained from South Africa or we can procure it through our agent who handles such, for us.**

**In both cases, you will need to make an upfront payment.**

**However, if you already have this document, then send the copy of the document to us immediately so that once you open the account, the funds will be lodged into the account and transferred to your account in the U.S.**

**In the meantime, please fill out the form from Citibank London, sign and send back so that we can commence the process.**

**Presently, your funds are kept in the vault of the Citibank. Please note that this arrangement of lodging these funds into the bank is entirely classified and is only being done for us due to the network we have with the bank.**

**I will therefore advise that you abide by our instruction strictly this time so that we can avoid a repetition of what happened during your trip to London.**

**I will await your response regarding the completed form and the drug clearance certificate.**

**Thanks. Yours faithfully,**

**John Tegi."**

Ian went back to the Board of Directors, and to Leonard Landerfeld, saying,

"Well isn't that a surprise? They want me to pay some up front money for a "Drug Clearance Certificate". Boy, that sounds expensive. I bet they want a lot of money for that!

Can you believe the nerve that these people have?"

Leonard answered, "You probably don't want to make these people mad."

"It's too late for that" Ian said, laughing.

"Maybe it's them that shouldn't make me mad!

Do you have any idea how many poor, old people these vermin prey on? How many trusting people who invest their life's blood and savings into a get rich quick scam like this, out of desperation because the stock market has fallen or their retirements have gone sour?

If I can save just a few old people's savings, so that their golden years can still be golden, it will be worth while for me, and for the time and money I have spent. I am so close to uncovering their intire scam.

Just one more week Lenard, and I will either get to the bottom of this thing or die trying."

Leonard said, "OK, one more week, but be careful. We don't want you to die trying, my man."

# CHAPTER 27

May 5, a phone call from Cindy in Wurzburg, Germany, to Ian in Eureka.

“I'm pretty far into your new book now” Cindy said, “It is very interesting.” She was referring to Ian’s last book; “Light and Shadow.”

“Thank you very much” Ian responded.

Cindy continued, “It was good to hear all your news in your last email. Talking to your own bank is a wise move. Can you imagine? Do you suppose there really is some money?

It was hard for me to believe before they treated you like they did in London. Then, I was sure it was a scam. Either this man is trying to protect himself by keeping you on the string longer until his tracks are clearly swept away or he is a nut who is playing a game, or there IS an inheritance.

But honestly, if there had been money it would have been in England when you were there.”

Ian said “Well, yes there could have been money at the holding company in London when I was there. The London connection was trying to play me for all that he could get. I just don‘t trust him.”

“They said the shipment was there, even gave you a shipping receipt. I see lie, on top of lie, don't you?” Cindy asked.

Ian said, "I have not really believed all this from the very beginning, but of course you would like to think that there is some truth involved as far as the money is concerned. It may well turn out that all they bequeath is the wind. They do seem to be full of a lot of hot air."

Ian continued with Cindy on the phone, "I knew that there was something that was not right, of course. I was hoping that the only thing illegal was them just trying to get this money out of South Africa."

"Anyway, what have you been up to?"

Cindy said, "I have been grading papers till eight o'clock, both Wednesday and Thursday nights. I did study some last night, toward my Master's Degree.

My girl friend, Angie and I are going out to dinner and then to a marriage seminar tonight. We decided we would be each other's date, and learn from Chaplain Robinson how to understand our future mate, if we happen to get one, that is.

So, I will take the test for my Master's this coming Saturday."

Ian said "Thanks for the phone call. Good luck on your test."

Ian didn't say anything about the marriage seminar, he felt like she was dropping a mighty big hint.

Cindy responded "Okay, I'll phone again this weekend when you have more available minutes on your phone. Good night."

Ian Bishop was not really ready to comment about the marriage seminar that Cindy had made a reference to, but all the same he thought that was a good sign. She must have been thinking about "marriage and how to understand her future mate."

Not that she could ever really fully understand Ian Bishop, if that was what she was thinking. He was doing good just to understand himself. When he wasn't thinking about the "Nigerian Scam", that is if it was a scam, he was thinking about Cindy or Jean, and how nice it would be to have someone to come home to. It had been a long time since Ian had unconditional love in his life, and he missed that. At the same time Ian Bishop was enjoying the freedom he had in his life right now. As for now he was not ready to commit to a one love relationship. When he was ready, they would know it, because Ian has never been one to beat around the bush.

Marriage was a subject that Ian Bishop understood. He was not only an adventurer but a lover. He was always ready to jump in where angels feared to tread. Ian felt that love was a chance worth taking.

As if Ian Bishop did not have enough things on his plate, he had been devoting more and more time to his writing and had begun working more on his new novel; "Bequeath the Wind". It seemed like a good title because he felt like the inheritance might very well be nothing more than hot air. Ian wanted to get down all the details before he forgot them, so he spent his days off of the Play putting down the skeleton of his plot. He would add the flesh later.

This however, was not the time for day dreaming. Ian Bishop was a dreamer, but for right now he had other things in which he needed to concentrate.

There were more pressing life and death decisions. The "Nigerian Scam" as it was called by the Development Bank of South Africa was a chess game that he had to win. He had not been playing the game this long to loose. Ian Bishop did not like draws. He wanted to beat these guys at their own game. He wanted to leave them holding the bag, an empty bag, for the last four months of work.

Ian Bishop had received the two page form from Citibank London, mentioned very briefly in the email from John Tegi.

*"In the meantime, please fill out the form from Citibank London, sign and send back so that we can commence the process."*

They wanted a complete credit history to open up what Ian noticed in fine print a "**Joint Account**" in London. A regular person may have either overlooked that little detail or figured that the account would have to be 'Joint' in order for them to move the money into your account or wire it out of London to your home bank. But, to Ian it looked like these people wanted a "power of attorney" over his finances, signed, sealed and delivered.

This two page document from Citibank London sent up all kinds of WARNINGS to Ian Bishop.

He decided to just send to London a signed letter with his permission to wire the funds from Citibank London into his local bank account in Eureka.

Then he would take this latest information directly to his bank personally, in Eureka Springs, U.S.A.

# Citibank Account **Application Form**

**For existing customers adding a joint applicant**

If you would like to add a joint applicant to an existing Citibank Account tick this box ☐

Please state the existing account number to be linked to a joint applicant ☐☐☐☐☐☐☐☐

Please complete the following sections:
For the Primary Applicant: Personal Details, Financial Details, Your Account Activity and sign at the end.
For the Joint Applicant: All Joint Applicant fields, US Tax Status and sign at the end.

All fields marked with a red triangle (➤) are mandatory, and must be completed. We will be unable to open your account(s) without this information. Please complete the application in BLOCK CAPITALS

## Step 1. Choose which account(s) you want to open

UK Current Accounts: ☐ Sterling Current Account

UK Savings Accounts: ☐ Instant Access Account ☐ 60 Day Direct Account ☐ Online Saver

Foreign Currency Current Accounts: ☐ US Dollar Current Account ☐ Euro Current Account

Foreign Currency Deposit Accounts (please specify currencies) ______ ______ ______ ______

## Step 2. Tell us about yourself

### Personal details

**PRIMARY APPLICANT**

➤ Title (Mr, Mrs, Miss, Ms etc) ______

➤ Surname ______

➤ Forename(s) ______

➤ Current residential address ______

______

______

______ Postcode ______

➤ At current address since (dd/mm/yy) ______

➤ Residential status ☐ Owner/Occupier ☐ Tenant ☐ Living with parents ☐ Other

If your surname or address has changed within the last 3 years, you must complete this section. You must provide all your addresses within the last 3 years (including non-UK addresses), attaching a separate sheet if necessary. We will be unable to open your account(s) without this information.

➤ Previous surname ______

➤ Previous address ______

______

______

______ Postcode ______

➤ Time at previous address ______ Years ______ Months

➤ Date of birth (dd/mm/yy) ______

➤ Nationality ______

➤ Country of permanent residence ______

➤ Marital status ☐ Married ☐ Single ☐ Living with partner ☐ Divorced/Separated ☐ Widowed

**JOINT APPLICANT**

➤ Title (Mr, Mrs, Miss, Ms etc) ______

➤ Surname ______

➤ Forename(s) ______

➤ Current residential address ______

______

______

______ Postcode ______

➤ At current address since (dd/mm/yy) ______

➤ Residential status ☐ Owner/Occupier ☐ Tenant ☐ Living with parents ☐ Other

If your surname or address has changed within the last 3 years, you must complete this section. You must provide all your addresses within the last 3 years (including non-UK addresses), attaching a separate sheet if necessary. We will be unable to open your account(s) without this information.

➤ Previous surname ______

➤ Previous address ______

______

______

______ Postcode ______

➤ Time at previous address ______ Years ______ Months

➤ Date of birth (dd/mm/yy) ______

➤ Nationality ______

➤ Country of permanent residence ______

➤ Marital status ☐ Married ☐ Single ☐ Living with partner ☐ Divorced/Separated ☐ Widowed

PLEASE REMEMBER TO SIGN AND RETURN THIS APPLICATION WITH YOUR IDENTIFICATION DOCUMENTS
OFFICE USE ONLY: REFERENCE NUMBER SOURCE CODE: OFFER CODE:

## Your account activity (continued)

Please estimate the value and number of transactions you are likely to undertake per month, for each of the transaction types listed in the table below.

| Type of transaction | Estimated monthly value of your transactions: Less than £5,000 | Between £5,000 & £10,000 | Between £10,000 & £25,000 | If £25,000 or more please state amount | Estimated number of transactions per month: 0-3 | 4-6 | If 7 or more please state amount |
|---|---|---|---|---|---|---|---|
| **Deposits** | | | | | | | |
| Cash | ☐ | ☐ | ☐ | ______ | ☐ | ☐ | ______ |
| Cheques | ☐ | ☐ | ☐ | ______ | ☐ | ☐ | ______ |
| Direct credits (including salary) | ☐ | ☐ | ☐ | ______ | ☐ | ☐ | ______ |
| Funds transfers in the UK | ☐ | ☐ | ☐ | ______ | ☐ | ☐ | ______ |
| International funds transfers | ☐ | ☐ | ☐ | ______ | ☐ | ☐ | ______ |
| Other (please specify below eg. travellers cheques, Drafts etc) | ☐ | ☐ | ☐ | ______ | ☐ | ☐ | ______ |
| **Withdrawals** | | | | | | | |
| Cash | ☐ | ☐ | ☐ | ______ | ☐ | ☐ | ______ |
| Cheques | ☐ | ☐ | ☐ | ______ | ☐ | ☐ | ______ |
| Direct Debits/Standing orders/Bill payments etc | ☐ | ☐ | ☐ | ______ | ☐ | ☐ | ______ |
| Funds transfers in the UK | ☐ | ☐ | ☐ | ______ | ☐ | ☐ | ______ |
| International funds transfers | ☐ | ☐ | ☐ | ______ | ☐ | ☐ | ______ |
| Other (please specify below eg. travellers cheques, Drafts etc) | ☐ | ☐ | ☐ | ______ | ☐ | ☐ | ______ |

### Step 4. Please read the declaration below and sign your application

#### Data protection notice and declaration

**DATA PROTECTION NOTICE**

(To be read in conjunction with the paragraph entitled "Information" in the General Terms and Conditions)

Citibank International plc is a member of the Citigroup Group of Companies and is the Data Controller. We will use your information to open and administer your account and for other business purposes, including the following: make any enquiries that we consider necessary to confirm your identity and for credit assessment purposes; use credit scoring techniques when considering your application, operating your account or making credit decisions (you have a right to make representations against any adverse decisions which have been taken on a solely automated basis) [illegible]

[illegible]

☐ [illegible]

☐ [illegible]

☐ [illegible]

[illegible]

**DECLARATION**

This must be signed by each applicant.

Note: When two or more people sign this Declaration, the following applies to each of them [illegible]

[illegible]

I accept you have the right to decline my application without giving an explanation.

#### Your signature

I have read and understood the Data Protection Notice and Declaration.

Primary applicant's signature ______________________ Joint applicant's signature ______________________

Date (dd/mm/yy) ______________________ Date (dd/mm/yy) ______________________

### Step 5. Please enclose your documentation as outlined in the section 'The documents we need to open your account'

The Security Officer at Ian's bank looked at these forms from Citibank London and knew immediately what these people wanted from Mr. Bishop.

❧

# CHAPTER 28

May 5th.

It was time to talk with his friend Leonard again. Ian phoned him.

"Leonard, I went to the bank today.

I laid out the whole plan (scam) from South Africa to London. My records from the last three months.

I was directed to the Bank's Security officer. She listened intently to my story. She had heard of many scams of different types, even lottery scams from out of South Africa and Mexico. But, she had never heard of anything this large before. This involved major bank fraud on an international level. My bank officer told me that the U.S. Secret Service would want to know about this because it involved many millions of U.S. dollars, supposedly moved by Diplomatic Courier from one continent to another."

All Leonard could say was "Oh my gosh!" as Ian continued his story.

"I had not figured out, that the information to wire money into my account (as a deposit slip) contained enough information that they could draft my account for the whole balance in that account. At this point they had my passport information, my bank account number, my birth date. If they thought there was any amount of money in that account they would have drafted a check and stolen it all."

Ian went on, as Leonard was caught up in his story.

"The scam really begins to sound plausible when you know that you have not put any money up front, but that's all part of the deception." Leonard said, "They sure had me fooled for a while."

Leonard called his wife, Laura to the phone, "Honey, you've got to hear this. Get on the extension."

As Ian continued "As it was, at this point they had changed their strategy to Identity Theft instead of just drafting my bank account. I had wondered why they continued this game even after they found out that I did not have any money in my bank account. I was probably worth about a half million dollars U.S., credit wise.

If I would have filled out the final papers they send to me, they would have had all the information they needed to make a complete run for my credit worth, as well as everything from every account that I had."

Laura said "Well, what did you do?"

"I closed my accounts and changed all my information at the bank and opened new accounts."

Ian went on, "I contacted the Social Security office, the theater where I work with direct deposit and automatic withdraws for my bills, and gave them my new information."

Leonard asked, "Where do you go from here?"

So Ian answered; "The bank told me that I needed to contact the United States Secret Service, Scotland Yard in London, Interpol and the Development Bank of South Africa.

I will have to file a complaint with the F.B.I. and make a report to a major credit report company, telling them, that my credit had been compromised."

"But what are you going to do about these people in London and Africa?" Laura and Leonard wanted to know.

Ian just simply said "Stay in contact with them, lead them on, as though I was still under their spell. That is until the proper authorities clamp down on their operation."

Laura said. "But what if some of them get away and come after you?"

Bishop was used to this kind of response from his friends. He went on, "The secret is . . .Always stay one step ahead in this chess game of moves and countermoves. Several times they had tried to move in for the kill and several times I made a counter move that had thrown them off.

This time they had made their final move to Checkmate. But I had made a counter move one step ahead of them.

I changed all my account numbers, and did not fill out their final two page information sheet from Citibank of London, that was suppose to finally wire the $25,600,000. to my bank in Eureka."

"A forced move was their mistake!"

# CHAPTER 29

This was a dangerous high stakes chess game, but this time the Bishop felt like he had **them** on their way to Checkmate.

Ian Bishop continued his phone call to Leonard and Laura.

"To catch the London Connection and the South African contact off guard", Ian said "I plan on communicating to them that my bank told me that they already had enough information to transfer the consignment monies from the Citibank, London Vault to my bank in Eureka.

I will tell John Tegi in London to; 'Please continue with the wire transfer.' They will think that I am still in the game, and if nothing else they will think that they can do a run on the bank account that I had already closed. They will think that, but they will be sadly mistaken and I am still at least one move ahead of the opponent."

This chess game was coming to a close. It was now a very aggressive, fast moving game and was running very close. But Bishop positioned himself to at least force a draw or maybe even Checkmate.

But, this part of the game was even more intense and the moves more critical than at the beginning. There could be no mistakes.

"More chess games have been lost by mistakes, than games won through intelligence!"

***Bane Maleke <@yahoo.com>*** Friday, May 5 wrote:

**"Dear Bishop,**

**I got your mail and you said something about a phone call. I did not call you and have not called you for a very long time now. Please mind who you communicate with, regarding this transaction. You know that what we are doing is a deal, so you have to lay very low, so nobody is put in any problems.**

**However, In your last mail you said you have contacted your bank regarding the transfer of your funds. You should not have done that in the first place. All this could cause internal problems. Has the transfer been made to your account?**

**Please advise me on how to get my share.**

**Regards, Bane Maleke"**

May 5, Email Reply from Bishop to Bane Maleke in South Africa:

**"Not to worry, Bane. I got the phone call from**

**John Tegi. John told me that he had everything he needs to make the wire transfer from the security company in London that is holding the consignment of funds. I will let you know when the transfer is complete."**

**"Dear Bishop,**

**Please keep me informed so that I can start making preparation for my trip to the United States. Did you speak with Mr. John Tegi regarding the transfer of the money?**

**We need to finalize this transaction by next week.**

**Regards, Bane Maleke."**

To John Tegi from Ian Bishop, on Saturday, May 6:

**"I will have to get back to you on Monday. I have been working 12 hour shifts at work. I will send you what you need to wire transfer my inheritance funds to my bank in Eureka Springs. You may not get it till Tuesday, because of the time difference."**

❧

Ian continued to play their game until the authorities caught up with these swindling fools. Meanwhile he wrote an email to his daughters and stayed in touch with his friends. He wrote to Cindy in Germany to keep her apprised of the situation.

Ian reminded them "They do not have my Social Security number and my accounts have been changed at the bank. I will be contacting the U.S. Secret Service tomorrow. Today is one of my 12 hour days at the theater."

***Cindy responded to Ian with this email***

**"Oh my goodness. Wow, I am sure glad you didn't give them the last information. Steal your**

**identity, Oh my, that would be a terrible thing.**

**Do you suppose you will be in danger forever, I mean as long as you are Ian Bishop?**

**I mean, can they pretend to be you, and search out new information about you?**

**Well anyway seems you are handling it the best way.**

**Isn't that going to be difficult, contacting the authorities in Africa and England? God bless you as you work this all out. I am so sorry there is not an inheritance.**

**Love, Cindy"**

Ian's daughter responded to his latest email on Saturday, May 6th.

**"Ahhhh, Yes, isn't that just like life, a chess game. I've often thought of that."**

**"Stems from all the games I played with you when I was a kid. I think I beat you once, but you probably let me win.**

**It sounds like you are just in the game to toy with them and have them cornered. I'm glad you're good at chess, I'd like to think I had a small hand in that since I played you so much when I was a kid. Who knows maybe chess will come in handy for me one of these days too.**

**I pray that nothing happens to you.**

**Can't wait to read your book, 'Bequeath the Wind'**

**signed, your loving daughter, Valinda."**

On Sunday, May 7th. Ian began to contact the authorities.

He called the United States Secret Service with the phone number that was given to him by the bank. There was no answer. So, Ian figured that The U.S. Secret Service does not work on Sunday. A recording said that they would be open at eight-thirty am on Monday.

Ian looked up the F.B.I. on the Net and filed a report with them and also looked up Scotland Yard in London and filed a full report with them including full documentation via email attachments.

ൟ

Bishop also notified The Development Bank of South Africa:

**"Dear Sirs,**

**The Nigerian Scam is continuing. Please follow through with investigation and turn this matter over to authorities. These phone numbers and email addresses are still being used by the perpetrators. Please be careful with this info so you don't just scare them away. I also intend to phone the U.S. Secret Service and Scotland Yard in London, U.K. because of the London contact as well.**

Dr. Bane Maleke, Regional Manager DBSA

@yahoo.com (still active)

Mr. John Tegi, Administration, ADB Organization, London Security Company?

@hotmail.com (still active) (LONDON, U.K.)

Phone numbers in London:

33-207-060-0057 or 0677-803-5763

Gold Card Membership PASS CODE; KK11WT

**I hope this information will help in apprehending these characters. I have complete email files on this scam if you need them. Please don't just scare them away. I also have their French bank account info for you.**

**I have a feeling they will go "underground" after this week. They seem to be running just a little afraid.**

**More documents to come under separate cover."**

Ian wanted to alert them as far as the bank fraud was concerned, and he knew that they would know more about the proper authorities to contact in South Africa, than he did.

Monday morning arrived. It was a beautiful day in North West Arkansas. Ian was going to be on the phone with the United States Secret Service most of the morning.

"United States Secret Service, How may I direct your call?" The lady asked on the other end of the line.

Ian reflected a moment, "Well, I need to speak with an agent regarding international bank fraud and inheritance scams, on three continents."

"Just a minute Sir, I will connect you with one of our agents." . . . . "Hello, this is Special Agent Henderson, what can I do for you?"

"Well, Sir, I think it is more what I can do for you, today. You are speaking with Ian Douglas Bishop in Eureka Springs. I want to report international bank fraud, an inheritance scam in the amount of twenty five million, six hundred thousand U.S. Dollars that covers three continents and attempted I.D. theft."

"Go ahead Sir, you have my full attention." the Agent exclaimed.

Ian Bishop explained it like this:

"I know that I have put myself in harm's way, but I just had to get to the bottom of this inheritance scam from out of South Africa to London, the United Kingdom. I had protected myself by making it known to them that there was complete files of all the phone numbers, names, dates and addresses with a friend in Germany and another friend in the States, with instructions to turn over these files to authorities if anything happened to me. First of all they seemed to be after the 'up front money'.

Since they could not get the 'up front money' they changed their plans to include wiping out my checking account.

I made it known to them that I did not have much money in my bank account. If they needed funds to pay for up front shipments or administrative charges, they would have to collect such funds from the banker in South Africa that I had been in contact with.

If I had filled out the final papers they wanted, in order to open a bank account in London and wire the money to my bank in Eureka, they would have had enough information to steal my identity and make off with a half million dollars U.S. worth of my credit."

Ian continued with his conversation with Special Agent Henderson. "I have kept complete files on everything from the beginning.

I have full documentation, addresses and phone numbers that are still in use. I have continued to lead these people on. They think that they still have me on a string."

Agent Henderson responded by saying, "We have been following this situation ourselves. It is called the "Nigerian Inheritance Scam" because it originated out of Nigeria, Africa. We used to have an office over there for a while but we could not get any cooperation from the Nigerian Government, so we closed that office. However, I feel like you are in real danger. People who have not been involved as deeply as you, have disappeared and some have been found dead."

To that Ian moaned "What should I do? I am closing my negotiations with them now. I wanted to keep them on line until you can follow through."

"Sir" the Agent said "Please send us your complete files with all the current, in use, phone numbers and addresses."

"Yes, Sir. I will do that. I have already filed this information with Scotland Yard, Metro in London and the F.B.I, as well as The Development Bank of South Africa."

Special Agent Henderson said "Mr. Bishop, thank you for all that you have done. We will move on this information and if we need more from you, **We know where you live!**

Well, I didn't mean for that to sound so ominous. We have your phone number and if we need further information from you, we will call. By the way, if I was you, I would be more careful."

"You have been messing around with some very treacherous people.

Also, if I was you, I would make myself very scarce for the next few months," concluded the agent.

"It's kind of difficult to make yourself scarce when you are on stage five nights a week."

❧

# CHAPTER 30

Ian Bishop called another meeting with the Board of Directors of the J.C. Foundation and shared with them what the Secret Service had said. Ian also confided in his friend, Leonard, "Maybe I should just kill myself !"

"W H AT ? !!" Leonard exclaimed.

Ian said, "I don't mean that literally. I just meant that if I want to really throw these unscrupulous people for a loop and get them off my trail, I should pretend to be dead."

Leonard was relieved to hear that, "Oh, you know, that might be a good idea. Let me know what you come up with."

"I will." Ian mumbled as he was already deep in thought about his next move.

&

On Tuesday, May 9th. A copy of an email sent out from the Development Bank of South Africa to Ian Bishop

**"To Whom It May Concern:**

**Could you please shut down the account below (malekeb@yahoo.com) as this account may be used for a Nigerian 419 scam."**

**"Regards, N. Weitz, Manager,**

**Internal Audit, Development Bank of South Africa"**

It would appear that the Development Bank was shutting the Nigerian Scam, down in South Africa.

Then, the New Scotland Yard responded to Ian's email;

**"Dear Ian,**

**Thank you for your email - this has been passed to the Fraud Squad.**

**Email; Office New Scotland Yard, London Metro."**

Ian wondered if the "Fraud Squad" was anything like the "Mod Squad" from the olden days of television? Well, that at least showed that he had not lost his sense of humor even when his life was in danger.

From Bane Maleke in South Africa, Monday, May 8

**"Dear Bishop,**

**Keep this transaction to yourself alone. from the mail you sent me it looks as if you have discussed it with your bank officials.**

**This is not good for this transaction, because every body's eyes will be on that money right now.**

**The money has been put in a safe deposit at Citibank London and I am sure the transfer has been made already.**

**I am a waiting your urgent reply,**

**Bane Maleke."**

**Email to John Tegi from Ian Bishop, on Monday, May 8th.**

**"Bane Maleke in South Africa told me that the money was in a safety deposit box at Citibank, London.**

**I hope we can get the transfer of the consignment finished today?**

**This attachment has my bank info on it. This is all you need to wire the funds to me.**

**Thank you, Ian Bishop."**

Of course all the bank information that Ian was sending was false information. All of his account numbers and information had been changed, and the bank had been alerted to the problem.

Tuesday, May 9th. Ian decided what he needed to do. He sent the following email to his friends and family as well as the Board of Directors of the J.C. Foundation. He didn't want to catch anyone off guard:

**"I have continued to play their game. I was in contact with London as well as South Africa this morning to keep them using the same email addresses and phone numbers, in hopes that the authorities can trace them.**

**I heard back from Scotland Yard as well as the**

**Bank in South Africa this morning and talked at length with the Secret Service.**

**Just in case, the authorities don't catch everyone involved in this scam. I am going to die of a heart attack. Actually that is a good idea. I think <u>I will write them right now, (and email it tomorrow) as if my daughter was notifying my email friends, going down my address list, telling them of my tragic, unexpected death.</u>**

**The U.S. Secret Service Agent said that "some people that have personally followed up on this scam have ended up dead or held hostage for money. I might add, I have kept "my angel" very busy during the past three months running interference for me."**

Ian Bishop then prepared the following email . . . .

THE SUBJECT line of the email had the explanation for his friends and family only, that this was a copy of what he would send out to South Africa and to London on the following day.

It was now **Wednesday, May 10th**. This was the ending of a long journey that had begun last November.

But, **sometimes** one has to look at death as a new beginning, not just an ending. As Ian had said many times, "I don't like goodbyes. Don't ever tell me goodbye, just say, Until we meet again."

**This is the email that was sent out to London and to South Africa:**

**"Dear Friends,**

**I regret to inform you that my Dad**

**(Ian Douglas Bishop) died of a heart attack while he was on the computer today. I do not know who he was communicating with, but figured that I would just send this message to all, on his address list.**

**If you knew him, you knew that he lived each day as though it was his last.**

**He left this world in peace and without any great amount of pain.**

**Thank you for being his friend. He will be missed by all, I am sure.**

**Most Sincerely,**

**Dorinda Lynne**

**His Loving Daughter"**

# CHAPTER 31

"You might think that this is a good place to end this book, but OH NO! When you have known Ian Bishop as long as I have, you are never quit sure what he is going to do. The unexpected is always what you should look for," Leonard said.

As you recall earlier, Ian said, "Sometimes one has to look at death as a new beginning, not just an ending, but a resurrection."

So on we go, to the new beginning.

Leonard and Laura Landerfeld, Members of the Board of Directors at the J.C. Foundation .

The Landerfeld's were celebrating their first wedding anniversary the night when the disturbing news came to them about Ian's death.

Laura had never in her life been so shocked. "He was in perfect health, just the day before". She received an email and she sat there at her desk reading it over and over. "Honey", she yelled to Leonard, "Come in here and read this!"

It was Ian's death notice.

She had not read the SUBJECT LINE but had gone straight to the body copy.

Leonard said "Honey, read the SUBJECT LINE."

She said "OHHH!" somewhat sheepishly, when she noticed that this was only a copy of what Bishop was going to send to the people running the scam, he had become so involved with over the past few months.

Leonard went on to explain to her that "Ian had to do this, as a matter of safety.

The U.S. Secret Service had recommended that he 'Lay Low, and what better way to lay low, than to die since he could not get into a witness protection program. Ian Bishop did not want to change his name or move away.

So, it was better if he just temporarily died."

Ian Bishop's oldest daughter, Valarie, phoned him and said "Dad, you freaked me out ! I even had bad dreams !"

Also it was at one-thirty in the morning, that same day when Leonard and Laura's phone rang;

"Ahhh, Hello?" Laura said sleepily as she just rolled out of bed.

On the other end of the line, all the way from Germany, Cindy exclaimed "IS IT TRUE? I S I T T R U E ?? "Between sobs.

"No, Cindy. It is not true. You need to read the subject line of that email."

"Is he still alive? Are you sure? Have you talked to him?"

Laura reassured Cindy "Yes, he is still alive. Don't worry Honey. Ian is fine. Take a deep breath and let it out slow. Stop crying and do what ever it is that you do at this time of day," Laura being woke up out of a sound sleep had no idea what time it was in Arkansas rather lone, figuring out what time it was in Germany.

Cindy said between crying, "Well, he won't be alive when I finish with him. I have never been so afraid in all my life."

The next day Ian received this email from his friend Leonard;

**"Dear Ian,**

**I regret to tell you that Cindy called us at about one-thirty a.m. and was sobbing and crying hysterically.**

**She kept asking Laura, "Is it true? Is it true?"**

**She was really beside herself with grief. I really believe that she cares for you. She, too, like Laura probably didn't read the SUBJECT line of the email first and just quickly went right to the text.**

**Oh, well, it was exciting. Like I said in the dressing room at the Play, Saturday night,**

**'There's never a dull moment with Ian.'**

**I am really enjoying our time together, now that the play has started. I look so forward to the times that we are in supporting roles and can talk.**

**Leonard"**

Ian Bishop thought that he better send another Email to Cindy

**"Dear Cindy, May 10th.**

**That last letter was sent out to London and Africa at ten this morning (Wednesday). I hope that it made THEM cry, but that's doubtful.**

**I apologize that you misunderstood, my death."**

**"I thought I had written to you before, saying that my death would be a good idea because the U.S. Secret Service had told me that people were being murdered and or abducted in regards to these people in Africa and also in London.**

**Actually if you killed me, I wouldn't have to die of a heart attack.**

**I didn't mean to upset you. I didn't even think I would be missed. Signed, Ian**

Bishop wrote this email explaining that he was sorry that Cindy was upset about his death notice and that he had told her about his plan in an earlier email. Ian apologized and Cindy had forgiven him;

**"I am sorry I said I was going to kill you. I am soooooo glad you are alive, I am still crying. I can't get over this scare. Please write as soon as you can. Laura says you are still alive. She was sleeping. I sure hope she is right. Cindy"**

Ian had no idea that his death would create such a stir. After all this is the first time he had ever died. He had been through a few close scrapes before but this was a new experience for him.

In the midst of everything that had been going on. The Play had begun on April the 28th. And the rest of Ian Bishop's life was still ahead of him and the biggest adventure of them all still to unfold!

☙

Laura had been best friends with Cindy for many years so she was always giving Ian pointers on how to handle Cindy. It was at the Play one night, back stage in the dressing room when Laura cornered Ian and said "You better not hurt my friend." She had said it with a smile on her face, but Ian knew a threat when he heard one.

Cindy told Ian on one of their long distance phone calls that his death made her realize how much she actually cared about him. He also explained to her that he was not going to answer his phone to anyone who was not on file in his phone list of friends. That way he could see who was calling before he answered.

Cindy wanted to know how long he would have to be dead.

☙

Ian Bishop was going to write some more in his newest book, “Bequeath the Wind”. He opened his computer to begin writing that day and decided to check his email.

That was a relief, no email from London or South Africa.

There was a welcome letter from Cindy waiting patiently in Ian’s email;

**“Dear Ian,**

**You don't ever have to worry about hurting me, I know you are not the type to want to hurt anyone. I am not thin skinned.**

**Anyway that is the main thing I like about you, you are not vengeful, you are not living in self pity. You don't need someone to help heal you. You are well already.**

**I don't know where this road is leading, but I am very glad to be traveling it, along with you.**

**It is real good to know that there is one good man in the world who cares for me, no matter how deeply, or how permanent.**

**I have to admit that I am not 20 anymore. No matter how young and healthy I feel, life will have to slow down - it just will. I don't know the future, and I am grateful that I don't.**

**Love, Cindy”**

☙

# CHAPTER 32

And, then it happened. An Email to a Dead Man.

Ian opened up his email and there it was!

**“Bishop,**

**Please do not play me, I need my money.**

**Regards,**

**Bane.”**

When Ian saw this email he thought he was in trouble. It made his heart race and his mind shifted into gear. Bishop punched Leonard’s number into his phone.

“Hello,” Laura said.

“Yes, this is Ian. Is Leonard there? I would like to talk with him, please.”

“Hi Ian, my man. How are you doin’?”

“Well, Leonard, I’ll tell you when I figure that out. We need to meet and I don’t want the girls to know about it. How about meeting me for lunch today, over at the Gazebo Restaurant?”

“OK, How about eleven am?” Leonard responded.

“Fine, I’ll see you there.” and Ian hung up.

Ian Bishop was thinking that Bane Maleke was either on a fishing expedition, just trying to find out if Ian was still alive, or he knew that Bishop was alive and was hot on his trail and very angry that Bishop had broken up his organization. “If that’s the case” Ian thought “I could be in grave trouble.”

Two hours later in front of the Gazebo Restaurant, Ian pulled up on his new Honda Shadow Motorcycle. Leonard had just set the lock on his car. They shook hands and slapped each other on the back as they headed for the restaurant door. The temperature was up near 90 degrees already which was kind of hot for the middle of April in the Ozarks.

It felt good to step into the air conditioning.

“What’s up Ian? With all the secrecy I thought maybe you were in some sort of trouble.” Leonard whispered into his friends ear as they walked through the lobby into the restaurant.

“Two for lunch, please” Ian mentioned to the hostess, as he turned to his friend and said softly “I may well be in a very dangerous situation. I need to talk about this and see where we should go from here. I didn’t want to upset or scare the girls with this latest information, but, South Africa may well know that I am still alive and well.”

“What makes you think so?” quizzed Leonard.

Ian answered after they were seated at their table over in the far corner. Ian always liked his back up against the wall, so he could people watch and see who was coming in and going out.

He was a people watcher even in normal mode. However, these circumstances were not normal and his life might be hanging in the balance. “Leonard, I need your council as to what to do. I got an email this morning from Bane Maleke, the banker from South Africa. I could not tell if he was mad or desperate, or both. I don’t know if he really knows that I am alive or just trying to see if I would respond to him, so he could find out.”

“What did he say?” Leonard questioned “And was he threatening you?”

“The email was rather ominous. He said that he needed his money. Now, I thought that was a funny thing to say. He also mentioned that I should ‘not Play Him’. Bane must have known that I did not have his money. Chances are, Scotland Yard moved in on his buddy in London and that he himself is in big trouble with the Development Bank of South Africa. That is assuming that he had actually ever worked for them.”

Leonard asked, “Ian, suppose the money is real and that part of this whole mess was true? Have you considered that as an option?”

“Oh, surely not!” Ian exclaimed “You don’t suppose that Bane was sincerely following through with the inheritance funds and moving those funds out of South Africa, do you?”

“If that was the case,” Ian puzzled, “He would have to go through me because my name was on all the paper work. His hands would be tied and he would not be able to touch that money without me. But, that’s too far fetched. How could that be?”

“Well, it could be if the man that was in charge of administration in London was crooked and was connected in some way with the diplomatic courier service out of Africa.” Leonard said.

“That could be a possibility, but where do we go from here? Should we share this information with the girls?”

'The girls' was a reference to Leonard's wife Laura and Ian's friend, Cindy who was best friends with Laura. What one gal knew, the other would soon find out. And, after all, Ian Bishop and everyone too close to him might be in great danger.

"No", Leonard responded, "There is no reason right now to upset the girls and make them worry. After all, there might be nothing to worry about. They might not really know after all, that you are alive and kicking. Maybe you should check this out with Scotland Yard or the Secret Service and see what they have to say. What do you think about that?"

Ian said, "I don't like keeping secrets from the girls, but it might be safer for them if they do not know what is happening. I will see you tonight at the Play and I suppose I will speak discreetly with the Yard and the Secret Service tomorrow. I will have to get up in the middle of the night to contact Scotland Yard at a proper hour in London. Thanks for your help and suggestions, Leonard. Two heads are better than one."

"Hey, that's what friends are for, my man." Leonard said as he turned with a big smile on his face, "Let me get the check." But, the waitress already had taken the money out of Ian's hand.

The Production Company that had hired Ian Bishop as an actor twelve years ago, was well pleased with Ian's ability to portray particular characters. Matter of fact everyone on set and off, knew his name and his reputation as a character, himself. Ian Bishop was an easy guy to like.

Ian Bishop liked the idea that even the Car Parkers and the Security People knew who he was as well as the Ticket Sellers and the Cashiers in the gift shops. He enjoyed the reputation he had made for himself in this small community and even restaurant waitresses knew who he was.

Ian Bishop had been waiting in line at the Wal Mart Pharmacy. It had been heavily raining outside. Ian wore his rain togs because he was riding the Honda Shadow, and was dripping on their floor. One of the employees noticed . . . .

"Ian Douglas Bishop as Simon Peter, Walking on the Water in The New Holy Land"

As the gal was going for a mop, she said "Simon Peter, if you would just stop falling in the water so much you could stop dripping on other people's floors."

The Wal Mart lady had seen Ian playing that role and falling into the waters of the Galilee.

The problem was, that if anyone was looking for Ian, he would be so easy to find. Under the present circumstances, it was not to his advantage to have such a high profile. If bad guys were looking for him, Ian was in real trouble.

Ian was talking to himself again (which he did often) "It is now the middle of May. Cindy will be back to the States from Germany around the middle of July and finishing her schooling in Florida, but that is a long way down the road. The Play can not get along without me for long, so that means that I can not just run off to Florida to meet Cindy. I am going to have to just stay here and face what ever comes."

It was now eleven pm. The Play was over for the night and Ian was changing out of his costume and back into his street clothes. Leonard had played opposite Ian in a supporting role that night. They always enjoyed each other's company and that gave them more chance to talk when they were in the dressing room between "stage calls".

There was a speaker system in their dressing room so they could also keep up with the progress of the Play. They did have to be careful not to get too involved with their personal conversations. It is a BIG NO NO, to miss your Cue lines and you NEVER wanted to miss a scene.

So this evening was over, and they would live to face another day, another Play.

Leonard said "Nite, Ian, Be safe with that motorcycle on your way home. Good job, tonight! We didn't miss any scenes or Cue lines." That was always a good thing!

The next weekend was going to be a big holiday weekend for the theater, "Memorial Day", and we had two extra performances that week. It would be nice to play to a packed theater.

It only took Ian Bishop about fifteen minutes to get home from the Play. Sometimes Cindy would phone around midnight so they could chat for a while. Bishop was finishing his day, but Cindy was just beginning her's. Tonight, however Cindy did not call. Just as well. He didn't want to worry her about having to get back in touch with the Secret Service or Scotland Yard.

Ian put a DVD movie into the slot and the machine pulled it out of his hand as though it was hungry to consume the upcoming movie with surround sound. He put some popcorn in the microwave, listened to it pop and headed for his easy chair to watch his movie on the big plasma screen.

❧

Two and a half hours later, Ian decided that it was about time for Scotland Yard to change the morning shift and begin a new day, so he phoned the Scotland Yard Agent in London.

"Agent Paul Dew, please" Ian said as soon as London was on the phone line.

"Yes, whom may I say is calling?" the operator inquired.

"This is Ian Bishop calling from the States in regards to the London Connection of the 'Nigerian Scam'."

"Yes Sir, Mr. Bishop, I will connect you right away to the Fraud Squad."

"Good morning to you Sir." answered Paul Dew of the Yard. "We have been busy in regards to the 'Nigerian Scam' as you reported it, last May 9th. In the past two weeks, thanks to you, we have arrested John Stegi. 'Stegi' was his real name. He was involved with several different scams in this area. He worked freelance, but he was involved with some real mean characters, most precarious men. Some of them, we are watching and some have slipped through our grasp. It would be a good idea for you to continue to lay low for the time being."

"Well Paul, that would be easier said than done", responded Ian "Because I am an actor on stage five nights a week. By the way, what have you heard about the South African end of this operation?"

Agent Dew said "We don't know anything from South Africa, except that we have discovered that the Government Diplomatic Courier organization was feeding John Stegi information on the side, for rather large monetary payoffs. It was the diplomatic courier service that probably put John

Stegi in touch with Bane Maleke down in Africa. Stegi ran his own operation which he called the ADB Holding Company. Sometimes he would call it a security company. He was the administrative head. He ran several different scams from the same location in London. We are breaking up that operation now."

Bishop questioned, "Have you come up with any connection between John Stegi and a Safety Deposit Box at Citibank in London?"

"No, we have not uncovered anything along that line but I will make a note to check into that and get back to you later. Thank you for the lead, as well as all the other information. May I be of any further assistance to you?"

"I don't think so, but if I hear anything else I will pass it on to you" Ian said.

"I appreciate all that you have been doing. I know that these men are very dangerous and I will try to be careful. Have a good day Agent Dew."

❧

# CHAPTER 33

Ian Bishop was exhausted. It was now three o'clock Friday morning, May 26th. He had a performance at the theater that night at seven-thirty and on Saturday and Sunday, he would be at the theater for two performances each day. Memorial Weekend. That would actually require his presence for thirteen hours a day.

With so much on his mind he figured that he better take a sleeping pill and "hit the hay."

Ian got up at eleven am Friday, fairly well rested and ready to face a new day. He was going to play opposite Leonard again that night. He always looked forward to that. Also, the theater was going to put on a "Feed" for the whole cast of one hundred fifty people on Sunday because of the Holiday. Cindy was on her way to Israel today for a respite, before she was going to head back to the States and an accelerated summer course at a University in Pensacola, Florida U.S.A.

At the Play that Friday night Leonard asked, "What did Scotland Yard say?"

Ian Bishop discussed all the new information and also said, "I am probably still in danger. Scotland Yard can really do nothing here in the U.S. or South Africa. The Secret Service even had to close their office in Nigeria, Africa because they could not get co-operation from the government.

I would think that maybe the South African Government may not cooperate fully either. Too many pay-offs in that part of the world, I would suspect."

"Well, my man, You better be extra careful and watch yourself. If Laura and I can do anything for you, just let us know."

"Does Laura know anything about that email I got from South Africa, after my death?" Ian asked Leonard.

"No, I told you that was our secret. I agree, there is no reason the girls should have to worry about this."

"Good." Ian said "Let's keep it that way for the time being. I have not re-contacted the Secret Service yet."

Laura came up to Leonard and Ian, saying "What's up Boys? You looked like you were in the middle of something deep."

Leonard answered "Well, Honey we were just talking about Cindy. You know that's a deep subject." he said with a smile on his face.

Laura turned to Ian and said, "You know Ian, this is not a business deal you are proposing to Cindy. You need to be romantic too."

Ian remarked, "That's just a little hard to do when you are 4,000 miles apart."

"Well, write her a poem, tell her you love her, whisper sweet nothings into the phone. Do something!" She had said all this with that coy look on her face, but Ian knew that she was right, at least he thought she was.

He had so much else on his mind it was difficult to think about anything else, but he also knew that he had been ignoring Cindy lately, not on purpose of course. All his thinking had gone to the vicarious situation he was facing, not knowing if the bad guys knew he was still alive.

Ian Bishop was also very serious about his acting and he could not let his personal life interfere with his performance. The novel he was writing had also taken on a life of it's own. Ian would spend hours at the computer keeping up with the flow of words and word pictures, as it was all unfolding before him.

As soon as Ian Bishop got home that night he sat in front of his computer. "Alright, I can do this. A poem. Where will I start? At the beginning, that's where all good stories start."

He faced a blank computer screen and nothing seemed to flow.

He had remembered one time someone had told him that "If you are having trouble sleeping, just picture a blank canvas."

Ian had told that man "That would never work for an artist. If an artist pictures a blank canvas, he will stay awake all night visualizing how to fill it."

Bishop began talking to himself again.

"Focus, think about the beginning of your relationship with Cindy and let it flow from that point to this present day.

Just see what happens. Follow the Spirit!"

"You came along when I was just living half an existence,

And, told me It is not good for man to be alone.

You showed me that I was not complete.

I had only gone the way of least resistance!

You entered as a song, a sweet melody without words.

And, before long your melody just lingered.

We are now adding the words to a new refrain.

Our spirits intermingle, unhindered.

Now with words and music you have filled me,

With faith, hope and love.

The greatest of these is love.

The best gifts are given from Above."

Ian Bishop decided since school was coming to a close, that he would email this to Cindy at her yahoo address instead of to her school address. He hoped that this was enough to show her that he cared. After all, it was her that had brought him out of his shell.

The hermit crab had come out of his shell and into the light of day.

Cindy called Ian the next day. He thought that she had received his poem but she did not say anything about it. Ian said, "Did you get the poem I sent you?" She said "No! You wrote me a poem? How very sweet of you."

Ian said "I sent it to your yahoo address, but if you like, I will read it to you."

"Oh YES, Please. I would love for you to read it to me." Ian asked if she was sitting down, knowing that she could become emotional.

So Ian said "Okay," and he began to read it to her. She started to sob, and then the sobs turned into a cry that would not stop. She was so moved that she could not hardly speak, at least not where Ian could understand her.

Ian apologized "I am sorry that I made you cry." Cindy

responded "That's Okay, sob, It is a good cry, SOB." They would have to talk later. She had to go for now.

Poor Cindy. He had scared her almost to death. This was totally unexpected. Ian had not divulged anything so direct to her before and she was actually caught way off guard.

Cindy had started Ian thinking about marriage. She had said several times "It is not good for man to be alone." She had probably thought that saying things like this to Ian, was like water off a duck's back.

It might take Ian Bishop a while to think about something before he responded to it. He had learned to handle himself this way. Earlier in his life he was always getting himself in trouble with his mouth because he would speak before he would think it through first. It was true that Cindy had started Ian, thinking about marriage, but not necessarily to her.

Ian even told people: "I have been fast to speak and slow to think, and that would always get me in a whole lot of trouble. By the time I had thought about something it was already out of my mouth."

Ian had grown accustomed to being alone, but was thinking that Cindy was right. Ian was beginning to think that maybe they were kindred spirits, longing for romance and adventure. Maybe they could explore Europe together, using Germany as a home base. Bishop figured that living in Europe could open up a new market for his art work as well as his books. Exploring can be more fun with two. Many new memories could be made on the road ahead.

One thing about Ian Bishop, was that he had to have his dose of adventure. He was not destined to live a mundane life in a rut, with a mortgage, insurance and property taxes in a sub-division of Suburbia.

Ian Bishop had just finished a twelve hour day at the summer playhouse. The Play had closed at ten-thirty pm and he was home by eleven pm. His pocket began to vibrate. Ian always set his phone on "vibrate mode" when he was at the Play. It would be embarrassing if his phone rang on set, in front of over a thousand people that were in the audience.

"Hello" Ian said knowing that it must be Cindy. She knew when to call him. It was eleven pm in Eureka Springs and six am in Germany.

"Yes, this is Cindy. How was your day today? What did you do?"

"I had a young boy on one of my tours today as I was playing the role of Simon Peter in the first person.

The boy asked me, "Simon Peter, Is it true that you are over two thousand years old?"

I started to ask him: "Do I look that old?", but decided against it. So instead, I said, "In light of eternity, what's a couple of thousand years?"

"I'm not sure the boy got the drift of my answer, but the adults that were standing around understood. I must have been very believable in the part to get that kind of question."

Then Cindy said, "I need to talk to you about something."

"Yes, what is it?"

"Well," Cindy hesitated, "I accepted a job offer in Kentucky. I have not been happy the last four years in Germany. I have many friends, but I don't even know how to read the phone book. I have been wanting to get back to the old terra firma of the United States and be close to my family. I know that you wanted to come and spend time in Germany and that it would be a great place for us to build wonderful memories, but I had to make the decision."

"I know that the new job is a lot less money and fewer benefits, but maybe the cost of living will be a little less too. Will you forgive me?"

"There's nothing to forgive. You had to make a decision that you would be happy with and you made it. I understand that you wanted to be closer to your family."

"It must seem to you that Kentucky is right next door to Houston, Texas and your son, since you have had to travel all the way from Germany to spend time with him and his family." Ian was remembering the time together last Christmas with her family in Houston.

"Are you still planning on coming to see me in Florida the last of July?" Cindy asked.

Ian thought about that for a moment and responded, "If I can find a replacement for myself at the Play. Our cast is short this season and the understudies are usually filling other needed roles because of sickness and emergencies."

"I know you must be tired after one of your long days." Cindy said, "Have a good night and I'll talk to you later on."

Ian said "And, you have a good day." because she was just starting her day in Germany.

Ian Bishop was thinking, that he should be happy for Cindy, coming back to the States. But, actually he was disappointed that he was not going to explore Europe with her.

He had wondered what it would have been like to live in Europe and sell his work there. Most of the subject matter that he liked to paint and write about was European.

Well, so much for the romance of Europe with Cindy, he was

thinking. For many years Ian Bishop had essentially become addicted to wild escapades and exploits across the globe. He desired at least one new quest a year and loved to venture out and explore new places.

Ian wondered how Cindy's choice would effect their relationship. She was going to move to Kentucky and he had already explored that state as well as the other forty-nine.

Ian had thought that his relationship with Cindy was growing into something more permanent, but evidently it was not. Now, she had started making major plans in her life that did not take him into consideration. Bishop had thought that her adventurous spirit would blend perfectly with his, but now he had cause for doubt.

❧

The next day he got up and there was an email waiting for him from Jean, his shipboard romance of last November. They had continued to stay in touch with email through the months since they had first met. She had even mentioned that she almost phoned him but figured that it was too late to call. She told him in an email, "My life has been very hectic. I don't even get home till eight at night, and that would be eleven in Arkansas."

Ian told her that it was eleven most nights when he finished with the Play.

Ian Bishop had also mentioned to her about the new novel that he had begun to write, "Bequeath the Wind".

"You see, this really is a true story that you are reading," and Ian has been writing it, as the story has unfolded in his life. "This has been like a journal."

Ian had told Jean, "I have really been impressed with you. I even wrote about our time together on board our cruise. I will always remember that time together with you and hold it as a cherished memory for the rest of my life."

Then this email arrived from Jean. She had not been very personal with her emails up to this point. There was much that Ian would have liked to share with Jean, but she was sort of like a timid little bird, and he didn't want to scare her off.

Jean said:

**"I would love to read your books.**

**I feel honored to have a spot in one of them. I enjoyed meeting you as well and agree that it added to the cruise.**

**Too bad it wasn't until the end of the cruise that we met. You were a very good sport to enter into all of the activities but I see now.**

**That is how you live your life - to the fullest.**

**I find that very fascinating. It would be nice to have a chance to meet up again one day, I enjoyed your energy & sensitivity and found our conversations very stimulating.**

**Have you done any more paintings?**

**What grand adventure will you embark upon next? It is always fun to hear about your adventures.**

**Loved hearing from you. Thanks for keeping in touch. Jean"**

The reason that this email gave Ian pause for thought was that he himself had been also coming out of that cocoon of grief after loosing his wife in death. Ian had closed himself up in half his house, not wanting to live in that other half of his life, that he and his wife had so happily shared together.

Cindy had a lot to do with bringing Ian out of his shell. He had been like a hermit, living alone, when he had met her and she showed him it was not good to be alone.

Now it was, like Jean was just beginning to come back into his life. What would Ian do with two different love interests? This was indeed another dangerous game and one that he really did not want to play. But, he would see how this all played out!

Could it be that Jean was becoming a beautiful butterfly and that she was flying into his life for a reason? Was there a chance for happiness and true love again? Ian was getting way out ahead of himself this time. Just the thought of her excited Ian. Maybe Ian was only in love with love.

Bishop also wondered, if he read too much into it. Could it be that she was really interested in Ian Bishop. Was this the beginning of a love triangle, or maybe just plain ol' love?

Time would tell and Ian was not in any hurry. However, Ian Bishop did not like the idea of stringing two relationships along at the same time. He had previously told Jean about Cindy, but there had been nothing to say to Cindy about Jean.

Ian needed to spend some time with both ladies and see what developed.

Ian continued to write down, the pages of his life in this new book like a diary, as it unfolded before him. He lived his dream and played the game of life as a chess game. When he says, "I can hardly wait to see what happens next". That is what he literally means.

He decided that he would send a segment of his book to Jean, to see what she had to say about his recollections of their time together on board "The Love Boat." This was after all, the same ship that was used on the television series by that name, and the cruise line liked to use that term.

Ian had to come back to earth, put his heart aside and his mind in gear, to take control of other matters at hand.

The time had come to phone the United States Secret Service, again.

"Hello, this is Ian Bishop calling from Eureka Springs. May I please speak with Special Agent Henderson?"

"Yes, Mr. Bishop, just one minute. He is on the other line. I will tell him you are waiting."

After waiting for a few minutes . . . "Mr. Bishop, it is good to hear from you. We have been collaborating with the F.B.I. on this matter that you brought to our attention. We have combined our files and we might also bring the C.I.A. in on this because we need more jurisdiction and more intelligence between Africa, the U.K. and here at home as well. I am afraid you have stirred up a hornet's nest. Honestly, I am concerned about your well being. It is not in our budget to give you protection, but I would recommend that you loose yourself for a while. I know Scotland Yard has made some arrests, and are working on trying to make a connection to South Africa, but as of now, their jurisdiction does not reach that far. They might pull in "Interpol." Have you had any further contact with these people Mr. Bishop?"

"Actually I have. Bane Maleke with the Bank in South Africa sent me an email thinking that I was dead, saying 'not to play him' and he said he 'needed his money'."

"Mr. Bishop, what made him think you were dead?" quarried the Special Agent.

Ian Bishop answered, "Well, I had actually sent an announcement of my death to London and to South Africa. I hope that was alright?"

Special Agent Henderson said that he thought that was a "capitol idea, under the present circumstances.

Hang low, Mr. Bishop and thank you again for all your assistance."

Bishop had just been off the phone for two minutes when Cindy called from Israel this time.

Cindy said "I am having a wonderful time. Jerusalem is truly an eternal city, and I feel like I just came home."

When Cindy had called Ian from Israel, he asked her to pick up one of those shirts that says "ISRAEL" across the top, with the "STAR OF DAVID" in the middle and under that it reads: "THE REAL LONE STAR STATE".

Ian knew that way back there someplace in Cindy's past was some Jewish blood, and said; "I am so happy that you are having such a good time. Remember when you are in the Garden of Gethsemane at the bottom of the Mount of Olives, that the original Roman cobble stone road that Jesus walked on from Bethany is just to the left side of the Garden."

"The guide will want you to go on the black top path to the right because it is easier to navigate. At least go over and see the original road.

Also, while you are in Jerusalem, be sure to see the house of Ciaphas, the High Priest. There are dungeons under the house where Jesus was jailed over night and the original Roman road still goes by the house."

Ian said "This is your chance to unwind and relax, slow down and enjoy all of it. This will be a trip you will always carry in your mind for the rest of your life.

Cindy said "Thanks so much for being there for me. I love you, Bye!"

"SHALOM! "Ian responded.

When Cindy spoke of love, Ian was not sure that she was speaking in the romantic sense. They had many talks about such things over the phone and email, but he was not sure that she knew what love was. Love included taking the other person into consideration when making future plans.

She had been in several failed marriages that were not her fault, but Ian would tread carefully.

# CHAPTER 34

It's now Monday, May $29^{th}$, Memorial Day. The long working weekend is behind Ian Bishop. Today, there is nothing to do but relax. Soon enough there will be two performances a day with 12 hour days at the Summer Play House. And, on his days off, he was writing his novel and taking care of business. Ian had to remind himself, "It is winter, when I have my vacation and time slows down" Right now he felt like he was going 100 miles an hour in a 35 speed limit zone. This past winter had been a whirlwind. Maybe next winter will be more relaxing.

☙

From time to time he thought about what it would have been like to be a wealthy man, and that line from "Fiddler on the Roof" . . ."Would it ruin some vast eternal plan if I were to become a wealthy man?"

☙

"Might as well forget about that!" Bishop felt he was still in danger from the London Connection even though John Stegi was now in jail. He understood that John Stegi was a very dangerous man even from prison. After all, he probably had people on the outside that would still work favors for him.

He felt like maybe he should check out the South African end of the investigation to see what was being done about Bane Maleke. After all it was Maleke who sent the mysterious email to a dead Bishop.

Ian didn't know if he should contact the bank in South Africa since he was suppose to be dead.

What if Bane still had friends at the bank that would tell him, that Bishop was not dead after all?

Ian decided that he would not call the bank, for now. It was so hard to just sit down and do nothing. Bishop was always a man of action. He would have to wait, and allow the authorities to do their job and sort things out. The bank in Africa had told Bishop that they had Bane's email address closed down.

Ian Bishop had his friends around him and had a very busy schedule, but he was feeling rather alone. He missed the time that he had with Cindy in Germany. She had told him that after she closed up her house in Wurzburg, Germany that she had stayed at a hotel with a restaurant that "had food to die for" and the place was even more romantic than the German Restaurant where they had spent many happy hours together.

Ian wished that he was with her right now, but that would have to wait.

Ian Bishop was not very good at waiting, and he even hated waiting in lines. He wanted everything right now. But, wait, he must.

❧

It was time to turn over a new calendar page and face the month of June. Summer was here. A full week had gone by since Ian Bishop called Scotland Yard.

It was now Friday, June 2nd. Bishop had returned home after the Play that night and was having a midnight snack before he went to bed. After watching a bit of late night TV, he was taking a shower when his phone rang.

&

"Shalom." Ian answered thinking it was Cindy on the other end.

"Is Mr. Bishop there please?" was the response. Truly this was not Cindy, for it was a man's voice with a British accent.

"I'm sorry," Ian said, "I thought you were someone else. This is Ian Bishop."

"That's quite all right Sir, Agent Paul Dew, here, with the New Scotland Yard, Fraud Squad. I have some news for you Sir."

"Well, I'll tell you what" Ian said, "I could use some *good* news right now."

Agent Dew replied "We caught up to another accomplice of John Stegi. Her name is Lynnette Robinson. She said you took her out for dinner one night when you were here in London. Is that correct?"

"Well, yes sir, that's right." answered Bishop, "But that's all there was to it. Mr. Stegi had sent her over to my hotel for a payoff, but I didn't give her one. I sent her home with a message for John Stegi: 'Thanks, but no thanks'."

"That checks out, Mr. Bishop. What I really wanted to discuss with you was another matter. We found a key on her person, and have discovered that it went to a Safety Deposit Box, over at Citibank, London. We have arrested her and when we opened the Safety Deposit Box, we discovered a Will with Letter of Probate made out in your name."

"Yes, I know about that." Ian said "This was the reason I mentioned the safety deposit box to you when we last spoke. That's why I was in London in the first place . . .to collect the monies from that Will. Was that all you found in the Deposit Box?"

Paul Dew said "Sir, are you sitting down?"

"Well, Yes, I am, but why do you ask? I just finished taking a shower." Ian said.

"Well Sir, we also found twenty five million United States Dollars in that Citibank Deposit Box with a shipping order from Development Bank of South Africa that says it belongs to you. We tabulate that it is six hundred thousand dollars short of the amount specified in the Will. However when we arrested John Stegi and seized his bank account, we found six hundred thousand dollars and some change, in his account.

We now feel that money belongs to you."

"I don't know what to say" Ian gasped, "I thought that the whole thing was just one big scam."

"Here's the crux of it, Sir. We actually do feel **that it was all one big fraud**."

"However, The papers and documents were all drawn out and legally notarized. That makes you the legal recipient of these funds, since they were found together. This money will be tied up with this court case for a while until we see if there are any other claims on these funds.

There may be others that were swindled by John Stegi that come forward and lay claim against this estate of John Cuthbertson from South Africa. We will see."

"Wow, I guess that means that we can proceed on this end

with our attorney and the "J.C. Foundation" to get everything operational. How long do you think that my money will be tied up in court?" asked Ian.

"Mr. Bishop, I wouldn't think that your money will be tied up any longer than six months.

Congratulations. Usually all of my fraud and scam cases end up with a lot of big losers. I am happy that this one is turning out different for you. Good luck on setting up your charitable foundation. The world needs more people like you.

I will continue to be in touch. It is partly because of all the documentation that you had done that makes the job of prosecuting this case easier. You may need to testify during the trials, but for a man of your means, that should not be a problem for you."

"Thank you so much for all the work you have done on this case and all the work that you have yet ahead of you. Sherlock Holmes would be proud of you." boasted Ian Bishop.

Needless to say, Ian Bishop did not get much sleep the night of that call from The New Scotland Yard, Metro Fraud Squad. Ian had lost quite a lot of sleep over the last eight months. Had it really been eight months? Actually to Bishop, it felt like more. One can do a lot of living in a short period of time. It's a matter of making every moment count for something.

❧

In this chess game, Ian had seen the pawns fall, the chess pieces give way to the Bishop and finally the Queen was captured and the King was deposed in London.

❧

# CHECKMATE !

❧

“Elementary“? No, far from it. This was a hard fought victory, of cunning and deception, of many moves and countermoves.

❧

Ian Bishop had that whole night to gloat. Even if he was by himself. He never missed out on an opportunity to celebrate. He even opened a bottle of “Dow’s Fine Ruby PORT from Oporto, Portugal. He had bought that bottle in Lisbon, way back at the beginning of this escapade, last November.

As he breathed in the soft bouquet and tasted the warmth of the wine, his thoughts drifted back to Cindy and the time they spent together in Germany.

Jean was there too, in spirit. The three of them would celebrate this event.

Ian wished that they were really with him now. But, as they say, “Wishin’ don’t make it so.” For tonight, Ian Bishop would be content to think of the soft bouquet of Cindy’s perfume and the sweet taste of Jean’s warm lips as he drifted off for a short sleep.

He faced a twelve hour work day on Saturday, but he would continue on as though nothing had changed.

The first thing that Ian Bishop thought about that next day was, “If money changes you, you have no rights to it. If life was good before, why should it change anything. Life will continue to be good, and I will live it to the fullest measure, just like I always have."

Ian Bishop knew who he was and he liked who he was. And, as his thoughts turned to Cindy once more, he knew that it didn't make any difference to her, if he was rich or poor and he also wondered how Jean would react to this latest news. Actually it didn't matter because it was not going to change Ian's lifestyle.

The money would go to the J.C. Foundation.

Ian continued to think about Jean. He checked his email and there was an email from Jean. She was in Monterrey, California, and had read that portion of his book about their adventure together last November.

**"Dear Ian,**

**It is one in the morning and I am working on my laptop at home, trying to catch up with work.**

**Your book came to mind and I decided that I was just too curious to wait any longer.**

**It really has me smiling. In some ways it is so real, actually, I can't believe the details you remembered ... but that is probably the artist in you.**

**Of course there were definitely parts that weren't real ... We both know the part about "they danced the night away" was pure fiction!**

**It was very fun to read it and re-live it. I am glad you sent it to me and now I am curious to see**

**what happens next. It is interesting that you said the same thing because I often thought writers did know what they were going to write about, before they started.**

**Well, I had to write immediately after reading your manuscript but it is so late and I have an early and long work day tomorrow.**

**I remember you said you used to lead tours to Israel. If you ever do it again, let me know. I do really want to go there one day.**

**Bye for now. Jean."**

Ian was thinking "Yeah, she was right", as he also looked back on their cruise together last November. Ian had said, "Would you like to dance?"

Jean responded, "I really don't know how to dance."

"I will teach you", Ian had said, but she was too unsure of herself or too shy, perhaps.

She promised Ian "I will learn and get back to you on that offer, after I have taken some lessons and practiced."

Ian didn't care how well she danced. He just wanted to hold her close and feel her heart beating against his. He hoped that he would later have that wish.

When Jean had said in her email: "*I am curious to see what happens next. It is interesting that you said the same thing because I often thought writers did know what they were going to write about, before they started.*"

She did not realize that this book was happening as he was

writing the manuscript. Did she not know that *she* was writing the end of his book, or was she?

*Was life imitating art or art imitating life? Ian Bishop had spent time in that dimension of dreams and visions. Could it be that his dreams and visions were so real that he didn't know what his own reality really was any more.*

*Perhaps Ian had played so many roles on this stage as an actor, that he didn't know who he was any longer. Was it Shakespeare who wrote: "The whole world is a stage and we are all but actors?"*

*The Spirit of the Living God appeared in one of Ian's visions and told him: "I have placed you center stage to see My eternal drama unfolding before your very eyes. With that privilege comes responsibility." Ian Bishop wanted to be responsible in this life.*

*This was a problem that he needed to figure out because his life was touching many others on a very personal and emotional level.*

*Was he actually writing this book or was the book leading him toward his destiny? "That's a scary thought!"*

*Our physical reality is but a shadow of spiritual truth.*

*With the spiritual realm sharing the same space with this physical realm, you just can not help but wonder, "Am I in control of this situation, or have I lost it?"*

*What if the only way we can truly be happy in this world, .is when our physical existence lines up with our spiritual life in that parallel dimension? Maybe that's where the old saying "Made in Heaven" came from.*

*"The closer I get to spiritual truth the more questions I have."*

*Was Ian Bishop, really the King of this chess game, or was he only a Bishop, or maybe just a pawn, to be sacrificed. NO, he would not accept that last option.*

*Who was to become his Queen?*

*Was he really in charge of moving the pieces around this board of life, or was someone else really moving the pieces? Maybe all he was doing was making "counter moves" to the situations that he faced in this chess game called life . . .*

Ian got caught up in his day dreaming remembering the rest of that magical evening with Jean. . . .It was a warm November night in the middle of the Gulf of Mexico. They were skimming across the waves reflecting the full moon. Jean and Ian felt like they were high and lifted up on gossamer wings to the highest heaven. Were they on their way to destiny or was this only a brief episode of life?

This is a true life venture . . . Ian had to remind himself. "Sometimes I have taken a few diversions down a different path. A path of fantasy. Life does not always take us the way that we want to go. It can be interesting to see where that other path may lead". . . . as you read in the Forward to this very book.

Cindy felt like she was still in "the valley of decision", but Ian was not invited into that valley with her. Which was okay with him because he preferred the mountain tops anyway. The view was much better, and one can see more clearly.

Ian Bishop really was very disappointed that Cindy was not going to stay in Germany. He had felt right at home the short time that he was there, even a kinship type of feeling with the land. Ian had always wondered what it would be like to actually live in Germany and not just visit. Then again, was he more interested in Germany or fascinated by Cindy?

Bishop was also a little upset with Cindy because he had voiced his opinion on wanting her to stay in Germany.

They could have made many more wonderful memories not only in Germany but in all the surrounding territories.

She chose not to take him into consideration with that decision. It made him also wonder about the future decisions that would have to be made.

Cindy had said that she couldn't even read a phone book in Germany. Maybe Ian should have told her that he had trouble reading a phone book in Kentucky. Maybe then, she would understand that 'the place' was important in deciding your future.

These were all questions that he had to figure out, with the rest of the "Players".

Ian Bishop was wondering who would finish the final chapter in this book for him? He was usually very decisive and knew which way to go. Ian Bishop was just going to have to take control of this situation and finish this book by himself.

Ian felt that this was just like, having had a wonderful meal and someone serves you two desserts.

*Which one do you choose, Banana Cream or Cherry Pie?*

*You love them both, but alas, you can not have both, you know.*

☙

Ian Bishop's thoughts went from the future to the past and he began wondering about Bane Maleke in South Africa.

He did not know if he would have to look over his shoulder for the rest of his life or if that part of his book could be closed.

Ian Bishop needed to find out what had happened to Bane.

☙

# CHAPTER 35

Bane Maleke was a nervous wreck. He had been working on this particular deal which involved Ian Bishop and the Cuthbertson Will, for too long. Normally he liked to get in and out fairly quick.

"I am getting too old for this!" he told himself as he was working at his desk in the small South African town of Midrand. Bane had worked his way up to a Regional Manager for Development Bank. The title was much more impressive than the job itself.

Bane Maleke knew poverty, because he was raised in the Sudan. He started working at Development Bank as a teenager, pushing a broom, which was a big job, with all the dusty roads. Bane was very good at running errands and could be trusted.

By the time he was twenty, they made him a Teller and on his twenty fifth birthday he was the local Manager. "His bank" (that was the way he liked to think about it.) was located on an intersection of two dirt roads. Lever Road and Headway Hill. The bank building itself was adobe and it was surrounded by a few old wooden buildings and a couple of scrub trees. There were also some small kiosk lean-tos that sold varied items in the area.

Right behind the bank was a small house where Bane lived with his wife, "Janet" and three kids.

Bane had always felt like he was never paid what he was

worth. To him it seemed like the rich got richer and the poor just continued to get poorer. Bane was now in charge of a couple other small branch offices of Development Bank in the bush country, but he was fast approaching his forties and some days he felt even ten years older than that.

About fifteen years ago, Bane had come across a bank scam out of Nigeria in connection with his work. Law enforcement did not seem to be interested in pursuing it when he had reported their activity in his area. Matter of fact, he had met one of the men involved by the name of Gif, and he kind of liked the guy.

Gif said “Bane, a man in your position at the bank could make a whole lot of money, and I could show you how to do it.”

“Really?” Bane exclaimed. He could see that he had a dead end job and knew that he would never work for Development Bank in Johannesburg, South Africa. That had been his dream, a high paying job in the big city. He loved his wife and children. He wanted to see his wife have fine things and his children schooled properly.

“Why sure, man.” Gif had said. “You and me, we make a good team!”

And, that was what started Bane on this path, that would lead him to either prosperity or destruction.

Gif had shown him how to work the old “Nigerian Scam” as it was known.

The scam could all be done by phone and email. The world was full of suckers and you could have your pick. Bane was a smart man and knew how to maneuver people. He decided to build his organization right then and there. “Why wait?”

Bane Maleke brought an underpaid bank attorney into this deal as well as his youngest brother, Alto, who was smart enough to do the leg work. Alto was also the good looking one in the family and could represent himself well, in anyone's company. And, that was the way it started.

Bane had a background in banking and knew how to move money around. He knew the ins and outs. He would add his own adaptations and improvements to the old Nigerian Scams and would make it fool proof. He figured if he worked it right, he could retire at the age of fifty with at least 30 Million U.S. Dollars. Bane's plan was to constantly build his reserves of cash, hiding the money within accounts that he could control. He would use names of his own depositors and open up coded accounts that only he could have access to and control.

He would do more than just run an inheritance scam. His plan would have many directions, and facets. Bane felt like he could take care of any contingencies that would come along. He would start out with a simple inheritance, where he could collect front money. If the front money did not materialize, he would attempt to get people's bank name and account numbers so he could draft their accounts and clean them out, using a false name. If the other plans did not work out he knew how to steal their identity and collect on their credit worth.

"They will never catch me." Bane told his brother, Alto. "I am too smart for them. All of my deals will be legal. I will have the cash to back them up and I have the bank's attorney in my pocket. All of the documents that I have drawn up will be legal. How smart is that?"

Alto said "Sounds pretty smart to me Bro. I'm in."

Gif wanted in on this deal also. He was not as smart as Bane, but he could make himself useful. He could do the grunt work and be the runner.

So there they were with the perfect scam. They had operated this scam for the last fifteen years and never came close to being caught. How, could they? It was legal up until the very end, where they would abscond with the other person's money. Then all they would do is change their email address and cell phone numbers, and be ready for the next "Mark" to come along. Simple!

&

Then there was Bishop. Bane had never dealt with anyone like Ian Bishop before. Maleke had built up his nest egg to more then twenty five million dollars. He had it safely stored in a dead man's coded account. The dead man had an account with his bank for many years and even had his Will stored in a safety deposit box at Bane's bank. The man's name was John Cuthbertson. It was a simple matter to find the right "Mark".

That mark was Ian Bishop. They had found him on a rich man's cruise in the Mediterranean last November. Actually, Alto had found him.

This was going to be a big score. Bane could feel it in his bones.

All Bane had to do to get the ball rolling was have his attorney change the Cuthbertson Will into Bishop's name and convince him that this was someone out of his past.

It was usually an easy thing, to convince someone that a stranger had left them millions of dollars. But the problem area for Bane was that he had left the Will and bank account in the name of John Cuthbertson too long. Development Bank of South Africa employed a man by the name of Norman Weitz. Norman was the manager of Internal Audit and had caught wind of this large sum of money. The Will should have been probated and the money moved out long before this, so he started to check into it.

Mr. Weitz created a big problem for Bane Maleke. His investigation had stirred up interest within the South African Government, because of all the questions he was asking. When they had found out about the twenty-five million dollars, they wanted to confiscate these funds because a beneficiary had not been found and the money was unclaimed.

Bane had to work fast to stay ahead of Internal Audit and the South African Government. He called a meeting with his brother Alto, the bank attorney and Gif. They had to come up with an answer to this problem or they would loose their twenty five million dollars.

Bane was a gambler or he would not have been able to run up a balance like this over the years, but now everything came down to this moment in time.

Alto asked "What's this all about?" and Gif chimed in "Yeah, what's up?"

The attorney just kept quiet and listened.

Bane exclaimed "We might be in big trouble. Development Bank has ordered an Internal Audit and the Government wants to confiscate all our funds."

Gif quarried "What is the auditors name? I can take care of him."

"No Gif, you can not take care of this problem in that way. There are already too many eyes on this situation."

Alto asked "What do you want me to do? I know some people over at the office of South African Finance. Do you want me to call in some favors?"

"That will not help us out of this situation, but thanks. Actually, I feel like I have lost control of the situation at hand. It has a mind of it's own and is running it's own course." Bane said to Alto.

"I have a suggestion." the attorney spoke for the first time in this meeting.

"Looking at this from the legal standpoint, there is not much choice. I understand that you have already named someone as beneficiary of the Cuthbertson Will?

Bane responded "Yes, an . . . Ian Douglas Bishop."

"Well, I suggest that you proceed in that direction as quickly as possible. Is Mr. Bishop willing to go with you on this matter? Is he willing to go over to Amsterdam, London or Switzerland to claim the inheritance?" the attorney asked.

Bane said "As far as I know. He said he was willing to travel."

"Fine, I will proceed with the probate and we will be able to move our funds out of South Africa before the government can confiscate our money. And, we will do it legally, where the Internal Audit can do nothing about it." And the attorney added, "POOPH! The problem goes away."

Alto asked "How can we be sure that Bishop will cooperate and fall into our plan?"

"Yeah, and How do you plan on moving that much money out of Africa?" Gif questioned.

"I can handle Bishop. He may be a problem, but he will be so confused when we finish with him that he will not be able to think straight. Before he knows it, we will have his up front money, his bank account, and a million dollars worth of his credit in our hands.

He already has his doubts that the money is real. It should not be a problem getting him to finally believe the inheritance is a scam and the money never existed. He will forget about the inheritance and we will reclaim the money as uncollected from the Courier Service."

Gif said, "Speaking of a Courier Service. Do you have anyone one in mind?"

"I have a list of some of the Services" Bane said, "My bank has used them in the past, but if you know of a good one that can be trusted with such a large sum of money, maybe we should use them? We will need a reliable service that can act quickly and not ask a lot of questions!"

"There is one in particular that I found to be good and very discreet." Gif continued, "It is called: The Government Freight Agency. They are the official Government Diplomatic Baggage Couriers. And, they already have a connection in London, United Kingdom, if you would be interested in traveling that route."

"Gentlemen, I think we have avoided a major catastrophe. Thank you for your assistance. Let's get right on it. Gif make contact with the courier service, and have them get in touch with me. Alto, stand by. I may need you to run some interference." And then he instructed the attorney to have the letter of probate on his desk as soon as possible.

Bane Maleke was pleased with himself for coming up with the answers that would satisfy Internal Audit and the government. This should safeguard his monetary funds in London and he will also take Bishop for all he is worth. All of this in one fell swoop.

&

Two days later, Government Freight Agency contacted Bane at his office.

“Mr. Maleke, I am Mike Crowe with GFA.

“Yes, Mr. Crowe, I have a shipment of precious gems that I need to move to the U.K. by April 12th. The consignment shall be in two secured silver colored containers. I understand that you deal with a John Tegi in London who represents ADB Security?”

“That is correct.” Mike stated, “Where would you like to have the consignment picked up and delivered?”

“The consignment is to be picked up at my bank, DBSA in Midrand, South Africa along with a copy of the Will of John Cuthbertson and letter of probate naming Ian Bishop as beneficiary. I want this delivered to John Tegi at ADB Holding, by way of his Security Company in London, U.K. by Wednesday, April 12th.”

“Yes sir, we can arrange that transport.” Mike said.

Including the documents, made the shipment legal as far as the government and internal audit would be concerned. It would also alleviate all responsibility off of Bane’s shoulders. Bane felt that this was a very smart maneuver. Sending the consignment under the name of “Gem Stones” was to help keep the courier service honest. Better if they didn’t know they had so much cash in their possession.

“What is the value of the consignment, Sir,?” Mike Crowe, from the Government Freight Agency asked.

Bane replied, “Precious Gems, Twenty five Million, Six Hundred Thousand United States Dollars worth.” as though he was talking about a grocery list.

"Thank you Sir. The consignment will be delivered as ordered. Our security fees, insurance and delivery will be 29,200. British Pounds Sterling. 6,500. British Pounds Sterling upon delivery in London. Is that satisfactory, Sir?"

Bane said, "That is satisfactory."

Mr. Maleke, your confirmation number is : FSA/FMV - FGN 045 WR KD 200. I will have a special detail pick up the consignment, which you will have ready to transport tomorrow morning, Friday, April 7th. The head of our security team will be James Jimytyme, along with two other security personnel, known as ; WR and KD."

~

Mike Crowe from the Government Freight Agency was back at Bane's bank the next day. Mike introduced his number one security man to Mr. Maleke.

"Bane, this is James Jimytyme. He will see to it that your shipment arrives safely at the other end. I will collect the front money of 22,700. Pounds Sterling. James will handle the rest for you."

"Mr. Crowe, I just wanted to make sure that you understand, I will expect to reclaim this consignment, just in case it is not claimed by Ian Bishop in London." Bane added.

"That is correct, Mr. Maleke. In a deal of this nature, that is understood."

The money was paid. Mike Crowe left and Bane relaxed in his office thinking that his problems were all over.

The consignment was already prepared and waiting for his

pick up from the vault of Bane's Bank. It consisted of two silver lock boxes.

The consignment was loaded in through the security door of the GFA armored truck parked curb side in front of the bank. Next stop London, or so they thought.

☙

So, the stage had been set and all was ready for Ian Bishop to fall into their trap. Bane Maleke had every contingency covered. What could possibly go wrong?

Bane continued to stay up with his emails to Ian Bishop. He constantly tried to keep Ian encouraged to follow through with his "deal." He had to continue to play Ian Bishop to the bitter end.

And, the bitter end had come.

It was Wednesday, May 10th.

In shock and unbelief, it seemed like Bane's world had tumbled down around him. He received the following email from a girl called Dorinda Lynne. She claimed to be Ian Bishop's daughter and she had said that he had died.

**"How can this be?"** he said to himself. **"I didn't plan for that contingency**. What do I do now? **All of my money is tied up in this deal. I am ruined."**

Maleke jumped on the phone to call Alto, "Alto, a terrible thing has happened. Ian Bishop has died.

Our money in London is in his name and it will be held in the estate of Ian Bishop, and tied up in the court system. I thought that I had all the bases covered, but I never planned that Bishop would die of natural causes before I reclaimed the funds."

Alto replied, "Slow down and think about this. All you have to do is call John Tegi in London and tell him to destroy all the paper work that has Bishop's name on it, and begin the withdrawal of the funds right away."

"Thanks, Alto. I'm all over this."

&

Bane directly phoned John Tegi in London. No answer!

&

He called the security company in London. No answer, and he dialed it again, no answer.

&

Bane decide to call the Government Freight Agency. He found out the consignment of his funds was delivered to John Tegi in London as promised.

&

Bane opened his computer and stared at Ian's death notice again. "Maybe Ian Bishop is playing games with me. Maybe he has run away with my money. Maybe he is a bigger crook and con man than I am."

"Maybe I have just been outsmarted?" Bane mused sadly.

Maleke sent out this email to Ian Bishop:

"Bishop,

Please do not play me, I need my money.

Regards,

Bane."

He tried to send out another email to John Tegi, but it was like his computer just shut down and froze up. He rebooted his computer, and tried to get back to his email, but there was an error on his screen. Something about his service has been interrupted. "What in the world does that mean?" he wondered.

~

Ian Bishop got on his computer and decided at this point to contact Norman Weitz at Development Bank of South Africa.

Weitz replied immediately. He happened to be on the computer in his office. He brought Ian up to speed on everything that had happened.

Bishop felt better as far as his safety was concerned, but kind of felt sorry for Bane Maleke who had been a victim of poverty and circumstances as well as his own devices.

In South Africa there was a knock on Bane Maleke's office door.

"Come in." Bane ordered!

To Bane Maleke's surprise it was Norman Weitz from his bank's headquarters in Johannesburg. There was also a police man in uniform and a nicely dressed government official.

The Official said "Bane Maleke, I arrest you in the matter of moving money illegally out of South Africa, running a Nigerian Inheritance Scam and Bank Fraud."

The police man moved in, to place cuffs on Maleke. Bane did not fight against them.

Bane was speechless. Which was just as well. He didn't want to get himself in deeper. He thought he had all of his bases covered and had done everything legally. He was led through the lobby of "his bank" to the surprise of all his customers and employees. There was a murmur in the bank as they paraded past, and out the front door into the waiting cars.

Bane Maleke sat in a dirty jail cell for almost a week before a court appointed attorney came to see him.

"It would appear" Bane's attorney said "that they can not make the charges stick pertaining to **Inheritance Scam,** because Ian Bishop was the legal beneficiary of the inheritance of John Cuthbertson and the money had been sent to London for his collection. Also for this same reason the government can not prosecute you for moving money illegally out of the country."

Bane breathed a sigh of relief. "I am glad to hear that!"

His court appointed attorney continued "However, they are still looking for some reason to detain you and they will not let you out on a bond because they don't trust you, and you have no real ties to this community."

Bane said "But I have a wife and kids and I work for Development Bank of South Africa."

"Not any more you don't" his attorney spoke to Bane solemnly. "Your wife has fled with the kids and you have been let go from your employment. Before the government is finished with you, you will be facing charges of some kind and most certainly will face prison time."

Bane could not believe that Ian Bishop had beat him at his own game.

☙

Alto, Bane's brother ran away with his wife, Janet and his three kids.

☙

Gif was caught and charged with conspiracy to commit fraud and was tied into an old Nigerian Inheritance Scam, that he had been hooked up with, before he met Bane.

The bank attorney still has his low paying job with the Development Bank of South Africa. All he did was draw up some legal papers for Bane Maleke.

Norman Weitz received a promotion at the bank.

☙

# CONCLUSION

It was now the first weekend in June. Weekends don't mean much to Ian Bishop. Even thought normal people get out and do things on the weekend, Ian had to work, two performances a day at the theater.

Six months later, Scotland Yard got back in touch with Bishop and told him that the $600,000 that had been in Stegi's bank account in London, was awarded to other victims but the twenty-five million of Ian's inheritance was clear and free. The trial was over and Stegi had received a fifty year prison term. John Stegi would not see the light of day until he was about 89 years old.

Ian was still balancing his relationship with Cindy and with Jean. That's what it is you know, when you have two friends and you like them both. It is a delicate balancing act. One false move and it all comes tumbling down like a house of cards, and a man could end up old and alone in the end. But, Ian truly did care about all concerned, including himself, and he did not want any more mistakes in his life.

Ian Bishop turned the J.C. Foundation over to Leonard and Laura Landerfeld to operate. He decided he liked his lifestyle the way it was for the time being, at least.

Another summer had come to the end and Ian once more had to scratch that travel "itch."

Ian Bishop had decided to head out for more adventures and more globe trotting, but before he left, everyone came together and gave him a Testimonial Dinner.

It was a great surprise for Ian to see his family and friends all gathered together in the Grand Ballroom of the Crescent Hotel. There was a sign across the wall behind the head table that read: "The J.C. Foundation," Chairman of the Board, Ian Bishop. Everyone had come to honor a man's man, a man who was not afraid to say what he thought. A man that was in touch with his spiritual side. Ian Bishop was a man who gave to everyone who knew him, a zest for life and even more important than showing them how to die, he showed them how to live a more abundant life.

When it is time for Ian to pass over to the other side, no doubt, he will also show us how to die, as well as he showed us how to live.

"What is death, but another adventure, another new beginning, after all!"

☙

Bane Maleke was set free from Prison in South Africa, after about eight months. He contacted Ian's old email address that was now being used by the J.C. Foundation.

Bane apologized and repented for his misdeeds. He was trying to set things straight.

Bane Maleke had lost everything, his wife and children, his brother, and his job at the bank. He was making a fresh start.

The J.C. foundation awarded Bane Maleke one million dollars and the right to open a branch of the foundation to help the poor people in Africa combat malaria, aids, and poverty. This was a cause close to Ian Bishop's heart. It was also a cause that was worthy of Bane Maleke's time because he came through that kind of poverty, himself. Now he would be in a position to do some good for his own people. He was so grateful for the opportunity to serve with the J.C. Foundation that he invested the money to create even more revenue in Africa.

He had discovered what Ian said was true: "It is the things that you do and are doing for each other that defines who you are."

If you ever find yourself in an inheritance scam or a scheme to help someone move large amounts of money from one continent to another, or just another get rich quick scheme,

Just say, **"Thanks, but no thanks."**

It could very well be that all those people will BEQUEATH to you is the WIND.

**That's the part of this story, that you better believe.**

Yours Truly,
Ian Douglas Bishop,
Chairman of the Board
Bishart@yahoo.com